fallon's hope

By michael a. gibbs

PUBLISH AMERICA

PublishAmerica
Baltimore

First printing

ISBN: 1-4137-3764-1
PUBLISHED BY PUBLISHAMERICA, LLLP
www.publishamerica.com
Baltimore

Printed in the United States of America

For Janey

part one

the tremors of winter

one

Born of me, for mine, and mine shall require no other nourishment.
        —Book of Morrigan

The ancient glacier gleamed with an icy blue pride of permanence, and boasted in frozen silence of its longevity. It left behind the evidence of its strength on a scoured landscape that was void of any good thing. With each snowstorm the glacier grew, its life blessed, its mass nurtured for eons by the frigid northern air. And then, almost imperceptibly, the frequency of storms began to diminish, and the air warmed, gnawing at the giant's surface. As the millenniums crawled across the earth, becoming ever gentler in terms of climate, the glacier reluctantly gave birth in the glaring light of midday to a crystalline trickle of bright melt water. From low on the ice mountain's southern slope, the tinkling tears widened into a silver flow that fell with others of its kind toward a distant sea it would never reach.

This seemingly innocuous gathering of small streams spilling freely from the vast and frozen desolation of Artinus soon became part of a thousand similar minuscule eruptions of murmuring and gurgling cascades. In the lower latitudes, that medley of moving sound melded into a crescendo, only to cease its music and become the silent aquamarine depths of the cold and living Fallon River. Now having descended across four hundred miles of barren ice and stone, the Fallon flowed into an inhabited valley of the same name. There, the river forked, and forked again, and yet again, until its five nourishing arms reached to embrace the scattered villages that lay along its courses.

The width and breadth of the valley were almost identical. Gentle slopes of forested solitude bestowed upon the depression the drainage that a passing visitor might believe was responsible for the successful agriculture that made the valley villages self-sustaining. Such a visitor, should one ever enter there, would indeed assume that the fecund bottomlands were the result of the natural geography. But should that visitor linger through the warm months, he would depart through the autumn foliage wondering at the three consecutive harvests from that one growing season. He would have seen that not one of the valley natives appeared older than fifty years of age, although some were grandparents many times over. The visitor in Fallon Valley would find little evidence of disease, past or present. Some of the marked graves on the hillsides were hundreds of years old, and the inscriptions on the individual gravestones referred almost invariably to either the deceased's extreme age or the accident responsible for his or her early demise. Because of the river and the blessings it held, the humans on this part of the Artinus continent were at peace among themselves and with the valley itself.

And so it was, and had been, since anyone alive here could remember. But still, the gift of peace was not taken for granted. The war-trained young men of Fallon ranged the woodlands and meadows of the entire valley year-round, always conscious that what their goddess had bestowed upon them was to be jealously guarded.

No visitor had entered the valley since the Great Migration, except for those rare occasions when a king's representative would arrive from Sogg. Such noblemen from the continental government were always welcomed with feasting and celebration, for if the Fallonese were anything, they were the people of King Alsandair. But his lands were wide, mostly uncharted, reaching across even the great ice flows, and only a few of the old ones in Fallon Valley could remember a royal visit. The ancient secrets of the river existed only for the people those waters nurtured, and the Book of Morrigan warned of the possible consequences of diluting the magic by imparting the knowledge of its existence to those outside. Even the speechless river undines knew as much.

Four of the Fallon's branches were named with respect toward the oldest of the tribe's families—those who could trace their bloodline to a time before the Great Migration, before sudden climatic changes had pushed the people south. The Aine, the widest, shallowest and the most western branch spread across mostly level lands of unnaturally rich soil that gave to the western clan the pride of producing enough for the entire tribe, which was hardly necessary given the evolved farming skills of the Fallonese.

It had not always been so. Among the more than two thousand pages of the Book of Morrigan, the origins of Fallon were set forth in a poetic vagueness that Priestess Oriana had made lucid to the present generation. Each citizen old enough to comprehend knew that the Fallon and its quiet power had not always existed. The river was born of the ice that had only in the last twelve thousand years begun to thaw. The melting ice—now the Fallon River—was at last giving back to the tribe of Fallon all it had taken when it forced the people south with its unforgiving ice flows that had steadily encroached across the landscape and the centuries.

But now it was melting, and someday, according to Oriana's interpretation of the Book, the last of the ice would disappear from the fertile northern lands that were in ages past the place of Fallon. The people would return. That was the promise of the Book of Morrigan, and none of Fallon blood doubted the truth of it. Except Bairre.

Mikael Sveinson sat on the straw by his mother's sleeping pallet, puzzling over the gray color of her face. Never had he been this close to pending death, and he could not recognize it.

Iona saw his distress. She spoke for the first time today. "I see your worry, Mikael. It's in the wrinkles above your brow, and in your eyes. You are so much like your father in that regard. He had blue eyes, too. Have I told you that before?"

"Many times, Mother. Sometimes I think I can see his face."

"He looked like you, child. The same strong and determined face. The same deep blue eyes, like pools of the Aine. And you have your father's fine yellow hair—baby hair, I used to tell him, and he would laugh. Of course I didn't know him at your age, but I suspect he was just as gangly." She smiled and reached to take his hand.

It was cold, her hand. She had no fever as he had suspected. Something else.

Her smile was not returned, and so she knew his anxiety. "You should ask Oriana, my son. She will tell you where I go. You haven't the age to understand. Oriana will explain. Seek her wisdom."

"Mother, how can you speak of going? You are too weak to even climb the steps of the hut."

He saw her gaze shift to the door. Indeed, the three steps leading to air not spoiled by hearth smoke and sickness would be too much for her.

MICHAEL A. GIBBS

"I do not speak of a mortal journey, Mikael. I want only for you to know that I must leave before the blossoms of spring are gone. I go to Fallon—to your father."

Surely, she spoke from a fevered mind. Was she not in Fallon now? Was it not she who told him that his father had been dead for fourteen years?

"Go now, son. Speak with Oriana. Ask your questions there. I must rest."

He left her then and stepped up and out of the sunken hut into the cold but brightening afternoon. Rain had turned the glaring snow to a melting mess of brown slush. The broken cloud cover permitted sporadic bits of sunlight into the village. He glanced toward the Aine and saw the green water high in its banks from the morning deluge. The clean smell of the river wafted to him on the dying winter breeze, and he needed no further invitation to avoid acting upon his mother's request. That could wait.

As he approached the water, a soft splash took his attention to midstream. Too late, he looked. Only the rippling remnant of something underwater existed there now. An undine perhaps? Probably not. They tended to avoid activity for some time after a storm.

He walked on, knowing the truth of his procrastination. Oriana would tell him things he didn't want to know. She would tell him something his mother had not the strength to say. Something terrible.

Another splash. This time he saw her. Almost fully exposed, she was, just for a second. Fionna, one of the prettiest. Might it be as the elders said, that the undines were aware of distress among the humans of Fallon?

"Fionna," he called.

She did not reappear. Perhaps she recognized him as only a youth, and surmised that his distress was insignificant. He sat down on a rock at the water's edge and let his feet dangle, and with the tip of a winter moccasin he made gentle concentric rings. He wondered if Fionna could detect that small disturbance.

His mind wandered, as a child's is prone to do. He considered Fionna and those of her kind. Were they as beautiful as legend held them? Perhaps some were not. Perhaps only the beautiful ones had ever broken the surface, and thus the legend. No, it could not be only legend. The undines' attributes were fully described in the Book of Morrigan.

Maybe he would have one as a mate, he mused. That would surely set him apart from any present day Fallonese. The Book mentioned only one such joining. A peasant of Fallon had fallen in love with an undine, and they were married. She bore him a child, and in doing so gained a soul for herself, a gift

10

from Morrigan to the mate of the human she loved.

Someday perhaps, he would ask Oriana why the water nymphs had no souls, and if it were true what people said about the water being pure because of the undines. He would ask her those things and about the many other mysterious properties of the Fallon. How was it that it healed his wounds? Why did it never become muddy, even after the heaviest storms? How was it that the people of Fallon and the undines withstood the cold of glacial waters? Above all else, he wanted to know why he was so drawn to the river. Why did it pull at his mind unceasingly? Almost, the waters spoke to him.

He thought of the many summer nights he had been awakened by that soundless call. On those occasions, he had left his pallet and his mother and the night noises of the village to go to the water and dive to its clear depths, down as far as his young lungs would allow, not knowing why, but needing to be as close as possible to the waters he loved. Never would he leave Fallon Valley.

"Mikael!"

He turned. Old Esras came sloshing toward him, smoke blending with his gray beard from the pipe that seemed to be a part of his anatomy. He wore what he always wore, loose canvas breeches secured at the waist with a length of twine, a soiled, once-green tunic large enough for two men, and a ragged muffin hat. Shaggy strands of hair the color of his beard fell from under the hat and beyond his shoulders. He supported himself with a thick staff, which he leaned on heavily with each forward movement of his right leg. Esras couldn't explain his limp. He was too old to remember the accident, he said.

"Mikael, how is Iona? I've brought her some venison." He reached inside his tunic and retrieved a small, paper-wrapped package. Grease had soaked through the course paper, and Mikael smelled the sourness of spoiled meat.

"She's not well, Esras. I'm on my way now to talk to Oriana about her."

"That bad, huh?" Esras put the meat back inside his tunic.

"What do you mean?"

"I mean, if she's sent you to the priestess, the time must be close."

"What time?"

Esras looked at him in surprise. He stuttered. Then, "How old are you, boy?"

"I'm seventeen, and a second year bowman and javelin warrior."

"Oh, I see," Esras said. "I don't suppose you know about such things yet. I was probably forty before I understood it. And now I'm closing in on two hundred, and I swear by Morrigan herself, I still don't fully comprehend it all."

"Oriana says we're not to swear by the Goddess—not ever."

"Yes, that's right, Mikael. Sorry. You go on over and talk to Oriana now. I'll check on your mother." And with that he was gone, limping across the soupy ground toward Iona's hut.

Angered now, Mikael stepped quickly toward the main village. Esras apparently thought him too immature to understand what was going on in his own home. If his mother was destined to lay ill for an indefinite period, he needed to know. Arrangements for such things were necessary.

His concern carried him to the outskirts of town to a place where he could see the sod roof of the temple. How would she receive him on a non-service day? Would she read to him from the Book? Surely not. This was not really a Fallon matter. It pertained only to his family. Or did it? Doubt settled inside him, and his determination faltered, but he fought that and continued along the thawing street that took him among the huts and longhouses.

The village of Fallon was cleaner than others in the valley. Mikael had been to only a few of them, but he had heard from the traveling traders of the unpleasant lifestyles that had developed in some of the outlying hamlets. In spite of the blessings bestowed by the river, many of the other villages were plagued with petty crime and localized political problems. Fallon, being the government seat of Fallon Valley, often had to intervene. Twice already this year, Mikael had seen delegations departing for some other settlement, paddling upstream toward the main stem of the river.

In Fallon, even the peasants took pride in the fact that the other villages answered to the constables and bailiffs here. Perhaps that pride was part of the reason the Fallon huts were regularly repaired with new thatching. Livestock was kept well away from the living areas, and maintenance of the sanitary facilities kept odors to a tolerable level. Even now, shop owners were spreading fresh straw in the muddy street.

Mikael walked on, speaking to those he knew, nodding to others. He passed the fishmongers shop and saw the little man inside preparing his nets for an afternoon of boating and wading in the cold waters of the Aine. Mikael wondered how many undines he had seen in his lifetime.

Slums were nonexistent in Fallon. The poor were fed, clothed and sometimes even housed, in a joint effort by those who could afford to help. Mikael and his mother had been helped in times past, and when they were able, they gave aid to those in need. Fallon life had been that way as long as any living resident could remember. Crops, meat and work were shared by all. Perhaps not always equally, but no family suffered if the need was recognized.

Although the village of Fallon had a council, there was little need for laws or enforcers of laws. Meetings were held regularly at the council house, conditions were discussed, and remedies worked out. Always, Oriana was present, to guide and advise, for she knew the desires of the Goddess Morrigan, and she could interpret the Book.

As Mikael approached the temple, he noted that the door was ajar. She would be inside. Only now did he realize that he had been hoping she would be absent—perhaps away at another village ministering to someone in need. He slowed his pace.

The structure was nothing more than an unadorned longhouse, large enough to contain the Fallon worshipers on the seventh day. It had been built at an angle to the street, so that the wide front might be visible to the entire village. In that, the temple exhibited a kind of permanent welcoming gesture.

Mikael was able to calm himself before stepping inside. He smelled the scented candles that burned at the altar. He saw her then.

She stood in the vague light from the one window, her hands folded in front of her, facing Mikael as if she had been expecting him. She wore a gown of slate-colored linen, which fell loosely from her shoulders to the floor. It was belted at the waist by a narrow sash of the same color, and the collar extended high about her slender neck. She smiled.

Oriana's age was not known. "Probably about eighty," he had heard his mother say. But the Goddess Morrigan had been kind to Oriana in that regard. The sable hair that fell across her gown had only the slightest tinge of silver. Certainly, her complexion gave no hint of age. Light skinned, she was, almost pale, and without blemish. Eighty was early middle age for the humans of Fallon Valley, because of the river, but Oriana appeared much younger, and only her demeanor spoke of dignified adulthood.

"Welcome, Mikael," she said, "to the House of Morrigan. She loves you, as do I."

At that, Mikael looked high on the wall behind the alter where the portrait of Morrigan had hung for as long as he could remember. The Book told of an uneasy death for anyone brazen enough to look upon the face of the Goddess, and so, the painting depicted Morrigan in a posture that gave the viewer no opportunity to destroy himself by gazing upon that which was too beautiful for mortals to comprehend. She sat upon her golden throne, but her head was turned, her hair was down, and her facial features were obscured. Morrigan's attire was a gown of purest white, which lay in billows covering her feet. The Fallon flowed in green splendor behind her, and perhaps it was that which she had turned to see.

13

Oriana spoke again. "You've not come to worship, Mikael. You've come to inquire. But do you not know that to learn is to worship as well? To know our Goddess better is to learn how to serve her, which is in itself worship."

"Yes, Oriana. I would ask you about my mother."

She stepped toward him then, her rustling gown like thunder in the hush of holiness. She stopped in front of him and offered her hand. Never had he been this close to Oriana. Always during the services, he sat toward the back of the temple. The gracefulness he had observed then, the pretty face, and her soothing voice all fell together in a harmony of features that he only now fully appreciated. Her large eyes were black, the lids almost half-closed as if her soul was filled with a permanent serenity. Being in her immediate presence, the small confidence that had allowed Mikael to enter, evaporated into the thin gulf that separated them.

He took her hand. As warm as sunlight, and as pale. He knelt and touched the back of her hand to his forehead. She ran her free hand through his honey-colored hair that too many of those his age had teased him about. "Baby hair," they called it, as his mother did, limp and fine. So he kept it short and away from his face. Mikael had a strong face, despite the almost feminine hair. Hours at the river had long ago taken any hint of paleness. His generous lips were firm and his calm eyes spoke to a viewer of honesty and confidence.

Suddenly, Mikael was ashamed of his unclean condition and his soiled canvas clothing. He hoped his unwashed hair had no offensive odor that Oriana would detect as he knelt before her.

"Walk with me, Mikael. Ask what you will."

Still holding his hand, she led him back outside into the light of day where he knew she would be able to clearly recognize his unkempt peasantry. If she saw it, she gave no hint of being repulsed. Even after they were seated on one of the benches in front of the temple, she continued to keep his hand pleasantly trapped inside her own.

"Iona is old, Mikael."

"I know that." It sounded defensive, and he hadn't intended that.

"She will die. Do you know about death?"

"No, Priestess, she will not die." Even in his denial, he felt the uncertainty. "All I know of death is on the hillside—the grave markers. And mother told me that father is dead."

"He is dead, child. I performed the service when you were but an infant. And I will be here for your mother, when it's her time."

"No," Mikael said. "I don't intend impertinence, but that cannot be.

14

Mother is ill, that's all. She speaks of going to Fallon, of seeing Father, but that is the fever. It will pass. I'll have her drink more of the barley water."

"She speaks of death," Oriana said. "She goes in spirit to the Fallon under the ice fields. She's older even than Esras. You must understand that it is her time. Bairre should be told."

"No," he said again, as calmly as before.

A sudden sadness crossed her visage. She released his hand. "Go home, Mikael. She leaves us now."

He ran. If any other had spoken those words, he would not have the fear that now clutched his heart. The mud slapped against his breeches with every stride. A dog barked, and someone called out after him as he raced by the shops, splashing mud and disturbing the freshly laid straw. In view of his hut now, he saw Esras standing outside, staring at the ground. The old man looked up at Mikael's approach.

"Wait, boy. Wait for the priestess." Esras held his arm across the doorway.

Mikael pushed his way inside and went to the pallet. His mother's ashen face had gone slack. Her eyes were open, dry and unfocused.

So, this was death. Could it be this simple—this matter of fact? Could such a permanent change take place so suddenly, after all the years of life?

Mikael, Son of Svein, fell upon her breast then, and wept as he had not wept since Bairre had left. He knew not how long he stayed with her, but when he arose and turned for the door, a glow from the darkness greeted him. An entire village of mourners stood in strictest silence, the grief on their faces made visible in the light of the lanterns and candles they held. Oriana was there. She stepped forward, her smile still in place. For the second time this day, she took his hand.

"It is as you said, Priestess."

"It is more than that, child."

She pulled him toward the Aine, away from the others. They stood in the subdued light of the quarter-moon that was reflected from the clear waters of the river. For a while, neither spoke. He heard the soft ripples of the undines as they swam near the surface of the calm water. They loved the night. Their legendary beauty existed in Fallon as reflections on canvas—remembrances of Fallon artists who had come too close and seen too much by the light of their lanterns. It was said that for a man to behold the beauty of an undine, up close, was to be forever stricken with her memory, and never would he be able to be at peace with a human mate.

Eventually, Oriana spoke. "Your grief will lessen, Mikael. You have learned tonight what most Fallon children don't understand until they are well into adulthood. Parents die. And with that understanding comes a large piece of maturity."

"I do not know about such things, Priestess. I wish not to learn."

She pulled him to her then, and with the warmth that seemed to be an eternal part of her hands, she pressed his face against her breast. A tear, not his, fell onto his face. He knew then that Oriana shared his grief, and that she cared for him. He wondered if the Goddess Morrigan that he was commanded to love, cared as much.

"My dear Mikael," she said, and pushed him away to arms length.

An undine broke the surface very near the bank, but Mikael did not take his eyes from Oriana's.

"Bairre," she said. "What of Bairre, your brother?"

"Priestess?"

"He must be told. Iona requires that. All of Fallon will require it. Bairre is one of us."

"He is not. For six years, he's not been of Fallon. Do you not remember how he blasphemed before he left? He hates us for what we believe. He wouldn't care that Mother's gone."

"That's not for you to judge. Can you see inside his heart? You will go to Sogg because it's your duty as his brother. It has been arranged."

"What?"

"Esras will go with you. When you arrive, go to the court of Prince Andres and state your purpose."

"Priestess, I cannot…"

"You can. You will. Esras will help you. He knows the way, and he will recognize Bairre."

"Esras can barely walk. How can he be of help? Even if he could, I will not leave Fallon Valley." His temper came upon him, and with that, confidence to defy. "All of Fallon believes you speak for Goddess Morrigan. For the first time in my life, I doubt that."

She didn't receive the unkind remark as hurtful, but recognized the youth from which it sprang. And she knew she had been right in deciding that he should be told no more until he was well away from the valley. She smiled easily at him, prompting him to finish his anger. He did.

"Bairre is no longer part of Fallon, or this valley," Mikael asserted. "It is ludicrous to send me forth, especially now. Winter is not done, and blizzards are possible. I will not go to Sogg."

two

And having fed my own, she will die, a continuous death in which there is no sorrow, as her birth is continuous, and a joyful thing under the sun.
—Book of Morrigan

Mikael's bedroll and his two woolen blankets did little to stop the frozen night from soaking through to his bones. He lay on his back as close to the fire as he dared. The evergreen boughs overhead shimmered in the light of the waxing moon, and occasionally, with the breeze from the north, a whisper would run through that dark canopy, and the boughs would shift, giving him a fleeting glimpse of the clear winter sky. It seemed he had not been warm since leaving Fallon two days earlier.

Esras had all but stopped trying to converse with him, and flatly told him just tonight that his indignation was childish. What did Esras know? Who was he to offer an opinion about another's faults, especially when he himself was wrong?

Now he listened to the old man's steady breathing, and he wondered at his ability to rest so easily under such harsh conditions. He wished Esras would suffer more, either from the cold or their lack of food. He deserved to suffer. Esras had conspired with Oriana to drag him to Sogg and away from Fallon. The two of them knew the hardships of winter travel, yet they had insisted the trip be undertaken. The two days of argument had come to the point that banishment was mentioned as an option if the Son of Svein failed to accomplish what the Goddess required. How dare they force such a thing upon him in the name of Morrigan? This was a family matter, and not a decision for Oriana, the village, and most certainly not a thing Esras should have a say in. Did they not consider that he needed time to grieve? Must he lie in the winter wilderness without comfort from any quarter, and see his mother's dying visage appear each night in the cold heavens? Cruel, it was. Cruel of Oriana the priestess, and cruel of Esras. He would always despise them both for thrusting these miseries upon him.

Perhaps tomorrow they would find game within shooting distance of the canoe. With that thought, he reached from under his blanket to touch his bow. He kept it strung, although Esras had said there was nothing to fear in the night woods. Had he not heard the wolves howling at dusk? Esras obviously knew nothing of the ways of the wild. He said wolves would not attack humans. That was ridiculous. A pack of the beasts could take a man down easily enough. Well, let them come. They would spill their own blood before taking any of his.

But surely, no predator would come near the fire. He would worry about wolves tomorrow. Tomorrow, Esras had said, they would hide the canoe and walk away from the river. He had made the statement calmly, as if he spoke of the weather. In that, Mikael knew that Esras did not feel, and probably had never felt, the attachment to the Fallon that possessed Mikael. The thought of leaving the river filled him with unexplained foreboding. Somehow he felt guilty, as if he were abandoning a loved one who needed him. But it was more than that; he needed the river. He wondered how he would manage his emotions when the moment was upon him.

After leaving the water, Esras had said, they would have to be on guard every minute. Had he not been full of indignation, he would have asked the old man just what it was they should be on guard against, and why Esras carried no bow or sword. Perhaps he should have asked. Such things would be good to know. Surely, Esras would tell him before they left the river behind.

Their walking away from the Fallon was a puzzle to Mikael, and would be so even without his attachment to the river. Sogg lay directly south of Fallon Valley, according to Esras. And the river flowed almost due south, so it made no sense to leave the river, unless she made some drastic change of direction he didn't know about. Perhaps she did. Mikael had never been this far south.

He listened to the Aine's gentle murmurs and thought of the undines' peaceful rest on the sandy bottom. In spite of the cold, he fell asleep.

He awakened, or almost so, to the smell of frying corncakes. Shivering from the cold, he thought momentarily that he was inside his mother's hut, that he had failed to keep the fire through the night, and that he would be scolded.

Esras gave him a glance, then turned back to the low fire. Mikael thought he heard the old man grunt, as if he held contempt for such a late sleeper.

"Esras, you're a liar," Mikael said.

"What?" Esras had not turned his head to look at him again.

"You told me last night you had no more cornmeal."

"No, I did not tell you that. I said I had no cornmeal for supper. This is breakfast."

The aroma of the four sweetened cakes in the iron skillet, and the emptiness of his stomach, stifled a testy reply from Mikael. He merely asked, "Are they ready?"

"Yes, but you'll not eat until you've washed. Go to the river, Son of Svein. Do not tell me that Iona taught you to eat without washing."

The old man had almost gone too far with that comment. His mother was not blood relative to Esras; he had no right to speak of family matters, especially during his time of grief. But Mikael checked himself. He would say nothing to anger Esras before he had shared his corncakes. He started for the river.

"And you might want to offer a prayer to the Fallon," Esras said to Mikael's back. "You'll not have her protection after today."

Even in his anger, Mikael considered that. Never in his life had he been more than a few hundred yards from the Fallon or one of her branches. What would it be like away from her? Was the comfort she gave only a childish notion he would forget someday? No, her nurturing qualities were real, and he would miss the river's quiet peace, especially now that he was an orphan.

The frost-laden leaves and litter crunched beneath his feet as he walked to the water. He knelt at the river's edge on a beach of round pebbles and splashed water onto his face, then dried himself on the sleeves of his woolen coat. He looked out across the moving blue-green expanse of the Aine, and thought for a moment on what he should ask for.

"Goddess Morrigan," he began, "keeper of the Fallon and the Fallon's people. And to you, Fallon, provider of all things. I offer praise and gratitude…"

He stopped, thinking of his mother's death, his infidel brother, and the forced journey. What reason did he have to praise or thank any entity? He had nothing but an empty hut, and not even that until he returned home. Even though none of that was the Fallon's fault, prayers of thanks seemed somehow inappropriate. He stood and walked back to the camp.

He found the fire out and two of the four cakes missing. Fighting his inclination to ask permission, he reached for the cakes. He felt Esras' eyes upon him as he stood over the dead coals and swallowed the too-hot cakes. Having seized what was his only by implication, he still could not bring himself to express gratitude. He should be home eating cakes he had cooked in his own hut.

Mikael turned away from the heated rocks of the recent fire to tend to his bedding. He was folding a blanket when Esras said, "The skillet. Bring it, clean it, stow it." Esras started toward the river, limping away from a haze of pipe smoke, leaning on his staff, and hoisting the strap of his bedroll to his shoulder.

"It's not mine, old man. Clean it yourself."

Esras stopped and turned. "I cooked your breakfast in the skillet. You ate from it. You'll clean it and stow it away."

"I ate your leftovers. You dirtied it, you clean it. Or leave it on the rocks. I don't care."

Mikael bent to get his other blanket. He didn't hear Esras' approach, and he would never know how the old man covered the distance between them so quickly. As he straightened himself, he found Esras at his side.

"I'll not tell you again, Son of Svein."

"What's the matter with you? Why do you keep referring to me by my father's name? You and Oriana have insisted from the beginning that I'm supposed to have some family motivation for this foolish journey. Well, I don't. As for your damn skillet..."

Esras hit him then, and he was unable to stand against it. He fell heavily across his bedroll. The entire left side of his face stung viciously, and he realized Esras had hit him with an open hand. He had not thought the old man capable of such quick and harsh action. By the time he sat up, Esras was limping out of sight toward the waiting canoe. Mikael glanced at the fire pit. The skillet was still there.

Burning with resentment, he hastily collected his bedding, then retrieved the still-warm skillet. He carried his load to where the canoe had been hidden, only to find that Esras had already launched it. Eras sat in the back, paddle in hand, waiting.

They didn't speak as Mikael cleaned the skillet with river sand. He put it away in the canvas sack that rested in the center of the canoe. The sack held other necessities, including flint and steel, a cooking pot, a short-handled axe, a sewing awl, and Esras' personal items. He took his seat in the front and used his paddle to push away from the beach.

The clear and warming morning was only two hours old when the Aine intersected with the main stem of the Fallon.

Esras' tone held no malice. "The Aine is the longest of the Fallon anabranches, Son of Svein. I teach you this thing now as we drift into the full flow of the Fallon. The other anabranches, having fed the valley, have already returned. I think that nowhere on the continent is there another river with so many branches, all of which come back to the main stream. Look there."

Mikael turned to see Esras pointing ahead.

"Do you see the gorge between the two mountains?" Esras asked.

Mikael lifted a hand to shade his eyes against the reflected glare. "I see it," he said.

"That marks the end of Fallon Valley. From there, we walk."

"Why?"

"You shall see."

By early afternoon, Mikael found little need to propel the canoe forward with his paddle. The current, dangerously swift, demanded only that he and Esras keep the craft pointed downstream. Any other posture meant probable capsizing. Occasionally, Mikael checked on their progress by gauging the distance to the two mountains that stood like sentinels on either side of the river. That distance was shrinking at an alarming rate. He resisted the urge to query Esras about their safety. He was relieved when the old man spoke.

"We'd better ease it over to the right. Look for a good landing."

Mikael's anxiety over the fast water was instantly replaced with the foreboding he earlier experienced. They were going to leave the Fallon.

He realized that a sound had been in the air for some time—a low groan or growl, like distant thunder. But not thunder, he reasoned, because it was constant. Now it was even louder.

"There!" Esras shouted. He was pointing toward the right bank.

A low, sandy beach, no longer than fifty paces, stretched out in the sun between the dark entanglements of shrubs and boulders that occupied every bit of shoreline in this area. They paddled furiously for that bright landing, intent on arriving there before the current swept them by. What had been a growl was now a thunderous roar, dead ahead. As Mikael thrust his paddle forward for another grip in Fallon water, he risked a glance downstream. At first, he thought smoke was rising from the center of the river. Then, he knew it to be a mist, and he saw the sunlit sparkle of tiny droplets as the Fallon met some major change in its determined flow.

"The falls," Elias shouted above the noise.

The canoe shot onto the sand at an angle, and with enough speed to take more than half of the craft out of the water. Mikael sprang from his seat in the front to grab on to the bow and pull Esras onto the beach. He let himself fall back to a seated position in the damp sand.

Between breaths, he asked, "Falls?"

Esras disembarked and sat down beside him. "I didn't tell you before because you wouldn't have believed me. This is where the Fallon ends."

"Ends? Do you mean this is where we leave the river? Is it too dangerous to proceed below the falls?"

"There is no river below the falls."

Mikael scooted around to where he was facing Esras. He looked into his eyes, searching.

"I don't think you're in your right mind now, Esras. Maybe we ought to make camp here."

Esras laughed then, loud and long, and in spite of himself, Mikael was warmed by the sound. Gaiety, even insane gaiety, was welcome after the long and tiring days of disagreement.

"What's so funny?"

"You, my friend, that's what's funny. I have a bit of news for you that you could not have accepted any sooner. You must see it for yourself. Come with me."

Esras arose, picked up the sack and his staff from the canoe, and ducked into the brush like a man half his age. Mikael grabbed his bow and quiver and followed. Almost immediately, Esras was out of sight in the thick tangle of vines and brush.

"Slow down, old man," Mikael shouted.

If not for the movement of disturbed vegetation ahead of him, he would have lost Esras altogether. They were moving across almost level ground on the west side of the river. Even at this early afternoon hour, it wouldn't be long before the sun disappeared behind the high and ragged cliffs to their right. On the opposite side, an identical cliff faced them. The appearance and grand scale of that gorge caused one to ponder its origin. Perhaps the two mountains had been one in centuries past, and the raging torrent that was the Fallon River had ripped it in twain.

The steady crashing of tons of violent water exploding over the rim of the falls was unlike anything Mikael had ever experienced. Deafening, like the Fallon had suddenly realized that her death was imminent, and she screamed her outrage. An unexplained sadness came over Mikael, almost like he was nearing his own death. He plunged ahead, crashing through the brush like a wounded bear, needing to know what was happening to his beloved Fallon.

By now the mist had changed from a white fog to a dark screen of soaking vapors almost as impenetrable as the brush. Had Esras not stopped, Mikael would not have found him.

Conversation, even in screams, was impossible. Esras took hold of his wrist and led him forward. Suddenly, they were descending. Boulders, gnarled trees and rotting logs barred their path as if warning the humans to go no farther.

Steeper now, and wetter. They slid more than walked down through the heavy uncertainty of the fog.

And then, almost as if the elements were joined in purpose, the descent, the noise and the fog began to lessen. Mikael found himself in a quiet glade where the bare limbs of sugar maples gleamed in the broken sunlight. Esras released his wrist.

"Esras, I don't understand. Where's the Fallon?"

"Will you never know your river, Son of Svein? Do you mock the Goddess Morrigan with your childish ignorance?" He smiled then and put his arm across Mikael's shoulder. "Come, sit with me. We shall eat, and we shall talk."

They sat on the grass, close together, their backs against maple trees. From the sack, Esras retrieved a smaller bag. From that, he produced a huge chunk of goat cheese, and bread that had to be stale.

"I've saved this until now. We'll need our strength for the remainder of the journey." He cut the cheese and returned his knife to its sheath at his waist. "Here, lad. And bread, too. It will not last another day. You will have to kill us something to eat with that bow of yours."

Mikael held his questions and ate, knowing Esras would not be hurried.

"We have no wine, Mikael. I should have remembered to bring a skin of wine. I'm sorry. We'll find water soon."

Mikael thought it odd that Esras had a need to find water. They had just left a river of water.

Something passed through the very edge of Mikael's peripheral vision, in the trees, and he jerked his head in that direction.

24

"What is it, lad?"

"I saw something there." He pointed.

"There is no threat here," Esras said. The spirits here are of Fallon. They are the Guardians, appointed by Morrigan. They came with the river when it was new, and a select few of the Fallon dead have joined them through the ages. They guard the place of the river's demise. They are your ancestors, and their mortal bones lie beneath the ice of Old Fallon. Do you know about the Fallon's beginning?"

Mikael was slow to answer. The notion of visible spirits so close at hand was unnerving. But Esras' calming tone left no room for a display of fear. "She began in the ice fields that cover Old Fallon. She is the melt-water from there," Mikael said.

"These are truths, Mikael, as old as time. The Book holds the records and the voices from our past. But not only that. The Book shows us the future of Fallon. Oriana told me you are ready for that truth."

"Oriana? When did she speak of me?"

"When Iona died. Oriana suspects that you are the One. If that be true, the spirits here have already recognized you."

"The one what?"

"I have much to tell you, Mikael Sveinson, and I must do so before leaving this place. We'll camp here, for darkness will be upon us before I'm finished."

"I must know about the river, Esras."

"And so you will. The river does not exist from this side. The Fallon is for the people of Fallon, and once it leaves our valley, Morrigan takes it. Some say it descends into a cavern, an abyss so deep that it swallows the river entirely. And that void in the earth will continue to drink until the last glacier has melted, and the people have returned to their northern home."

Esras pulled his pipe and pouch from a coat pocket, then flint and steel and tinder. But instead of creating the needed sparks, he began to talk. He looked beyond the tree line to the north, as if remembering something long ago and far away.

"Before the Book was written, and for many years afterward, the Fallonese were people of the sword. Their way of life was war. In the far north, they had no farms and knew nothing of growing. They were hunters and warriors, a fierce tribe, but just, and not to be trifled with." He stopped and struck flint to steel. The tinder didn't catch.

"And then the ice came. Not suddenly, not in a year, and not in a thousand.

But it came, steadily and surely. As the great glaciers and ice fields formed, the people moved, and moved again, and again, until they came to the valley you know. That was the Great Migration, and it lasted for countless generations."

"And then the river came," Mikael said.

"Yes and no. The people settled in the valley and began to hunt, and to make war on the clans that were already in place in and around the valley. Their fighting instincts and abilities made them victorious over each tribe, including even the Elkana. Do you know about the Elkana?"

"I have heard the name."

"The Elkana, for the most part, are a peaceful race that live in scattered villages across the southern parts of the continent. I say 'villages,' but actually, they live in a system of caves and dens that they dig by hand. Their hands are more like claws. They have a tendency to avoid the sun, so by night they toil, hunt and fish."

Another strike of the flint produced sufficient sparks for the tinder to catch, and Esras quickly had enough flame to light his pipe. He inhaled and closed his eyes. Mikael understood that the journey had wearied him.

"The Goddess Morrigan saw that the people did not prosper. They fought and they survived, but gained little else. So she gave them the river. How many times have you heard Oriana recite the passage?"

Mikael quoted the verse he had learned before he could read. "I, Morrigan, the keeper of time, the giver of life, the Goddess of Fallon, will sustain you, my people, until your land be renewed, and you return to dwell therein. I will nourish my own, but no others, unless incidentally."

"And what does 'no others' mean to you, Son of Svein?"

"You ask me for that simple truth? It means that Goddess Morrigan is Fallon's goddess, and no others."

"Your vision is limited. The passage tells us more. The promised nourishment is the Fallon, and it is for our people only. That's the very reason it flows no farther than Fallon Valley, and that's the reason it's been guarded by man and spirit since it began to flow. Contamination by wicked outsiders, even downstream contamination, will spoil the gift along its entire course."

Mikael gazed at the old man without speaking, and wondered at the things he said.

"We rest and eat and smoke on holy ground today, lad. If you are indeed the One, you must learn this and more, for there are those who seek to raise the Fallon in an attempt to partake of what is ours."

***

Hulda's coven sat facing her on crude three-legged stools, forming a half-circle among the dead trees. She had held their strict attention through the cold night, since before midnight, and now not even the brightening of the eastern skyline created any restlessness among them. They were hers fully, except Zienna.

Pausing in her tirade for effect, she studied the ten faces glowing in the flickering light of the fire that blazed between her and them. All were young, Kattrin the youngest. But Kattrin showed the most promise. Already her family had turned her out as an incorrigible child-demon. Her natural abilities at witchery exceeded even Hulda's when Hulda was that age. She would take the child into her den when the time was right.

Hulda asked them again as she brushed thin strands of breeze-driven black hair from her eyes, "Will you leave this thing to me? Will you cower in your dens while I summon the forest forces forth? No, it shall not be. I tell you now that nine of you are born tonight into darkness. I can teach you little more. Your authority is full upon you. You require only my guidance and critiques."

Not one answered her. They and she knew that verbalization of their loyalty was beyond unnecessary; an obvious response would indicate a frailty kin to humankind.

Hulda's tone softened. "Zienna, come to me."

Zienna of Ranga, obviously startled, did not immediately rise. Her yellow eyes darted among the solemn, pale green faces of the others. Then she stepped forward, her hooded, black robe hanging from underneath the blanket that she wore against the cold. The robe dragged across the leaves, and that rustling was the only sound within hearing of the group as she made her way to Hulda. Zienna stopped within arms length, her back to the coven.

Hulda looked at the other nine, not at Zienna. "You, Zienna, are the proof that one Elkana's witch power is sometimes insufficient, and to succeed in some endeavors, such as we've discussed tonight, even a queen requires a certain synergy… no, harmony, I think, of purpose.

"Queen?"

"Do you wear the sign?"

"Of course, Queen. I am yours."

Zienna let the blanket fall below her slender shoulders to expose the heavy medallion hanging on a leather cord from her rough-skinned neck. Almost as large as the four-digit hand of an adult Elkana, it had been forged into a circle, divided into three segments by a raised bar, as in relief carving. The segments were engraved with the likeness of a star, the moon and a river.

"Turn and show your sisters."

Zienna turned. Constructed of polished iron, the large medallion reflected the firelight, and Hulda saw that all eyes were upon it.

"Zienna, why do you wear it?"

Zienna turned back. "I have earned it. I have proven myself to be above my kind. I am one of the coven."

"Stand there." Queen Hulda pointed to a rotting tree trunk that stood ten paces from her, to the coven's left.

Zienna obeyed. With no words exchanged, Kattrin arose and stepped forward.

"Tie her," Hulda said, and held out a length of twine that no eye within the coven had seen previously.

Without hesitation, Kattrin went to Zienna, whose face had gone slack. She put her hand to Zienna's breast and pushed her back against the remains of the long-dead tree. Without having to be told, Zienna reached back to embrace the tree behind her. Kattrin tied her wrists. Hulda had no need to check the knot. She knew it would hold.

"Stand with me, child," Hulda said to Kattrin, "and face our sisters."

"Zienna, daughter of Hannes the blasphemer," Hulda said without looking at the frightened girl, "have you renounced your village, your family?"

Zienna's voice quavered. "Yes, Queen."

"Why, then, do you report to your father after each coven gathering?"

"Who says such a thing, Queen? Name them; I will burn their lying hearts."

Hulda allowed the silence to permeate the night. An owl called, as if to restate Zienna's question.

"Three of this coven. Would you question their fidelity?"

Zienna's next few words were unintelligible. Then, "No, Queen, I would not. We are sisters, we eleven. They are simply mistaken. I have told you, and I have sworn that I am yours."

The coven heard that, and a murmur arose among them. They knew. Only a deceiver would say a thing unnecessarily. All in attendance had heard Zienna's previous oath of fealty.

From the folds of her own black gown, Hulda produce a bone-handled flint knife. The shiny blackness of the long blade gleamed in the increasing light of dawn. She stepped away from Kattrin toward Zienna. Zienna gasped.

"Queen, I beg you. Do not do this. I am…"

Hulda's knife hand darted forward, and the medallion fell. The blood soaking through Zienna's gown was all but invisible in the gathering dawn.

"My queen, you have wounded me without cause. You must stop this."

"Your mother is human, is that not correct, Zienna?" Hulda didn't wait for an answer. "Before today's light fails, Hannes will learn one more thing about me, and the price of sending a spy among us."

Hulda retrieved the fallen pendant and walked to the fire. Discarding the slashed cord, she held the iron in the flames until it glowed red. All three of her leathery fingers and her thumb were in contact with the metal, but caused her no apparent distress. A hushed gasp escaped the thin, pinkish lips of all in the coven. Hulda took the metal to Zienna and held it in front of her eyes. Zienna recoiled from the radiated heat, pushing her head back against the half-rotten wood. She screamed, a high-pitched and pitiful wail, as Hulda pressed the hot iron to her forehead. A thick and sickly smoke lifted from the burned flesh, and was dissipated in the breathless air before Hulda removed the torment.

"Kattrin," Hulda whispered.

Kattrin went to her.

"Burn this half-human disease with the power."

Kattrin eyes did not meet her queen's, but Hulda knew they were more green than yellow. A remarkable trait, those eyes, not to be dismissed as simply a mark of beauty. Kattrin was born to be what she was fast becoming. Her back was straight, and only seldom did she use her hands to walk. "Queen Hulda," she said, "I have not that gift. I am but twenty summers."

"Then select an assistant."

"Trella," Kattrin said.

An impossibly slender female stepped forward. Her animal-like posture was suggestive of the reddish cats of the forest. Tall for her age, Trella was considered beautiful by the Elkana. Her thin, auburn hair fell almost to her shoulders, and grew not at all from the back of her neck, as it did on most Elkana females.

Kattrin and Trella, their hoods thrown back, stood with their queen, facing the remaining seated Elkana witches.

"All of you have seen a burning," Hulda said. "In this same place, you watched as your queen destroyed the human outsider that ventured too near our secrets. Not one among you, not one in all of Alsandair's realm other than your queen, has that power as an individual. Kattrin knows that. Kattrin, our youngest, is our hope. I have no doubt that she is my successor. Without Kattrin, I do not believe the other nine of us could accomplish our purpose."

Hulda paused and glanced at Zienna. "I have said that to say this: I will tolerate no jealousies among you. I will maintain discipline and obedience at any cost. As of this moment, Kattrin is my second. You will obey her as you do me. I am your queen. She is your princess."

"Queen," Kattrin said, "I am but your student. I ask you to chose another."

"There is no other." Hulda turned to face her directly. "The coven needs you as my second, and so will you serve. Are you prepared for the burning?"

Zienna's wail escalated into a howling scream. It trailed off into sobs as Kattrin and Trella took their positions directly in front of her.

"You filthy, swampland demons!" Zienna screamed. "I admit that I'm not one of you, you godless vermin! You will pay a thousand times over for what you do. Have you not heard of the One from Fallon? The One that even the human king will respect?" She lunged forward, jerking her arms against the ties. "He comes from the north, pushed upon you by the moving ice. He was chosen centuries before…"

"Silence, blasphemer!" Hulda's voice was a weapon not to be ignored. "Do you think any of us here hold with the humans' religion? Your father has warped you, Zienna, and brought you to this death. Save your screams for the fire."

"I will not be silenced while I live, queen slut. Burn me if you can." Zienna's tone was cold now, and her steady glare at Hulda held a conviction that few of the coven missed. "You are right that I've done my father's bidding, but gladly would I have come among you without his asking. He knows the truth of you, and you will not conceal that truth by what you do here. The One from Fallon lives now. From childhood, he will come among you. It's not me or my father you must defeat, but him."

Hulda spoke one word, and that so softly only the intended heard. "Kattrin."

The coven saw the trembling of Kattrin and Trella, joined together now by minds that worked as one. Their eyes were focused on Zienna's breast. Trella shuddered slightly as she accepted that part of Kattrin's power she would need. From their mouths came words they had never spoken, and would not remember. Zienna's screams filled the brightening wood lot, and then faded again into sobs.

At the same instant that the winter sun spilled across the dead trees into the coven's forest, the hem of Zienna's gown began to smoke. She thrashed against the cord that held her at death's swinging gate. As the yellow light touched her face, she ceased resisting and gazed into her last sunrise, resigned to her fate.

She didn't scream when her gown and blanket exploded with fire. When the flames caught her hair, she found Hulda's eyes. "He comes," she said, and died.

three

My own know me, they hear me, and walk accordingly. But others, beyond mine, know my paths, and they wait for me through storm and hunger, that they might be comforted.
                                                    —Book of Morrigan

Mikael had little leisure to dwell upon his newfound knowledge of the Fallon. Having left the place of the river's demise, he followed close behind Esras on a southerly course that took them through tangled masses of brush, vines and briars. Each step required that they remain attentive to the clawing vegetation that seemed determined to take their possessions and clothing. Had the bitterness of the forced journey not still been fresh in his mind, he would have asked a thousand questions more of Esras before attacking the choking jungle. Without a doubt, he would have eventually learned of the Fallon's end without Esras having brought him to the physical place. Perhaps he would have discovered it on his own when the winter snows were finished and spring called him to the waterways.

Now they were clear of that hell, and they stepped into open and level hardwood timberlands. The great oaks and beeches stood with their naked branches thrust outward and upward against the dimming southern skyline as if welcoming them to kinder environs.

Mikael knew relief and concern at once. With the fresh and unobstructed view of the sky, he saw the rolling and bunching gray puffs of clouds that promised snow within a day. He stepped up even with Esras, and then beyond, taking in the lay of the land and almost smelling the fresh meat that surely browsed this forest.

Esras grabbed the nape of his coat, effectively halting his progress. "Easy, lad," he said as he let him go. "You haven't an inkling of what you're walking into."

Resentment filled Mikael instantly. The old man had actually reined him in like a plough horse that was bound to do his master's bidding. "Who are you to lay hands on me? Shall a hoary weasel like you presume to walk ahead of me always? I'll step where I please, old man."

"It would serve you well to keep your voice low, Son of Svein." Esras was scanning the forest, not looking at him as he talked. "When I told Oriana I would see you to Sogg, I spoke of getting you there alive. Have I not already warned you of what we can expect after leaving the Fallon?"

"And what specifically might we expect, old man? Your warnings have been suspiciously vague. Perhaps you merely wish to prolong my misery by slowing our pace."

"Yes, vague, and deliberately so, knowing your obstinate manner," Esras replied. "Always, your mind is closed to those parts of reality that are…shall we say, inconvenient. I thought it best for you to see for yourself what is true and what is real. However, having reached this point, there are certain things you must be told even if you cannot accept them."

"Like what? Some other torment arranged by you and the priestess?"

Esras ignored that. "King Alsandair knows some of our secrets. Back through the rein of his ancestors, our ways have been respected, and the Fallon has remained pure."

"What secrets?" Mikael asked.

"Think you that others live as we do? Don't you know that humans outside the valley are fortunate to live even sixty years? You attend services, but you don't listen, and if you do listen, you don't absorb. Sometimes I wonder that Morrigan chose you."

"Chose me? No one chose me for anything. You're daft."

Esras took him by the arm, despite Mikael's earlier warning, and pulled him back toward the cover of the thickness they had just escaped. "Listen to me, as an adult would listen. Learn from me, or die without saving the Fallon and its people."

Mikael felt the black eyes bore into him and through him. He shuddered, knowing he must hear what Esras would tell him. Even not wanting to hear, the black eyes told him he must. He sat down without speaking, and in that way he showed the elder a meeker side.

"War has not entered Fallon Valley since the Great Migration. Those driven from the valley by Fallonese warriors were of no consequence. Elkana mostly. Their resistance was nearly nonexistent because they understood whom it was that came among them—the people of the Goddess Morrigan and the warriors of the north.

Esras studied him then, searching his eyes, obviously trying to ascertain if his student was listening. Apparently satisfied, he continued.

"Why have you trained from early youth with the bow, Mikael? And with the spear and sword? Why does the temple hold chain mail and helmets? And why does Fallon have instructors to teach the ways of war? Do you know?"

"It's our custom. It's tradition."

"Yes, Son of Svein. It is both custom and tradition, but more. We are a fighting people, and none on the earth were stronger before the ice came. I fear we have grown weak since the Great Migration, and that the continued training is not enough. The need for the old ways is at hand."

"What need?"

"Your ancestors brought the Book here. Before the ice began to melt, the people knew it would. Before the river, before the undines, before the fish, and before the charmed water that pushes our wheat and barley out of the ground thrice each season, they knew those things were forthcoming." They knew because Morrigan gave us the Book."

"Yes, so I have been taught since childhood." Mikael's tone was patient now, not hostile.

"The Elkana hold no grudge. Through the centuries, they've not attempted to come among the Fallonese, or to take back what they once had. Seeing that her people were settled, and in need, Morrigan melted the ice that lay upon Old Fallon."

"So what has changed, Esras? The river is the same, the people are the same."

"It's not what has changed, but what *will* change if not prevented. Morrigan tells us of a vileness brewing just outside the valley, possibly in the place we now sit."

"Say what you mean."

"Oriana resumed her father's studies of the Book of Morrigan. Still, she studies and prays for wisdom, and for the ability to comprehend the unnumbered verses. Only the elders of our people and those that hold Oriana's trust know of her findings. Never in the history of the Fallonese has the Book revealed as much as it has to Oriana." Esras stopped speaking suddenly, as if he had said too much.

"Alsandair is not aware. Neither is anyone in his kingdom. I tell you now because you are probably the One."

"The one what? You keep saying that."

"Mikael, if I should die before you enter Sogg, you must gain admission into the king's castle. Your best chance is through Prince Andres. You must tell the king personally, as a Fallonese, what I tell you now. If he can be convinced that you are from Fallon, he will see you. He holds that much respect for our people, and for Oriana."

"I thought we were going there to see Bairre."

"We are indeed. But there is a more pressing matter. I've told you already that there are those who would raise the Fallon and destroy it. Alsandair will help you prevent that."

Mikael suddenly remembered what Esras had said earlier about the spread of downstream pollution. What of the undines? Fionna and her kind?

A weight of responsibility that he did not want pressed down, locking in a coldness, making him sick. He had been duped. Esras, acting for Oriana, had waited until now to tell him that he was somehow the hope of Fallon. Surely, they were wrong. Either the priestess had misinterpreted the Book, or she had selected him for some reason, maybe because he was an orphan. Maybe she thought he was young enough to be molded into whomever or whatever it was she thought could stop the vileness she saw coming to destroy the river.

He stood. "I will return to Fallon, alone if I must. Oriana will explain all this to me. I will require that."

"What is it you wish to know, Son of Svein? Ask me."

"You are obviously convinced that the priestess is correct in her interpretations. I am not. I'm not even certain she has seen what she claims. I will question her, not you."

"All right, Mikael. I will agree to your return, if you'll answer one question truthfully. But if your answer is 'yes,' you must agree to reconsider."

"Ask your question."

"Does the Fallon speak to you?"

The question startled him. How might Esras have guessed? Never had he spoken to anyone about his attachment to the river. Perhaps Esras was asking something else.

"What do you mean?" He gave nothing away with that.

"I'm asking if you've had communication with the Fallon? Not verbally, of course, but… inwardly. Do you feel as if you're part of her? Does she know you personally?"

"That's insane. What are you getting at?"

"Answer the question, Son of Svein."

He did not. He could not. Whatever it was that Esras knew, he could not possibly understand his relationship to the Fallon. Yes, it was personal. Deeply personal. Too personal to discuss, and too complicated to explain.

He wept then. The confusion of that emotional response carried him to the ground where he sat at Esras' feet and tried in vain to control himself. The sobs came, and he knew not why. He wanted away from the responsibility that somehow was becoming his. Who had done this to him? Esras? Oriana? The river?

Through his distress, he saw Oriana's face and the kindness in her eyes when she had held him. He felt her warm hands, and her truth. She knew.

"Esras, I am confused."

Esras closed his eyes as if collecting his thoughts. Then, "These are Morrigan's words, not mine. 'In the twelfth generation after the Great Migration, even before my crystal purity of life is threatened, an orphaned child from Fallon's poor will come of age and take upon himself the arrows of ash given to my own in the beginning, and saved from the ice for Fallon's protection even before Fallon's birth.'"

Esras knelt on one knee. From his bedroll, he removed a long, rolled piece of white calfskin Mikael had never seen. Gently, reverently, Esras untied the lashing and loosed the folds. In his hands now were numerous arrows of white ash fletched in white. The tips were of white flint. He held the arrows toward Mikael.

Hannes sat with his human mate, Tessa, in the deepest recess of his den, rubbing ashes into every crevice of his leathery skin. He scooped another handful from the outer edge of the all but dead fire that struggled to stay alive in the stale air.

Tessa spoke. "Let us go out into the light. All of Ranga waits to see us. There are those who would share our grief."

"Our neighbors don't care, Tessa." He gestured with his head toward the nearest exit. "Do you think any of the colony will go against Hulda? No, they will justify Zienna's murder by saying Hulda had a right to kill a spy. They justify the witchcraft because they're afraid of it." He reached his clawed fingers for more ashes. "No, I'll not go up. I'm ashamed of the colony for their cowardice. I don't want their false sympathy."

Tessa was silent for a while. Then she took Hannes' arm and pulled him to his feet. Hannes knew his wife well enough to know the futility of resistance. He stopped near the entrance to let his vertical pupils adjust to the light of day. Upon stepping out, he and Tessa found about thirty Elkana, most of the colony, squatted on their hindquarters, waiting. Tessa stepped forward intending to speak, but Hannes' voice carried across her shoulders into the crowd.

"What seek you here? An apology? You'll not have that. It's my loss more than yours, and gladly I would send my daughter among the witches again. I suspect that her death is the fault of one of you more than it is mine."

A hushed gasp arose from the Elkana. Some stood. Tessa whispered a warning that he ignored.

"One of you let it be known to the coven that Zienna was reporting back to me. Which of you would do that?" He let that settle on their minds, and he waited for the answer he knew would not come. The lizard-like faces were solemn, and most of the eyes looked elsewhere, not at him.

"This much I tell you, so that you'll know your cowardice is wasted upon Hulda and those that would follow her. Zienna learned…"

"Hannes, don't tell them," Tessa whispered. "It's your grief that speaks now. For our sakes, keep silent. They won't believe you anyway."

Hannes was not deterred. "Zienna learned that Hulda intends to make war on the Fallonese." He heard murmurs and outright laughter.

"How this is to be done, I do not know. It has something to do with the river that the Fallonese were given by their god. But there is more—something written in their book of prophesies that my father and his discussed only in secret, but I heard. I speak now of those same prophesies that the Elkana did not believe, even when the Fallonese were driven to their valley by the ice flows."

A hateful male voice from the back of the crowd: "It's not their valley. They took it by force. It is the Elkana's."

Hannes ignored the heckler, suspecting that he may have been the one who leaked information to the coven. "There is one from Fallon who will come. His childhood will vanish with the acceptance of his task. He and his king will fight the coven, and should they be victorious, those who have supported Hulda through their cowardice will likely die. That's all I have to tell you." Hannes turned abruptly, stalked past Tessa, and disappeared into the darkness of the den.

***

Bairre Sveinson, his dirty yellow hair falling into his eyes, bent over an inverted front hoof in the royal stable. When the white mare nipped his shoulder, Bairre swung his scraper at it, but the playful horse anticipated the move and bolted to the other side of the stable. The other horses stamped about in their stalls at the commotion they couldn't see.

"By the Gods of the Nine Worlds," Bairre screamed, "I'll turn that beast out of here one of these days. The whole herd can go to hell for all I care."

Matthias entered by the main door just at that moment, a wooden keg in his arms. He kicked the door shut against the killing chill that had ridden the frozen wind for two days. "Bairre, that temper of yours will get you turned out long before the horse is gone. Have I not warned you before? That's royal property you're cursing. Should the prince hear you, he'll hang us both."

"Then *you* trim her damn hoofs, Matthias. See if you can do it and keep your sanity."

"Give her a minute, let her calm. Here, sit with me. I've got beer; not very cold, I'm afraid." He lowered the keg to the earthen floor and ran a hand through his black, curly hair before seating his stout frame on a stool. He pulled another stool close for Bairre.

Bairre stepped quickly to his sleeping quarters behind the stacked hay that reached to the ceiling. He retrieved his horn cup and returned. Matthias was working at the keg's plug with a knife that seemed too large for the task.

"A gift from the royal kitchen," Matthias said. "I'll warrant Rebecca has taken chances to keep me stocked with beer and cheese. I wonder why that is."

Matthias's grin betrayed his sarcasm. Bairre had been awakened too many nights to the giggling and grunting coming from Matthias's pallet on the other side of the stable. Not that he blamed him. He had often been tempted to approach the cook's helper himself. But he worked too closely with Matthias to let some castle slut come between them. Anyway, a shortage of girls had not been a problem for Bairre since he arrived in Sogg six years earlier. His six-foot height and his blazing blue eyes were the topic of nighttime conversation in many of the huts that lay in the shadow of the royal castle. Even now, he knew of at least two barmaids who would be expecting to see his wiry torso coming through the doorway tonight. One would serve his supper and he would tell her of Fallon things that she wouldn't believe, and then he would leave her to see the other buxom girl who would serve him beer as long as he cared to indulge. Then that one would lead him to her room above the tavern, or come with him back here to the stables.

He held his cup out as Matthias tilted the keg. The dark golden ale overran the cup and splashed across his hand. He waited until Matthias had poured some for himself. Then they lifted their cups and touched them together, spilling even more of the lukewarm liquid.

"To King Alsandair and his son," Matthias said. "May they never know a Fallonese sleeps within the castle walls."

"That's not funny, Matthias."

Matthias chuckled. "Sorry, friend Bairre. But should the prince have believed you those years ago, with whom would I share my beer today? You would be wearing the king's own colors, walking his halls, eating his pheasants, and drinking his wine. Nay, I would rather watch you shoveling the royal horse droppings, and share in your misery than not have your company."

Bairre could not help but laugh himself. He had accepted his fate long ago. Too late to wish again that he had brought some token from Fallon—some proof that he was from there. With such proof, Prince Andres would have very likely taken him in. Only when he had abandoned his attempts to convince the prince did Andres take pity on him and give him work in the stables. And here he had been for six years. But he knew he deserved no better, and no better would he ever have. He had abandoned Fallon, and in doing so, he accepted his fate. One could not hope to keep family advantages when he did not share family values. He had dismissed the Fallon values well before his departure. In their innocence and ignorance, the people of Fallon clung to the words of a nonexistent goddess—words in a book written long ago that promised prosperity from waters that could be nothing more than the result of northern climatic changes.

The Book. The precious Book that all of Fallon believed to be either the handwriting of Morrigan herself or those inspired by her. But Bairre knew better. Too many generations had passed for the Book's origin to be confirmed. Only the Book itself stood as evidence of how it came to be written. And that was no evidence at all. Occurrences to date that seemed to fulfill the Book's prophesies were nothing more than coincidence born of time. Time in itself is the mother of all happenings, and if sufficient time elapses, most things will come to pass sooner or later. Only the ignorant believed otherwise.

He had to number his mother among the believers. She and Mikael. And old Esras. He had come to love the old man, much like he had loved his father, who had died too young. Iona had endured the grief of Svein's passing, and then the suffering of a widowed mother responsible for two hungry sons. The combined tragedies that fell upon her should have been proof enough to her and the entire clan that no goddess looked after them. But the poverty was not the reason he had left. No, it was much deeper than that. Poverty, he could have survived. If there was any good thing that came from the misdirected lives of the Fallonese, it was that the Book prohibited the people from allowing one of their numbers to suffer starvation, cold, or sickness, if remedies were available. Bairre missed that. How starkly different were the unforgiving slums of Sogg compared to Fallon Valley.

But he had made his choice, and here he would stay. He could not live the lie that Oriana forced upon the valley people. To partake of their goodness and to accept their charity while not being weak-minded enough to believe the fabricated teachings had been far too oppressive. The force of that had pushed him from his own home, and away from his needful mother and doting brother.

How cruel he had felt the day he left while Mikael pleaded with him to stay. Cruel indeed it had been to abandon the child and his mother, to leave them to whatever means of support they could design. Iona understood; he had seen that in her eyes. "Too much like your father," she had said. Perhaps she had explained it to Mikael. Perhaps Mikael saw it more clearly now. Perhaps not. Either way, the thing was done, and in six years time, surely they had adjusted. Even if Mikael remembered him unkindly, he would have adjusted by now. He probably still spent the afternoons sitting by the river, trying to fathom the mysteries that Oriana and his mother had said lived in its depths.

The river—a gift, if one were inclined to believe Oriana, but in reality the emerald-green flow was no more than melt water from the northern sector of a warming continent. Certainly, it belonged to the people of Fallon, but not by divine right. Humans and Elkana held land and water rights because of political boundaries, nothing more. And those rights and boundaries were no stronger than the people that held them, or the fear that kept others away. If the Fallonese were strong, or if their neighbors were weak, it had nothing to do with gods or books or rivers. Politics alone controlled the destiny of any race. The fact that Alsandair believed Morrigan existed was simply another political advantage the Fallonese held. Should they lose that...who knew what would happen?

ꜰoᴜʀ

The silent depths of hope, and the holdings thereof, shall be more to him than to any other, for her blood is in him. And he shall come to that knowledge.
—Book of Morrigan

Mikael felt the tremors before he saw the witches. The ground trembled sufficiently to crack the ice in the creek that he and Esras had just stepped across. The several witches, all robed in white, knelt in a circle, leaning back with their arms interlocked. They appeared to be sitting on their feet.

In the center of the circle stood two Elkana women, their faces plainly visible in the afternoon light that filtered through the branches. One was definitely older than the other. The elder's robe was hoodless, unlike those of the coven that knelt around her. She held an athame, a black, double-edged dagger, which she moved in a circular motion above her head. She was tall and slim, and her thin black hair shown even on this overcast day. All eyes were closed, and all faces were raised toward the gray sky. A low and steady murmur, like moving water, arose from the circle and fused naturally with the permanent sounds of the forest.

Mikael stood transfixed, not seventy-five paces from the witches. Never had he seen the like, and never had he seen an Elkana, much less an Elkana witch. Esras jerked him toward dense brush and then pulled him to the ground.

"They're doing that," Esras whispered. "They're making the ground move."

"Why?"

"I don't know, but you can bet it's got a purpose. This is a dangerous place to be. Come." He started backing away on his hands and knees.

"No, wait, Esras. Let's see what they're up to."

"We don't care what they're up to," Esras said. "It's not our concern. Unless…"

At that instant the older witch spotted them. How she saw them through the thick brush, neither Mikael nor Esras could tell.

"Intruders!" she cried. "Spies!"

Mikael nocked an ash arrow to his bowstring. "Are we in danger here?" he asked Esras, but Esras was no longer there to hear him. Mikael turned to look for him, momentarily taking his eyes off the upset witch. "Damn you, old man," he said aloud.

He turned back to face the white-robed women and was shocked to see them moving toward him. All of them. Maybe they were mad at him for breaking up their ceremony. He stood his ground and elevated the bow to make sure they saw it. If they did, they were not deterred. Fifty paces away now, and spreading out, making their way through and around the intervening scrub brush.

Esras had retreated, and Mikael now wondered if he should do the same. Thirty paces now. The tall one, the oldest, would be upon him in seconds. As she turned her head to check the progress of those with her, Mikael observed that her snout was longer than the others, and that trait gave her more of an animal-like appearance. Her black eyes were on him now.

At ten paces, she stopped and signaled with an uplifted and clawed hand that the others should approach no farther.

"Are you a spy, human?"

This close, Mikael saw the moisture at her nostrils. He quickly calculated his chances if it came to a fight. He faced about a dozen women. Girls, really. Most were no older than himself. But who could say what magic they possessed? He would kill the older one first if the need arose to defend himself.

"No," he said, deliberately lowering the pitch of his voice.

"Then what?"

"A traveler."

"To where?"

To answer another question would indicate weakness on his part. "Who's asking? And for what reason?"

"I am called Hulda, and I ask because spies don't live long in my company."

Her voice was raspy, even raw, but resonant. It held a terror he could not name. He would have to bluff her.

"You're more of a lizard than I am a spy, and I don't excuse myself to lizards. However, since you take me for a trespasser, and since I don't know upon whose lands I walk, I will take my leave of you."

"You'll leave when I permit it," Hulda said. "You've not answered my questions. Unless you do, I shall deal with you as I would a spy. Perhaps you should have fled with your friend."

"He didn't flee, lizard. He and the others with me are watching you now. I suggest that you return to whatever it is lizards do in the daytime, and leave us alone."

Hulda smiled at him through short, pointed teeth. "I can kill you with a word."

"Speak it, lizard." Mikael raised his bow to eye level. "It shall be your last."

The coven was gathering now, coming closer to Hulda, forming up for something. Mikael didn't wait to find out what that might be. He launched a white-tipped arrow at the mass of witches, only to see it pass harmlessly between two of them, the white fletching disappearing in the air among the snowflakes that had just started to fill the air. So much for gifts from goddesses. He turned and ran the way he supposed Esras had gone. But his strides were restricted somehow, as in a dream. His chest tightened, and he weakened. But still he ran, and he must have had sufficient lead on whatever it was the coven was trying to kill him with, for with distance, came relief. And then speed. By the time he slowed to a walk, the open places were white with fresh snow.

The witches could track him easily if they were so inclined. But they had no real reason to want him now, unless Hulda thought he should pay for shooting at them. Probably not though. His priority now was to find Esras. He would tell Esras in clear terms that a friend didn't abandon a friend in times of need. What had possessed the old man to run off like that?

He stopped and leaned against a leafless oak. His course had taken him back toward the river, but he had no idea how close he might be. Perhaps he should find the river and follow it upstream to Fallon. Yes, that was the thing to do, now that Esras had abandoned him in the wilderness. Even Oriana would understand him returning home.

"What took you so long?" Esras asked from a tangle of vines and saplings.

"Esras! You cowardly scoundrel! You left me to die. They were witches, and they would have killed me."

"But they didn't, Son of Svein. You're as alive as I."

"By my own wits, you old fool." Even in his anger, he was glad to have Esras back with him. "And thanks for the holy arrows of Morrigan, you witless twit. I missed the whole lot of them."

"Because you shot at the whole lot of them." Esras seemed not at all bothered by Mikael's insults. "The arrows are joined to your specific intent, and you had none when you wasted that arrow. You should have selected a specific target, not an entire coven of witches."

"I don't believe that."

"You will," Esras said as he stepped toward him. "In time, you'll believe that and so much more that your immaturity will not let you accept now." He stopped in front of Mikael. "But we've no time for that now. It's good that you didn't shoot one of them, or they would have followed you to avenge the loss. As it is, they've something else on their mind, more important than a boy with a bow."

"Like what?"

"I know now," Esras said. "I know what they were doing. They were practicing. At least I hope it was practice."

"For what?"

"To raise the Fallon. To steal it, or pollute it." Esras sat down in the light snow, looking back in the direction from which they'd just come.

"What are you talking about, Esras? It was just a small earthquake. We've felt those at home."

"Yes, small. That's why I say it was only practice. But if they can make the earth move a little, perhaps they can make it move a lot. Perhaps enough to raise the river."

"That's ridiculous," Mikael said. "I'm surprised at you. I thought you had some measure of common sense."

"Mikael, listen." Esras stood. "We've got to get to Alsandair. He must know of this. Perhaps he can stop it."

"Are we not returning home? Have you not had enough of these godless lands? Even Oriana would advise you to return."

"She would not, and she has not. We've already spoken."

"Spoken? When?"

"While we ran. It's more than you can understand now, Mikael. But believe me, she's aware of the witches and their purpose. She tells me to get to Sogg and Alsandair with all speed. Only when this matter is concluded will we have time to search for Bairre."

Mikael simply stood and stared. What could he say to such as that? Esras actually believed he had been in contact with Oriana, and that Oriana had explained their situation to him.

Apparently reading his thoughts, Esras said, "It's a gift. Some of the elders possess it. Oriana is the youngest known to me who has it. Perhaps the Goddess Morrigan gave it to her because of her station. I don't know. I know only that I've had it since I was eighty. I expect, because you are the One, you will attain it at an early age. Perhaps even sooner than Oriana did."

Mikael shook his head as if to rid himself of Esras' foolish talk.

"We'll circle the witches," Esras said. "Apparently, they didn't consider us worth pursuing. Because you lingered among them, they're certain that we're human, but they don't know we're from Fallon, or we'd be dead. Come now, we're still several days from Sogg."

At dusk, Mikael and Esras inadvertently walked into Ranga, that hilly country of Elkana dens. Some of the den entrances were out in the open on the sides of ridges, plainly visible now by the light from the clearing but dying western sky. Others dens were less conspicuous. Some had been dug at the base of massive trees, while others had been deliberately constructed behind screens of vines and brush. The smell of freshly turned earth and disturbed forest floor litter permeated the breezeless air. If not for the footprints in the soft soil, one would think the town was abandoned.

"Why do they hide?" Mikael asked.

"They don't hide, Son of Svein. They are simply at home. Did you expect a greeting?"

"I expect the respect due a human of Fallon. I'll have that or I'll not linger here. What do I care to talk to an Elkana?"

"You are from Fallon?" The voice was behind him.

Mikael turned. Although startled, he was thankful he hadn't jumped. Seated on his haunches at the entrance to a den was the first Elkana Mikael had ever seen, other than the witches. This one was three-quarter-human size. Mikael noted its short snout, like that of a lizard. The slick, moist skin of its face seemed a contradiction to the dry and leather-like hide of its exposed neck and arms. It wore trousers and a kind of shirt constructed of a canvas-like material, and no shoes. It seemed oblivious to the chill of the fading day.

Esras stepped between Mikael and the lizard and bowed. "Yes, we came down the river to its end. We have walked from there, traveling to Sogg. Please forgive the trespass."

Mikael heard the meekness in Esras' tone, and was angered, but he said nothing, not wanting correction in front of a stranger, even an Elkana.

"Introductions first, please," said the Elkana. He scooted off the diggings and took one step toward Esras. "I am Hannes."

Mikael could read nothing in Hannes' face. Perhaps the Elkana had no physical expressions.

"I am Esras Aronson. This is my companion, Mikael Sveinson."

Hannes tilted his head slightly. "You have two names each?

"It is our way," Esras said. "A means to keep track of families."

Hannes seated himself, cross-legged in the dirt. "I do not understand. Do you not know your families?" Hannes blinked his eyes, and Mikael saw that his eyelids were a pale yellow. Tiny wrinkles appeared under those eyes, and Mikael interpreted that as an expression of puzzlement.

Esras sat down in a like fashion. When Mikael did not, Hannes looked directly at him, the wrinkles now more prominent. Only when Esras turned his head back toward Mikael did he take the hint and sit down. He felt foolish. Why bother with this dirt digger?

"My father's name was Aron," Esras said. My name is Esras. I am Esras, Son of Aron. Esras Aronson. Do you see?"

"I have heard that humans are unnecessarily complicated. Did your father carry such a burden?"

"We don't think of it as complicated. But yes, my father was Aron Langason, or Aron, Son of Langa. We keep the names as a token of respect, and as a means of recording our ancestry."

Hannes nodded at Mikael. "So you are Mikael, Son of Svein. Mikael Sveinson."

"Yes." *Enough of such talk*, he thought.

"Mikael Sveinson, are you the promised one?"

The question struck him with hard surprise. Why would an Elkana ask that? What could one of his race know of human religions? And how could Esras, Oriana, and now this Elkana, have the same ridiculous notion? He could not verbalize a response.

"It is believed that he is," Esras said. "If he is, he has much to learn."

"Esras, that's enough. You've told this man…this creature, where we're from and where we go. Will you insult me now in his presence? It's time we go."

Esras kept his tone even, his voice steady. "Do you see, Hannes? It's a matter of maturity, I think. He is young."

"Ah, youth," Hannes replied. "A splendid time. I remember well." He smiled.

Mikael saw the gray lips part, revealing pointed teeth. He hated the lizard for agreeing with Esras.

"It's from youth," Hannes said, "that the promised one will come. My father and his spoke of such a savior. But many of my race have forgotten. Only a few of the others believe it to be more than a myth. But I know. That's why I sent Zienna among the witches."

"Zienna?" Esras asked.

"My daughter. They killed her, but not before she discovered their vile intentions. Their plans tell me it's time for the promised one."

Mikael shivered. He wanted to hear no more. How could it be that the Elkana knew of the so-called promised one for generations past, yet he had only recently heard of such a person being mentioned in the Book? There was some trickery afoot by Oriana and Esras, and now the lizard.

"They plan to raise your river," Hannes said. "They want the Fallon for their own, to pollute it, to exploit it, to steal its power. With that power, they will go against the kingdom. Should that occur, we are all lost to the ages, except for the intervention of the promised one."

He looked at Mikael then, and his eyes darkened. "Seek the wisdom of your elders, Son of Svein. Accept the flow and the weight of your river. Give yourself to her, for without you she will die, as shall we all."

Esras was nodding his head, like he was hearing something he had known all along. That was too much. Mikael exploded.

"Esras, you're a fool! A gullible and witless fool. Either that, or the master of lies. I've been lied to time and again since my mother's death. I'll travel with you no farther unless you explain this deceit."

"There's no deceit, Son of Svein. You've felt it yourself, yet you continue to deny. The Fallon is inside you, Mikael. It's part of who you are, and you cannot flee from that. Are you so afraid of the responsibility?"

Mikael rose to his feet and stalked away, leaving Esras and Hannes in the darkening glade.

***

His rage carried him through woods and meadows unknown, deep into the starless night that became blacker than his mood. The expected chill was less severe because of the cloud cover that held the day's minimal warmth close to the earth. But still, Mikael wished he had his bedroll. He had been stupid to leave it with Esras. The lizard probably owned it now.

He would go home. He would let Esras fend for himself; the old fool deserved no better. At Fallon, Mikael would take possession of his mother's hut and he would keep himself away from the temple and Oriana. When she learned of his return, he would tell her plainly to leave him alone and to not count him among her congregation, for he no longer trusted her, and he would tell her that even though he did not as yet know her motive, he recognized her deceit.

He sat at the base of an evergreen and leaned against it. He would sleep. Tomorrow, the dawn skyline would give him direction. He closed his eyes, but the sleep he needed would not come. The wildwood chirped, hooted and rustled from every direction. These sounds he knew, and there was no concern, except that he was alone. Esras had been close by before when their camps were made and the music of night settled in. The sounds had been a comfort then, but only now did he realize it. Alone he was, and lost—lost in a darkness that came not only from the hour, but also from his losses. His mother dead, his friend estranged, and his religion toppled. Perhaps the Goddess Morrigan did not exist. Perhaps the Book was the work of Oriana, or those of her kind. Perhaps Bairre was right.

Embracing that thought, he slept. He felt Oriana's touch in his sleep, and he followed Esras toward Sogg. Hannes, the Elkana, appeared too many times in his dreams before the late dawn allowed him to open his eyes to a drab grayness that lay over the woods like the blanket he did not have. Hunger and eagerness to be away pulled him to his feet. Too early, he thought, for the sun to lighten the eastern sky. Minutes later, he realized the overcast day would become no brighter. A light drizzle started—the kind of unmoving winter drizzle that lingered for days.

He had made a mistake to come here without thought of direction, and without provisions. He had his bow and his quiver of arrows, including those of ash that Esras had given him. One of those he had fired at the coven. Nineteen remained. If he could find game, and the temperature held, he would survive until the weather cleared. Then, with the sun to give him direction, he would know where the Fallon flowed, and once upon her banks, it would be a simple matter to follow her upstream to the valley.

Yes, the Fallon would take him home. The Fallon was his hope now. Mikael let his mind see her sunlit depths, and he longed for her. He thought of her clarity, her purity, and the comfort he owned in her presence. She was his provider, his reality, his lover. He needed her, and never had he felt that need as strongly as he did now, standing drenched and alone in a gray wilderness that offered no pity and no avenue of escape.

"Fallon," he whimpered, "lead me."

And suddenly he knew. The Fallon lay to his right, many leagues distant. He saw her and felt her clearly now, her silent depths and her nourishing chill. But she did not beckon. Then why did she show herself to him in his mind? Why would she give him a glimpse of her loveliness and her location, and not invite him to come? Did she not know he was absent and in need?

"No." He heard the word as clearly as if it had been audible. Through his clearing thoughts came the Fallon's need, and it was he that she needed, but not where her purling flow cut the wildwood. Somewhere else then. Where? Sogg? Mikael fell to his knees on the sodden forest floor.

"Fallon, do not send me there. I am not the One. I cannot be. I'm but a peasant of your valley, an orphan of no means even to support myself. What can I do for my people, or for you, that another with resources and courage could not do better?"

The silent evergreens, motionless in the breezeless air, whispered nothing at all to him. The naked limbs of the hardwoods stretched out, upward and away from him, offering nothing. Even the soft drizzle made no sound as it fell and covered the woods that seemed void of any life. But in that silence the possibility of his true identity screamed at him, deafening his mind to all else. Maybe he was the One. The burden of that fell around him here, where he was alone, soaked, cold and hungry, and it was too much for his mind to bear. He fell from his knees to his face, and the wet leaves and the smell of rot made his misery complete.

Why him? Why not Esras, or Oriana, or one of the Fallon warriors who had proven himself to be above the ordinary?

"I cannot," he said aloud as he pushed his face away from the cold ground. He stood and turned his face toward the Fallon. "I'll fall before I've even risen to the cause. Choose another, Morrigan. Not me. Not me."

Silence answered him a second time. The standing and fallen timber, the rotted stumps, and the boulders took a shape not their own. Through the mist he saw Esras, Hannes and horses. The air stirred and pushed falling moisture at his face. A squirrel scurried across the leaves from one tree to another, bringing just enough disturbance to the silence to terminate the apparition. Mikael came to understand in that moment that dead silence was the key to communication. He would find Esras, and Esras would have horses. How it was he understood that, he did not know, but even in this desolate place he no longer felt alone.

He walked with renewed strength toward the trees and boulders that were now only that.

By early afternoon, the dark and heavy sky had lightened enough for Mikael to know he was headed west. That fact meant nothing now because he no longer required compass direction. He was headed toward Esras, and that was enough. He came upon him by nightfall under a wind-torn sky that was thick with stars.

Esras sat by a low fire that was shielded from the wind by a bank of logs that still clung to their rough bark. He was cooking something, and the smell of it reminded Mikael he had not eaten today.

"I'm back, Esras," he said.

"I can see that, Son of Svein. And sooner that I expected."

"Expected?"

"Yes, it was a necessary delay for us."

"Perhaps."

"What have you learned, Mikael, in your absence?"

"Learned?" He somehow could not give the old man the satisfaction of being right again.

"Yes, learned. What do you know that you didn't know when you left me?"

"I've learned nothing, except that you would have left me out there to starve."

"Sit, my friend. Eat. It's some sort of fowl. Hannes gave it to me."

"Hannes? Is he nearby?"

"Of course. His den is there." Esras pointed through the dark with the stick he had been using to tend the fire.

"This is the Elkana town?"

"The same. I waited here, knowing you would return, knowing the Fallon would lead you back."

They sat without speaking for a while, and Esras shared his meal. He pretended to have had enough before the bird was finished, understanding Mikael's hunger.

Esras asked, "If you've learned nothing, how is it you found me in the dark?"

"All right, Esras. I did come to a certain understanding of my situation. Perhaps there is something to this threat against the Fallon. Perhaps we can do something about it." He would give him no more than that for now. "Are there horses here?"

"Horses?" Esras grinned. "Why would you ask that? Don't you know Elkana have no use for horses? The Elkana can run nearly as fast as horses, and they have no possessions to carry. Why do you think there might be horses here?"

His widening grin was maddening.

"Horses or not, Esras? Can you not answer a simple question?"

"No, there are no horses here. They're close by, though. Half-wild horses. We'll probably have to break them, but even with that delay, we'll save time. It's still quite a distance to Sogg."

Before Mikael could respond, a great shaking of the earth occurred. The fire disappeared into a chasm that suddenly opened up between Mikael and Esras. Through the almost total dark, Mikael heard tree branches clattering against one another, stones rolling, and water gushing. Suddenly, the forest in the immediate area was full of light, and Mikael saw that many Elkana stood outside their dens holding torches. As difficult as it had been for Mikael to read expression in Hanne's features, there could be no question now that each of the Elkana was filled with fear. Their eyes darted from one sector of the forest to another as if they might see the source of terror. They trembled, and many, especially the younger ones, clung to their neighbors. Muffled screams came from some of the dens, and he knew that not all of the lizard folk would survive.

Esras' voice was as calm as before. "Hulda's coven is practicing again. It would seem they've improved. We haven't much time."

The new day had only vaguely lightened the woods when Esras awakened Mikael. "Hannes has prepared a breakfast," Esras said. His voice was low, soothing. "He's not slept. Through the night he dug into sunken dens for the dead. Yet he shows no emotion."

Mikael came fully awake, remembering the quake and the concerns he had slept with. "How many were lost?" he asked.

"Five are confirmed dead. One is missing. A child."

51

"What can we do for them?" Mikael asked, his concern genuine.

"Nothing, it seems. They don't grieve like humans. They accept death as an end that cannot be altered."

"Esras, we need to talk. Just what is it I'm expected to do? And just exactly who is Hulda?"

"We'll talk later, Son of Svein. Hurry now." Esras left him.

Mikael sat up to see Hannes and an Elkana female bent over the dying ashes of a fire. Hannes stirred something in a blackened tin pot, and the pungent aroma wafted to Mikael. Certainly, he had not smelled anything like it before. Perhaps he would pass on breakfast.

As he finished stowing his bedroll, Hannes came to him with the pot in one hand, and a horn cup in the other. Steam rose from both containers and dissipated in the morning chill.

"You have slept on frozen ground, my friend," Hannes said. "You will need these to restore your body and to see you through the day." He held the vessels toward Mikael.

"I'm sorry for your losses," Mikael said, and the statement felt weak. He accepted the vessels, but not with his mind made up to partake of the contents. "What is it?"

"It is strength, and it is our best. You honor me by being here, but even more so by eating and drinking with me."

He wondered how his presence might honor Hannes, but he let it go. He asked again, "What is it? I don't mean to be rude, but..."

"It is kralene and scandeele. Our best." He gestured to indicate which was which.

"I usually eat alone."

"Certainly. A human custom. I understand." Hannes walked away.

Mikael held the cup to his nose. Some sort of tea, he surmised. He sipped, and sipped again, finding it not objectionable. He drank it down as quickly as the temperature allowed and then turned his attention to the tin. Upon tilting the pot back and forth, the thick, yellow liquid sloshed over chunks of some kind of dark meat. He tasted the liquid and was reminded of the strong flavor of boiled sheep that his mother had prepared in years past. He fished the meat out with his fingers and devoured it. He was ready to go.

Mikael and Esras were out of the town within minutes, Hannes leading by several paces. Hannes carried a length of rope that Mikael assumed would be used to capture the horses. Esras walked with Mikael.

"Mikael, I must tell you some things you'll need to know."

"No kidding."

"About the horses…"

"Forget that for now," Mikael interrupted. "There are more important matters."

"No, no. This you must hear now, before we arrive."

"Arrive where?"

"At the village of Andor."

"Never heard of it," Mikael said quickly, anxious for Esras to get on with whatever he had to say.

"It's a small village much like Fallon, but without its benefits. Humans live there. Andor is their leader and he will object to our presence."

"Why?" Mikael immediately became suspicious that Esras was again leading him into something he would have trouble understanding.

"The horses are his, or rather they are in the territory he claims."

"You intend to steal them?"

"No, Son of Svein. 'Take' is a better word. We have the authority from Oriana, and thus from Morrigan. The mission comes first, even before honor."

"You've communicated again with Oriana?"

"Yes. She confirmed the horses are there. They are for our use."

"Are you lying to me, Esras? Would you say this directive is from Oriana just to gain my cooperation in capturing the horses?"

"I will forgive your blasphemy. You are young and you will learn. You've learned some things already, am I correct?"

"I've reconsidered things. Can we leave it at that?"

"As you wish. But before we go too deeply into what must be accomplished, you must trust your inner self. I think you've begun to do that."

"What about this Andor? Will he resist?"

Esras stopped and confronted him directly. "Hannes is sure that he will, if he sees us. The village is several warriors strong. He and his men will fight to keep what they believe is theirs."

"As would we, Esras. It's a matter of honor." Immediately he remembered what Esras had just said about honor. "How far do you intend to go to secure the horses? What if it comes to bloodshed?"

"We'll not leave without two good horses. Be clear about that. We'll do whatever is necessary to that end. If it's any consolation, Andor and his followers are not people who recognize King Alsandair as their sovereign. He governs his own, unsanctioned by the realm. Heathens, Hannes has said, without religion of any kind. And you need to recognize that we not only have the need, we have the means."

"What means? You're saying we'll kill, aren't you?"

"Yes. Have you forgotten the arrows of ash?"

"What of them?"

"When you shoot, think of killing that which you shoot at. Think of nothing else. The arrows will fly true for you."

"For me?"

"For no one else. It is the gift of Morrigan to Fallon's hope."

A lie, Mikael thought, to bolster his confidence should the need arise. Perhaps it would not be such an evil thing to take wild horses which really belonged to no one. But how could he fight strangers, especially human strangers, for horses he hadn't even known existed until last night? Was their mission so important? Then he thought of the earthquakes and Esras' concern. Yes, he would kill humans to save the river.

They walked until the sun was halfway through its arc before Hannes halted. "The herd is just ahead," he said. "I can smell them." His black nostrils open and closed several times. "I believe they're in a meadow, or perhaps a marsh. We will go in together, and as soon as they spot us, I will give chase while you stand guard."

Hannes looked first at Esras, then at Mikael, as if asking for assurance that they understood. "If the humans see me, or you, they will attack. Guard me well."

Mikael pulled one of the ash arrows from his quiver. Archery had not been one of his better endeavors during training at Fallon. Never had he thought he would aim his bow at another man.

They proceeded at a much slower pace, Hannes still leading. He stopped them again at the edge of a sun-painted clearing. Marshy it was, and overgrown with shrubs and young trees. Seven or eight dark colored horses grazed on the upper end of the clearing. The one stallion continually raised his head, checking for danger.

Hannes crept forward, keeping low. Mikael tested the wind and found it to be in the lizard-man's favor. He followed Esras into the clearing, and suddenly, he smelled smoke, then he saw it at tree level. Simultaneously, he and Esras realized they were positioned between the horses and what was probably Andor's village.

Hannes singled out a gelding, which was now eyeing him suspiciously. The stallion snorted, and the herd was in a run all at once, toward the smoke.

Perhaps they knew somehow that Hannes was an intruder, and that safety lay closer to the humans they were accustomed to seeing.

Hannes sprang toward the young gelding. Mikael momentarily forgot his duty to keep watch as the pursuit played out. Unbelievably, the lizard-man was faster than the horse. The gelding swerved toward the tree line on its left, but too late. The noose settled around its neck and drew tight. In moments, Hannes had the animal tethered to a tree. As he bolted for the one other mount that was needed, several arrows struck the ground Hannes had just traversed. The village warriors had apparently been alerted. Mikael saw the archers a good hundred paces away, coming out of the trees, too far away to hit anything. But they were advancing.

Whether he wanted it or not, Mikael was now on the defensive. An arrow nicked his shirt, and another whistled close overhead. Esras was worrying with what appeared to be a foot wound. Why was he here anyway? He had no weapon. The fool would get himself killed.

A second wave of warriors stepped through the ranks of those who had just released their arrows. These had spears, and they were charging. The distance decreased rapidly while Mikael's thoughts raced. He nocked the ash arrow to his bowstring as he came to a decision. Whether or not he should have been involved in the horse stealing was a mute point. The situation now was kill or be killed.

He drew his bow fully, his eyes locked on a running warrior seventy yards distant, and apparently one of the leaders, as he was out front. Just as he released the string, the warrior stepped to one side, obviously having seen the shot. The white, helical fletching gleamed under the noonday sun, its course doomed to failure because of the warrior's quick wit. But then it seemed to Mikael that his arrow grazed an invisible obstacle in midair, because it changed direction slightly, and a second later, the charging warrior lay dying, both hands on the ash shaft that protruded from his chest.

A slight tremor of hesitation slowed the attack. Instantly, Mikael had another arrow on its way across the sixty yards that separated him from death.

This one split the heart of a tall man who was raising his slim, stone-tipped spear as he ran. A third arrow streaked against the blue sky, and a third heart beat no more. The rush of men stopped. As he placed a fourth on the string, Mikael saw that the attack was over, at least for now, as the warriors were fleeing back toward the smoke.

Esras was on his feet and limping toward him. Hannes and the horses were nowhere in sight.

"To the woods, Mikael! The woods!" Esras was screaming.

But Mikael waited until he could lay hands on the old man, so that he might help him to be away.

"Where is Hannes? Did he get the horses?" Mikael asked.

They entered the protective darkness of the thick woods and half-ran and half-walked away from the clearing. Almost immediately, they found Hannes holding the gelding and a mare. The animals, nearly identical in height, snorted and pulled at the ropes. Their eyes were open wildly wide. The gelding tried to rear at Mikael and Esras' approach, but Hannes held it.

"They smell blood. Is one of you wounded?"

"I am, slightly," said Esras. "My foot. It is nothing."

"You've no time now to see to it." Hannes looked at Mikael. "Are you trained to ride? Can you handle horses as wild as these?"

"Is there a choice?" Mikael asked. He was surprised at his own calmness. "Help me get Esras astride the mare. She looks somewhat gentler. You can ride with me."

"No. I will return home. The humans will seek retribution, but not in blood. They will know the horses were not for me or for any Elkana, as my people have no use for animals of any kind, except for food. As for you, I would not linger here." He went to Esras and helped him to the mare's back. It sidestepped, bucked once, and was quiet.

"I am proud," Hannes said, "to have been able to serve you, Mikael Sveinson, for I know you. Godspeed."

And with that, he was gone. Mikael last glimpsed him as he jumped a wide deadfall with the grace of a deer. As Mikael leaped astride the gelding, the ground moved.

five

And a certain few of the valiant dead shall watch for the living.
—Book of Morrigan

Demon, Mikael named the gelding, because of the torment it inflicted upon him by its ornery nature. He could understand the independence and spirit of a stallion causing a certain measure of problems for its would-be master, but those traits should not be so prominent in a gelding. Demon bit him, pushed him, and disobeyed him continually. Perhaps he had associated the earthquake with being mounted by Mikael because the two events had occurred simultaneously.

That third quake had been much worse than the two previous ones, although not as close. Even now, three days later, he and Esras were still seeing evidence of the witches' improving prowess. Huge boulders now rested far from where they had stood like sentinels for hundreds of human generations. Some of the root balls created by falling trees were higher than Oriana's temple. Creeks ran where there had been no creeks before, and some smaller streams had disappeared altogether.

"It will be easier for the coven," Esras said, "when the ground has completely thawed. "Their strength must be formidable indeed for them to move and rend as much of the earth as they have succeeded in doing. But still, Hulda will need many times the power they have shown, if they are to raise the Fallon."

Esras' mare broke the thin ice of one of the newly created streams as the horse carried him across into denser timber that reached toward a clearing sky. The gentle mare was almost as dark in color as Demon. She was by far more graceful in her moves, and more respectful to her human master. Esras had begun to show an emotional attachment in the short time he and the horse had been together. He brushed her longer in the evenings than necessary, and twice Mikael had overheard him talking to her as if she could understand his words of affection. Over and over Esras used the name Elsa, and Mikael wondered at that.

The smell of the horses and the late-winter air brought a peaceful contentment to Mikael that he had not felt since before the loss of his mother. If not for the weight of their mission, he might be simply following Esras on a hunting expedition, or returning home from such a foray.

Home. How far away it seemed, and how simple his life had been before. He had tended to his mother's needs and kept their home in good repair. He trained for the conflicts that no one expected to come. He hunted and gathered, and he prepared meat and collected foodstuffs for storage. That was all he had been responsible for, which left him time aplenty to sit by the Fallon, or immerse himself in her wonders, which now were threatened, according to Esras and Hannes.

"Esras, I need to know about Hulda and her kind. What have you learned?"

"Hannes told me all that his daughter told him. Hulda is apparently possessed by an evil beyond mortal comprehension. How many of the ash arrows have you?"

"Sixteen. Why?"

"The coven is ten in number, including Hulda. By now, there may be more. You must be careful with the arrows, Mikael."

"I had no opportunity to recover the ones I used. But I saw the magic they possess. The shafts followed my thoughts."

"It's not magic, Son of Svein. Learn that. It's far more than any wizard or witch's concoction. It is the gift of Morrigan to her own—an ancient power held until now. Do not waste it."

"Have I intentionally wasted the four arrows I no longer hold?" Mikael's question was not sarcasm. He had seen the arrows' power, and his concern was genuine.

"From what I saw, Mikael, you did what was necessary. But I pray that our future encounters with those we must fight will be less costly."

They rode on, Esras leading. The day warmed, and a few of the spring birds hopped and chattered among the branches that still showed no signs of budding. Mikael knew that Esras had not answered his question about Hulda, but he also knew that Esras would not forget his need to know. Esras interrupted that very thought.

"Hulda, Hannes said, is tall for an Elkana woman. And she is lean, even skinny. It is believed she eats little, and takes her nourishment from her powers of magic. She has a longer snout than most of those of her kind, and longer hair. It extends from the sides and back of her head and neck down beyond her shoulders. Black, it is, and much thinner than what one might expect on an Elkana. She is pretty by their standards. Her skin is smooth and not so leathery. Does that describe the woman you met?"

"Indeed it does. Do you know where Hulda is now—where she stays?"

"No. Hannes knew only the location of the coven's meeting place, which undoubtedly has changed since his daughter's death. We can't find Hulda without assistance from the realm. We go there first."

"Can't Oriana help us? You said that you have contact with her."

Esras turned his head toward Mikael and let the mare pick her way through the sunless forest.

"Even the priestess' knowledge is limited in that regard. The task is ours." He leaned forward then and whispered into the mare's ear, as if the two of them held a secret about the matter. "And then there's Kattrin. We must not underestimate her abilities. Hannes thinks her power almost equals that of Hulda's."

"Kattrin?"

"An Elkana witch, second only to Hulda. You'll know her by her green eyes, a very rare occurrence among the Elkana."

Mikael tried to recall the appearance of the hooded witches with Hulda, but he remembered none with green eyes. Having been face-to-face with Hulda, his doubts had lessened to the point that he now listened intently to Esras' description of the witches. The witches and the danger to the Fallon and its people were all too real, and he must start now to absorb as much information as possible about his enemies. Yet, his childhood pulled at him, wanting the entire matter to go away. Why could this thing not be put off until he was grown and had received full warrior status? Then perhaps he would have the confidence he needed and the eagerness to do battle. But not now. He thought of the undines and their peaceful existence. To be with them now and be shed of this burden was his wish. But then it was partly for the water creatures that he must continue toward Sogg.

Sogg. How much farther? How would he and Esras be received? He considered Bairre, and the possibility that he had already introduced himself to the prince, maybe even Alsandair himself, which would be a great advantage to Mikael and Esras. If the king held Fallon in high regard like his mother had said, then Bairre probably had no problem in finding a place for himself within the castle. He wondered how Bairre would take the news of Iona's passing? Likely, he would wave the matter aside; her death could be of little consequence to him. Bairre had left his mother and the valley, proof enough that he had little attachment to home and family. Perhaps he shouldn't depend on Bairre for anything at all.

Fully a third of Artinus was affected in one way or another by the latest earthquake. In Sogg and throughout all the villages of human and Elkana, citizens went about repairing what damage that could be repaired. The event was considered a natural occurrence, for few had reason to suspect a coven of witches was determined to take what Hulda thought belonged to the Elkana species. But deep inside Ranga dens, Hannes and others who believed the reports of the now-dead Zienna discussed the matter at length.

Such discussions and the resulting smoldering suspicions were not something to be contained. Whispered rumors provided the fuel needed for concerned parents of pre-adult females to become disquieted by the possibility that their daughters might succumb to the intrigue of Hulda's power. A potential witch need not be inherently evil; wayward and gullible were characteristics that would suffice for Hulda's purposes. She could sway them once they were recruited. It was the numbers she needed most now, not permanent loyalty.

And eventually they came. Giggling juveniles and young women afraid of how little their futures held, came to Hulda. Like earthworms surfacing in moist soil, the Elkana females slithered through the warming nights to the secret coven meetings. A few human girls, glassy-eyed and bedraggled, arrived from some of the impoverished and disease-laden hamlets that were scattered across Artinus. How many had come, Hulda wondered, just to get away and to be part of something less dismal than the lives they had led thus far?

The half-circle of young faces glowing in the firelight and surrounding the queen and her princess soon became a full circle, and that circle steadily increased in diameter until Hulda felt confident she had the number she needed, considering that many would be eliminated during training. She must expect that some were here merely out of curiosity, and some would change their fickle, girlish minds before they could be turned to the dark side long enough for the deed to be accomplished. The third part of the more than forty she now had would probably attempt to turn back to the safety of their dens and huts. Depending on what those examples of failure learned in the interim, they may have to be killed. So be it. Another Zienna would prove disastrous.

Already, the meetings had been moved several times. The Great Swamp of Artinus was unending and unforgiving, a treacherous and watery desolation in summer, and a vast, unmarked and unmoving flatness of ice and trees in winter. Only Kattrin and a handful of trusted others were informed of the meeting locations. In that way, when the young Elkana women emerged from their dens to meet on the outskirts of their villages, they had no clue as to where they were being led, and thus no chance to inform those who might seek to thwart Hulda and the aspiring witches that she shaped to fit the singular design of her purpose. And as they scattered through the dawn woods when the meetings were adjourned, they were fully aware the next gathering would be held in an entirely different section of the dead and soggy lowlands. As it was tonight.

The assemblage of cold-skinned Elkana sat on stools, their clawed feet half buried in the cold mud. They gave little thought to their damp environs. Most dens were deep enough to be continually wet. Eons of evolution had made such conditions not just tolerable, but welcome. The few human girls shivered and huddled close to each other. Excluding human eyes, more than eighty vertically slit pupils were fixed on the black-robed Hulda and Kattrin, who stood by a fire in the center of a circle that had been formed by the humanoid lizards.

"A test for you tonight, children," Hulda said, her voice as calm and pregnant as the rustlings of the night swamp. "Some of you have been tried already, and have proven to be fit for advancement toward the end that is inevitable. I speak of power beyond your present pitiful comprehensions. I speak of honor and reward unimagined for those of you worthy to be partakers of my glory. A birthright, actually, for those who are truly mine."

Whispers wafted through the women like a night breeze, and by that, Hulda recognized that her grasp on them was yet insufficient.

"Do you imagine that I color reality? Or do you suspect I pervert the only truth that matters?" She let that settle. "You will know tonight, children, who among you will abandon childhood and family dens to be part of what I offer." She paused again.

"And what is my offer?" she asked them. "It's power, prestige and influence that no Elkana has ever known. It's position above the Fallonese, and it's authority over the rulers at Sogg."

No wind of inattention moved through them now. No girl consulted with any other. Each mind was hers, at least for the moment. She would anchor them now with something visual. She turned where she stood, pretending to scan the greenish faces within the circle of potential witches, but actually looking for the weak and crippled Elkana girl with lazy eyes whose limping arrival she had earlier observed.

"You," she said, pointing at the overweight youth. "Give me your staff."

"My walking stick, Miss Hulda? Why would you want it?"

The question represented nothing more than childish curiosity, a spontaneous inquiry, the result of surprise, and without intended disrespect, but Hulda seized the opportunity.

"You slothful pig!" she screamed. "Bring me the staff!"

The frightened girl lurched to her feet and stumbled. She fell heavily, splashing muddy slush onto those closest. She crawled to Hulda, holding the staff toward the unmoving queen.

"What is your name, child?" Hulda asked. No residue of unkindness marked her tone.

The girl stood erect, and Hulda accepted the maple staff. It was an inch in diameter, well seasoned, and as straight as a moonbeam.

"Mya, of Ranga," she answered.

"Mya, why do you need a staff?"

"My leg, Queen, is not straight. A birth defect. I must lean on the staff."

"Stand away from me, Mya." Hulda spoke so softly that only Mya heard.

Mya took two steps back and stood between the seated coven and Hulda. Hulda turned to Kattrin.

"What do you see, Princess?" Hulda held the staff toward Kattrin at arms length.

Kattrin didn't hesitate. "A serpent, Queen."

She cast the staff to the ground, and it slithered away from the heat of the fire. Straight for the startled Mya it crawled, and then it buried its fangs into the calf of her defective leg.

The coven gasped, shocked more by Hulda's power than by the swamp snake's attack. Some stood, and two rushed to Mya's aid, kicking at the snake that was now nothing but a maple stick.

"Leave her!" Hulda commanded. "Was it not my authority that caused the serpent to strike? Would you undo what I have done?" She rotated herself so that each girl might see her face. "For you new arrivals, this is your first test and your first lesson."

Mya sat in the mud, holding the stricken member, crying.

"Mya has no substance. She's weak, and would never be able to execute my commands. Nor would she be able to stand against attack, as you have seen. I have no need of weakness. Be seated."

All but one obeyed. A tall human girl Hulda had not seen before stood over Mya. Her greasy, matted hair spilled from under her hooded cloak as she bent over the wounded girl. She spoke.

"Queen, forgive me, but I know the snake. Its venom is deadly. The girl will die without aid."

Hulda recognized the girl's insincerity. Her movements were a little too dramatic, and her voice too steady. She wanted attention, nothing more.

"Identify yourself," Hulda said.

"I am Olafia, of Hitara. She stood erect and looked directly into Hulda's eyes, as if she were worthy of notice.

"Are all the women of Hitara as insolent as you? I made the snake, you stupid child. Think you there is something about it I don't know?"

Olafia's posture slackened some at that, and Mya's crying grew louder, her pleading sobs a pitiful sound in the near-dark swamp. The human girl stepped away from her and found a seat.

"There are those here," Hulda continued, "who already know they have made a mistake by coming. You cannot accept the death you see occurring before you now. You have been tested and you have failed. You know who you are. You cannot serve me. Although you may have the capacity to take upon yourselves the craft I teach, you cannot implement its practice, which occasionally means death to others. Those of you of whom I speak, leave this place now. I grant you that."

The whispers came again, among some. One rose, and then another, and another, until fewer than twenty girls remained seated, including the nine loyal young witches who had been with her through the winter. Those that stood, turned their backs on the queen and were absorbed by the swamp's blackness. Hulda noted that the tall human girl remained seated. Impertinent perhaps, but that could be adjusted.

Hulda counted. Including Kattrin and herself, they now numbered nineteen. That was enough, if the newcomers caught on quickly. The usual training period for full coven status was a year and a day, but Hulda had not that much time. So, the new arrivals would receive that part of witchcraft training necessary for the accomplishment of Hulda's purpose, and no more. They were disposable.

Those that had departed had nothing to report short of the murder done tonight, except of course that Hulda had some purpose for the group. That much she had revealed, but only that. Only Zienna had spoken of the Fallon, and likely, no one believed her. The Elkana would consider such an event impossible. And surely, if word ever reached Sogg, none of the royalty there would seriously consider that such a rumor might be true.

Even if someone did take it seriously, time itself prohibited interference. Alsandair had not time to find Hulda, much less stop her before these new recruits could be trained and the necessary spells cast that would give them some part of the tremendous power they would need. None of the coven, not even Kattrin, knew the full design of her plan. The Fallon was only part of it.

Hulda had worked it out in her mind many times over, and she had no doubt that when the earth calmed itself from the disruption she would achieve, the matter would be settled. If anyone knew now the specifics of her intent, the expected end result would very likely be considered unattainable, even unrealistic to some of the coven, perhaps even to Kattrin. That would not do. Hulda needed their full power, collectively, or else she would fail.

Already there were murmurings about Zienna's ridiculous prophesy of a child from Fallon intervening. No human had ever lived who could stand against an Elkana witch, much less an entire coven.

How ironic. Hulda's own kin at Ranga now despised her, and it was she who would give them back the valley. It belonged to them, but the generations of continued weakness had established a seemingly permanent acceptance of their existence. The valley was theirs, the Elkana, and through Hulda's endeavors, they would possess it. To their shame, the Elkana people would never be grateful to her for that, because in their weakness they saw her only as a murderous witch, not the redeemer that she was. So be it. She and a select few of the coven would govern them, necessarily.

She gazed out at the unknowing faces of the young women, seeing not what they were, but what they would be.

Then, she dismissed the coven with instructions to be ready at any time to be called into service. Soon, she told them, they would leave their families and their home dens forever to be one with their queen. That lie would hold their loyalty until the deed was done. She waited until they were gone, and all sounds of their sloshing steps had been drowned by distance. Then Hulda led

Kattrin deeper into the swamp, to her den.

They lay together, Hulda and young Kattrin, in the candle-lit dampness, deep beneath the anchoring roots of an oak. The milky reproduction slime exuding from their bellies thickened and dried between them, wasted because of the matching gender. Hulda stroked the child's leathery body with her darting tongue, and voiced her pleasure with the almost inaudible grunts of a mating female Elkana. Kattrin offered neither resistance nor assistance, but lay limp, her green eyes closed, accepting. She accepted Hulda as dominant, in sex as well as political position. It was enough for Kattrin, Hulda knew, that she would someday replace Hulda as queen. Not only witch queen, but queen of all Artinus.

Instinctively, Hulda knew like any of her kind would know, when dawn arrived. The recesses of a completed Elkana den, constructed partly by the owner's individual design preference, and partly by necessity, received no natural light. The den tunnels were constructed in a series of turns and sharp angles, so that no enemy or predator could traverse the corridors without some degree of confusion, which would slow its progress and give the resident Elkana time to prepare for battle or flee through a secret exit. Recently, because of the earthquakes, Hulda had reshaped the passageway to the main living area where Kattrin now lay sleeping.

Hulda replaced the spent candle with a fresh one. From a waterproof oilcloth, she produced flint, steel and tinder. She lit the candle from the resulting tiny fire, and the blackness receded into the moist dirt walls of the den to await the candle's demise. Kattrin stirred, but did not wake. Hulda gazed upon the young witch's face, and wondered at the beauty. Elkana were not lovely, even to each other. But Kattrin, even with her scaled eyelids closed over the green depths of luminous fascination that had first attracted Hulda, was comely indeed. Her overly full lips, more pink than gray, seemed perpetually to be pouting, and contrasted pleasingly with the faintest hint of dimples that teased and questioned, creating a mysterious intrigue. Her moist and smooth facial skin faded half way down her graceful neck, melding smoothly with the soft, leathery jacket of protective skin that covered her body. She was not slim, but full-bodied. Even at rest, she projected a healthy vigor and a certain calmness born of confidence.

Hulda allowed herself to imagine, perhaps believe, that her love was returned, that Kattrin saw beyond her queen's age and station to the strengths and wisdom of maturity. Surely, Kattrin knew that she was in Hulda's thoughts continually, that Hulda would care for her as no other could. With

Hulda, Kattrin would be secure and free to develop her natural abilities without interference.

Hulda arose, and touched the girl's hair before going up to recite her vows to the rising sun. She found the March morning not as warm as the previous few, and she stared not a little at the northern sky, where clouds gathered like frightened sheep, except these were gray, rolling together, becoming darker. Sunlight would not brighten the wildwood for long today. Unlike the other Elkana, Hulda would have welcomed it. Perhaps, she thought as she pulled her cloak tightly around her neck, there would be snow.

She walked eastward from her den to the clearing that allowed a full view of the brighter eastern skyline. She knelt and gazed directly into the early sun that the clouds would soon hide. The sun was the mother of the elements Hulda served and from which she drew her strength. Today was the first equinox of the year. Before the second, her purpose would be accomplished.

As the late spring blizzards of Artinus were prone to do, this one struck with sufficient raging fury to be remembered as the last of the season. The blast of frozen arctic air was a shrill lamentation, coming in gusts, bawling and wailing, bemoaning the ending winter. Ahead of the wind and driven by it, an eighty-mile-wide wall of snow obliterated everything. What had been visible was no more. Even if a man could stand against the screaming onslaught long enough to peer through the seemingly solid barricade of whiteness, he would see nothing. The violence of the storm and the turbulence that had taken hold on this part of the world might appear deceptively less than reality due to the lack of contrasts, for contrasts are few and barely discernible where white is the only color.

The gurgling and whispering waters of the river competed not at all in volume with the cyclonic wind that tore through the darkening Fallon Valley. The muffled human voices under the snow, indeed below ground level, were not pitched with despair, or even with anxiety. The Fallonese, people of the north lands that they were, knew how to cope with winter and winter storms. Well provisioned, they were, and content to wait it out. Such were their lives; some sun, some snow. This was nothing they hadn't seen many times before, and nothing they would not see again.

Only one risked the wind-tortured upper quarters of her abode. Oriana. She knelt before the painting of the Goddess Morrigan, her mind closed to the howling raw and bitter killer that violently demanded entrance through the north wall. She didn't hear the storm's shrieks of rage as it clawed at the timbers that trembled in terror, but stood firm. Oriana's trance, self-induced and solidly fixed, held her in place on the quivering oaken floorboards. Her gaze, a calmness flowing from half-open black eyes, bonded with the turned head of Morrigan, and gave no hint of the urgency that tore at her mind like the blizzard she could not hear. The Book lay open on the floor, and Oriana's fingers caressed the ancient lines that her eyes had read many times over.

"Where is my failure, Goddess?" she asked. Her words were whipped away from her lips by the snowstorm's clamor. But she continued, knowing that Morrigan received not the pitifully inadequate human sounds, but the songs of the minds and souls of her children. "You have shown me their refuge, but prevented my communication. How, Goddess, will they survive to fulfill your purpose? Did I not send them forth on your authority? Will you abandon me now, and leave them to die? Oh, Morrigan, I pray that you would turn your face to me, that I might look full upon you, and perish, but save him alive who would save Fallon."

She wept then, not for herself, but for Fallon. For Mikael and Esras, she wept, her tears falling upon and staining Morrigan's written words of hope that seemed to hold nothing now but the cold, the frozen tears, and the unholy icy flakes of slow death that had penetrated the sanctuary. She brushed all but the cold from the pages, closed the Book, and tried again to reach Esras.

One couldn't help but become wise in the ways of nature, having lived two hundred years beneath a sky that held written warnings of approaching weather. In his wisdom, Esras saw the blizzard in the afternoon sky before it struck. Behind the deceptive pale-blue clarity, darkening clouds tumbled together, combining strengths, laying claim to the entire sky. Between the bunched hoards of pregnant power, he saw patches of pinkish-green light, but the clouds soon took that, too. But even Esras could not predict the storm's severity. He led Mikael in a direction not consistent with their ultimate destination, and he found a deep ravine, a chasm some twenty feet deep, and more than a hundred paces in length. Here, at least they would have some protection against the coming winds. They settled Demon and Elsa in among the gray boulders, and stored their few possessions as best they could. Then Esras walked away, without a word, and Mikael left him to his private moments.

Esras sat on the frozen ground, and leaning back against a wall of rock, he released his mind to cross sixty miles of wilderness, searching for Oriana.

Not finding her, he assumed that the approaching storm was not as ferocious as the threatening sky and the changing air promised. Oriana would know if he and Mikael were in danger. He returned to Mikael, and found him sleeping.

Esras set about preparing a meal as the snow began to lay itself across the hostile terrain like a white curse. This would be their last full meal until game could be found and harvested. His tiny flame sprang up from the tinder, and he nourished it with bits of dry material from the ravine's floor. Just as he felt comfortable in feeding the little fire with substantial pieces of wood, the wind came. It arrived suddenly, like a cold and violent death, and the bright and living fire was killed. In that moment, Esras understood that the storm had already arrived in Fallon, and that the turbulence separating him and Oriana had prevented contact.

Mikael woke with a start. "Esras, what is it?"

"A flurry perhaps," he lied. "Maybe more."

"Have we anything to eat? I'm hungry." Mikael shivered, and crossed his arms over a chest protected by nothing heavier than his canvas shirt.

"We've a little raw venison, Mikael. But I doubt that we'll be able to cook it."

"You mean until the wind dies, right?"

Not answering the question directly, Esras said, "You'd best get your coat from the pack."

In the loaded silence that followed, Mikael realized the approaching front was in fact more than a flurry, and panic began to rise in his bosom. He retrieved his sealskin jacket from the ever-present canvas sack. He stood to don it, but no sooner was it on than he knew it would not be enough. He shivered again, and looked at Elias to find him staring.

"What?" Mikael asked.

"You must help me, Son of Svein." With that statement, Esras rose from the unborn fire and came to him. His gray beard, filled now with hardened snow crystals, moved not at all in the increasing wind. His pipe seemed frozen into his beard. "Sit with me, Mikael. Very close, facing me, and take my hands."

"Are you ill, old man? Do you jest?"

"I have lost contact with Oriana, Mikael. Can you understand that? The storm is too powerful. It prevents the link. We must try together, as one."

His old eyes were bright with intent. He sat down, cross-legged, and reached both hands toward Mikael. This was the second time Esras had mentioned contact with Oriana, but not yet did Mikael believe. Probably, he should humor Esras, give him what he wanted, for this might be their last hour. He sat, facing him, and received the offered hands into his own. He felt the coldness of those hands, the dryness, and the bulging joints of old age. He suddenly felt sorry for Esras. He would do this thing for him.

"Close your eyes, Mikael. Don't think of the wind or the cold, or of me. Forget your hunger and your fear. Think only of Oriana. Only Oriana. Can you remember her face, Mikael?"

Esras' voice, barely audible in the roar of air through the ravine, soothed Mikael somehow. Indeed, he could remember Oriana's features, her smile, her warmth, her touch. He let himself go into that, not for the contact he didn't believe in, but for himself. She had sent him away, but still, the love and calm assurance she had displayed came back to him now, and he clung to it. He closed his eyes against the pelting snow, and saw her clearly. It was not Esras' cold hands he held, but the warms hands of Oriana.

Her warmth faded somewhat. He saw her still, but not as clearly. She seemed farther away, and in the space that separated them, and deep within the storm, he saw snow-covered huts, the dwelling place of humans. Fallon? No, the arrangement was wrong. Somewhere else. She led him beneath the snow, inside the huts, to one in particular now, where a family sat together in front of their hearth. The sweet serenity of the scene left him then, with only that one glimpse, and was replaced now by the wind-driven snow.

Still entranced, now he saw himself and Esras in the ravine, yet no light gave him the picture. He left the comparative comfort of the ravine with Esras, riding Demon not into the wind, but with it. The distance was short— less than a mile. Then, like a snow-laden pine bough, the vision cracked, was severed, and was gone.

Mikael opened his eyes to total darkness. How long had he sat here? He still held Elias' hands, and the storm still raged. Esras moved, then shouted.

"Did you see it, Mikael? Did you see the village?"

"I saw... something."

Esras stood, and pulled Mikael up with him. "It's that way," Esras screamed, as if Mikael could see him pointing. "With the wind. We go with the wind."

And with that, Esras was handing Demon's rein to Mikael, and then Esras and Elsa climbed out of the ditch, up into the killing ferocity of the blizzard. Mikael followed, pulling cruelly on the rein, coaxing the baulking Demon to blindly leave what little security the ravine offered. The depth of the snow surprised him. Two feet, at least. Again, Mikael wondered how long the vision had lasted.

Verbal communication with Esras was impossible, as was riding. Mikael would not have been able to see Esras even in daylight hours; such was the ferocity of the blizzard. They led the horses, and Mikael clung to Esras with his free hand. They let the wind push them to the southwest. Many times they stumbled and fell, and once they were separated momentarily, by inches or yards, Mikael would never know. But Esras found him, and Mikael's renewed grip on him was more like an embrace.

Two hundred paces from the ravine, the cold began to slash at their lives. It cut through coats and clothing, skin and muscle, bone and thickening blood. Mikael no longer felt Demon's rein in his hand; only by the pull against his arm did he know he still led the horse. He no longer felt the bruises inflicted by the numerous stones he fell against. The slapping, frozen branches of the wind-maddened trees pained him not at all as they slammed into his face and torso. He tasted blood momentarily, but then lost even that to the cold. He stumbled on, his mind frozen, except for the vision of the family at the hearth.

SÍX

But know a certain truth. Powers on earth, below the earth, and above,
are not all mine. So watch, children, and be ye vigilant.
—Book of Morrigan

Aingeal Zanesdottir, her hands and face black with soot, poked again at the chimney flu with a broom handle. Her mother fretted around her like a mosquito, moving in close for a look at her child's endeavors, and then backing away to avoid the falling ash and the heat from the low fire.

"It's stuck," Aingeal reported as she backed away from the hearth. "We'll have to get at it from the roof after the storm. It's not smoking too badly now, is it?"

As she turned, little Setanta, eleven years younger than his fifteen-year-old sister, squealed when he saw Aingeal's blackened face. Recovering quickly from his fright, he laughed.

"No, it'll be all right for now," Johanna said. "I don't like you working over the fire like that anyway. It's a wonder you didn't set yourself afire."

Aingeal tossed her head to clear her vision of fallen auburn hair. Almost red, it was, and too long and straight for a working girl doing the chores that were her father's before his death. She sat down on the raised stone hearth. The heat felt good against her back. "I'll need to go out for more wood before morning."

"Maybe not," her mother said. "You get ready for bed. If we need more wood, I'll get it."

Aingeal smiled. She glanced at the four pieces of dried oak beside her on

71

the hearth, and she knew they'd need more. The fireplace would hold ten such logs. Johanna would step into the blizzard if necessary to keep them warm, and that knowledge was a comfort, but Aingeal would be the one to go. Her youth gave her the needed strength, and even beyond that, she had what her mother lacked—confidence in her ability. Johanna lost more than her husband when Zane died. No longer did she have the zest for living that Aingeal remembered. Johanna doubted now. She doubted her own strengths, and she doubted that she'd be able to adequately care for her children.

Some of the more charitable citizens of the poverty-stricken hamlet of Hitara diminished Johanna's insecurities somewhat by providing for her and the children when need was greatest, but always, Johanna failed to completely mentally grasp those small gifts that in reality ensured the family's survival. She needed Zane, not because her husband had been a wizard of considerable talent, but because he had loved her, and now without that, she waited to die, wilting and withering like a winter garden.

Aingeal stepped around Setanta on her way to the front of the sunken hut. The boy giggled and grabbed at the hem of her dirty canvas skirt. At the door, she took her father's long and heavy wolf-skin coat from its peg.

"You'd best take a lantern," her mother said, "or you'll not find your way back."

"Don't you hear the wind, Mother?" She slipped the elongated hickory buttons through their leather loops. "A lantern wouldn't stay lit. I'll just keep a hand against the hut until I come to the barn. There's a lantern just inside the barn door that I can use to get the wood. And I need to check on Rose, so I'll be a few minutes getting back."

Setanta squealed again as the rush of night air swept into the hut, bringing more than a little snow. Aingeal would have laughed at that, but it took all her strength to close the pinewood door against the wind. She braced her moccasins in the knee-deep snow to keep from being blown away from the door as her fumbling fingers found and worked at the crude latch. Only then did she realize she'd have to fight and find her way back, straight into the wind and in total darkness, with her arms full of wood. The screaming wind warned her to go back inside. It pulled her long hair straight out from her head, scolding her for not wearing a hat. For a moment, she considered abandoning the chore, but no, her mother would want the fuel for the breakfast fire even if they didn't need it that night.

Keeping her right hand against the thatching of the hut, she pushed through the deepening snow toward the stable. Now she faced an interval of about twenty feet where there would be nothing but the wind's direction to guide her, because the hut and the barn were that far apart. She hesitated there, thinking maybe she'd hear the animals, and then almost laughed, knowing she'd hear nothing above the roar of the blizzard.

Confident that the wind's direction was constant, she let herself be carried away from the hut. Not having its support, she fell. For an instant, she was under the snow and out of the wind. Then, she was up and moving. A minute later, her outstretched hands found the barn. Weakened now by her efforts and the cold, she fell hard against the structure, pushed cruelly by the unrelenting wind. Once inside, she thought, she'd have to rest a short while before heading back.

The vertical boards of the barn told her that she had not arrived at the door as she should have. Left or right? She tried to remember if her fall had caused her to veer one way or the other. Guessing, she sidestepped to the left, searching the rough boards with bare and freezing hands for the door's latch. How foolish she had been to come out with no more than a coat.

Aingeal came to the end of the barn without finding the door. She'd gone the wrong way. She started back the other way and found that she could barely move her feet. How odd. Were her legs that cold? Then she was on her knees, the snow almost level with her chin. Perhaps she would rest a moment. So sleepy now. Someone touching her, lifting her. She reached and felt a bearded face. Father?

Yellow lantern light flickered against the stacks of hay. Rose pushed at her with a cold muzzle. A fine horse, Aingeal thought, and the only thing she had that her father had given her. Not yet fully awake, and so cold, she reached to stroke his reddish muzzle. She saw two other horses with Rose, and she wondered if she were dreaming. The dream showed her an elderly man kneeling at her feet, bending over, working at something. Rubbing her feet, he was. She sat up, and he looked fully into her face. She saw the gray beard and the smokeless pipe.

"You're not my father." The words were out before she thought.

"Not as far as I know, my lady. My name's Esras. The boy on the floor there, that's Mikael."

She looked then at the bloody face of a boy she'd never seen. "What happened to him?"

"We had a difficult time finding shelter. This barn was the first thing we came to. Hope you don't mind."

"No, not at all. But I thought…I mean how did I…"

"I bumped into you about the same time I found the barn. Stepped on you, I did. You would have been frozen in another minute or two. What in the name of the Nine Worlds were you doing out there, dressed like this?"

"I went out to get some wood. I live here."

"In a barn?"

"No, no, in a house. Right there." She pointed toward the door.

"I think we must have walked right past it in the dark. I'll help you get back to your house."

"What about your friend? Is he all right?"

Esras turned to look at Mikael. "He needs to rest. I doubt if we could wake him if we tried. How far to your house?"

"About ten paces. I can find it."

Esras smiled at her. "Ten paces is a long way tonight. We'll wait until dawn."

Aingeal marveled vaguely at the authority with which the old man spoke. She wondered where he and Mikael had come from, but she didn't ask. Maybe she would when she wasn't so tired. Her last thought before sleep took her was that her mother would be worried.

Daylight arrived gray and cold. The wind had fallen off by half, and the snow had stopped. Mikael stirred, and Esras went to him.

"Wake up, Son of Svein. We are needed."

"What? Needed for what?" Mikael sat up and saw the sleeping girl. He stood. "That's the dirtiest girl I've ever seen."

"You don't look so fair yourself," Esras said. "We've got to get her to her house, a few steps from here, I think. Grab some of that wood." He pointed at the large pile of split logs.

When Esras lifted Aingeal, she woke.

"Put me down!" She kicked her feet and tried to squirm her way out of his arms. "What are you doing?"

"I carried you in here, my lady. I suppose I can carry you out."

She remembered then, and stopped fighting. Mikael went first, carrying a armload of wood and pushing his way through the drifted snow and breaking a trail for Esras and the girl he carried. Johanna opened the door as Esras worked the latch.

***

Two days after the storm had passed, sunlight fell suddenly into the open doorway of Johanna's hut, brightening the morning scene therein. Setanta had attached himself to Esras, and the two sat on the floor playing with a wooden toy the boy's father had made as he lay ill during his last days. Esras' pipe was lit, and the fragrant smoke wafted out the door into the unseasonably warm air. Johanna sat at the big table near them, peeling potatoes. A slight smile flickered in her eyes.

"We'll have a fine supper if Mikael is successful," she said. "It's been a long time since we've had fresh meat."

Esras didn't respond. He worried about Mikael and the girl being off alone, supposedly hunting. The look on the boy's face after Aingeal had washed and changed her clothes was unmistakable. He was smitten for sure. The very round hazel eyes, the auburn hair that fell around her face, and the just-scrubbed pink complexion of youth had struck the boy hard.

Understandable, that, but travel time was too precious to waste. The heavy snow had probably stalled Hulda, but the respite wouldn't last. This warming trend would bring the witches together all too soon. He suddenly realized Johanna was still talking.

"Alsandair himself should eat as well," she said.

"Do the people of Hitara serve the king, then?" Esras asked.

"Why, yes, of course. But there's little we can do for His Majesty. We're too far from Sogg even to be taxed. We have no representative. Zane, he…" her voice trailed off. She walked to the door and flung the potato peelings outside. She stood there a moment, obviously composing herself.

Esras said nothing, giving her time. He poked a finger at Setanta's stomach. The lad giggled.

Johanna turned. "It's been hard without Zane. He was a wizard, you know. Not well known. He didn't want that. Hitara knew him, and often asked him for help with births, crops, things of that sort." She walked back to the table and sat down. "I was about to tell you that he journeyed to Sogg once, not long after Aingeal was born. He said he wanted to offer his services to the king. He didn't even get into the castle. They laughed at him, he said."

Esras searched for the right words. "I'm sure he would have rather been here with his family." The statement sounded shallow, even stupid.

"I suppose," she said. He taught Aingeal…things, before he died. She never speaks of that, and I don't ask. But I think his instructions continue."

"Continue?" Esras asked.

Johanna turned her chair to face him directly. "You're from Fallon. I've heard about your valley and your river. It's said that water people live in the river there, and that you have more than one growing season each year. And other things I've heard, that I believe, but some others don't. So maybe you'll understand what I've told no one else."

"What is it, Johanna?" Esras stood, then limped to the table where he pulled out a chair and sat. He took one of her hands into both of his. "Tell me."

"Zane comes back occasionally, at night, when it's warm out. I've heard Aingeal talking to him in the barn. She talks to his ghost, Esras. She learns things."

They rode into the lingering morning, Mikael and Aingeal, side by side, talking openly about many things, all of it pertaining to the youth they shared. Demon took every advantage of Mikael's inattention to snatch at the tufts of dead grass where the snow had melted enough to make it visible in sun-sprinkled woodlots. Mikael had to constantly jerk at the reins to keep up with Aingeal riding her well-behaved Rose. A pretty mare, to be sure, and graceful. She stepped high even where the snow barely covered her hooves.

The moist ground released musty smells that reminded Mikael of the grassy banks of the Aine, but for the first time since leaving home he was glad to be where he was. Aingeal, although not as comely as many of the girls he had favored in Fallon, had somehow touched that secret and hidden part of his inner being where the pooled water of the Fallon rested, cooling his soul. He should resent that intrusion, probably, but he did not. In fact, he welcomed it. Aingeal's round eyes held a light that had flooded through him, like the Fallon. He saw intelligence in her face, and a mysterious confidence that issued from some reservoir he would probably never know about. Her straight but relaxed posture on Rose's back accentuated her already apparent self-assurance. Odd, really. One wouldn't expect such a sophisticated bearing from a backwoods peasant girl, especially one of her age. She still possessed traces of a little girl look, but that would change within a year, Mikael surmised.

They rode on toward a depression in the landscape that she called Bright Valley. The locals had always called it that, she said, because it was never shaded. On all sides, the forest stood back from the little valley, and no part of it was darkened by shadow. There would be deer there today, she promised, lured by the warmth that offered a respite from the higher elevations and the deeper snow.

"About another half-mile" she said. "I don't have to tell you we'll need to approach against the breeze. I'm sure you and Esras must hunt to survive." Her eyes flashed, like a sudden glare from the snow.

She was asking him to tell her why he and Esras had left Fallon. He was tempted, but he fought it, knowing Esras' wrath. "Yes," he said, and added nothing. Suddenly, he became worried that he would fail in the hunt, and she would think less of him.

They dismounted before leaving the shelter of the trees, and tied the horses' reins to saplings. Mikael did remember to check the wind, and to alter his approach accordingly, Aingeal following close behind. They were in full sunlight now, but in brush heavy enough to offer concealment. The wet ground allowed them to creep forward without sound.

And then they were there. Not less than thirty deer grazed warily eighty paces away in the rich bottomland of the little valley. Mikael knelt in the high grass and removed a hickory arrow from the quiver on his back.

"You can't shoot from here, silly," Aingeal whispered. She knelt beside him.

Aingeal was too close. Her breath touched his face, as did her warmth. The shifting breeze carried soft strands of auburn allure across his vision. Was she deliberately trying to addle him?

Although he had not intended to launch an arrow from this distance, her spoken warning reminded him that he had the means not to fail. Not only would he not fail, but he would also make himself a wonder in her eyes. He sighted down the hickory shaft as if examining it for straightness. He continued his deception by running a thumb across the edges of the gray flint arrowhead. Frowning, he returned the arrow to his quiver and drew one of the precious ash arrows.

Without speaking, he again went through the examination process, but now he nocked the arrow to the string. He looked directly into her calm eyes before standing.

So there would be no mistaking his intent, he said, "The buck grazing alone, on the far side, to the left." And then he thrust Aingeal from his mind in order to give his full attention to the deer and the shot. He came to full draw, anchoring his right ring finger in the corner of his mouth. Looking down the length of the ash shaft to the gleaming white tip, he let his mind see the calmly beating heart of the buck. Then the arrow was away, climbing in an arc across the deep blue of the spring sky, and then gradually leveling out, and maintaining the horizontal only briefly before the tip fell, almost imperceptibly. The sun caught the white helical fletching, which spun the arrow as it sped across the valley.

During the arrow's flight, the buck raised its head and looked directly toward Mikael, as if it had known all along the intruders were there, but felt confident of its safety due to the distance. The white flint entered just behind its right shoulder, and sank between ribs and on into the center of its heart. Mikael saw sunlight on the antlers as the buck bounded toward the forest, and he saw the white feathers protruding just above a spurting line of scarlet. The herd scattered.

Mikael turned then to look at Aingeal, and receive her praise. He didn't find the round eyes ablaze with astonishment and wonder, but they had dimmed, darker now with a hazel contempt.

"You're a fool," she said.

"What?"

"An immature fool. What were you thinking? To impress? To boast?"

Mikael fought for words. Aingeal spoke as if she knew of the magic ingrained in the ash arrows. But how could she? He stuttered and stepped one step backward and away from her.

"How many do you have now?"

"How many what? Arrows?"

"White tipped arrows, fool. How many?"

"Uh, sixteen, when I recover the one from the deer. Why do you ask me that?"

Her anger seemed to fade somewhat. She looked at the fletched end of the arrows visible behind his shoulder.

"Come," she said. We'll find your deer."

She took his hand then, as if he were a child, a foolish child, and led him through the grass down to the soggy valley floor. They found blood in the snow, and they followed it toward the trees, Aingeal leading. Entering thicker brush, she bent and reached to the ground. Turning, she handed him that part of the arrow Mikael had seen protruding from the buck's side.

"Fifteen, Mikael. Not sixteen."

A few steps more, and there lay the buck, its legs curled under it as if it slept.

"Gut it," she said, and Mikael reached for his knife to obey, uncertain about the wisdom and authority the young girl seemed to posses.

In the heart, he found the arrowhead. Out of habit, he turned it in his bloody fingers, looking for damage. Aingeal jerked it from his hand without comment, and hid it away somewhere in the folds of her dead father's coat. Mikael finished his chore, stood, and grasped the massive antlers to begin the drag back to where Demon and Rose were tied.

Aingeal moved in beside him to take the other side, and together they started out of the little depression, dragging the still-warm carcass across the snow patches and wet ground of Aingeal's Bright Valley. She spoke not at all as they entered the timber, and there in the shaded wood lots where the sun's glare from the snow became less harsh, and even welcomed as a contrast to the forest darkness, Mikael considered the pretty and silent peasant girl struggling beside him. Two years younger than himself, but yet she owned something of maturity that he could not comprehend.

His own silence was deafening, screaming to the wildwood of his guilt. They were not half way to the horses when he knew he had to ask.

"How did you know about the arrows?"

"I should not say. I've never told anyone. I don't think you're someone I can trust. I don't even know why you're here."

He thought about that at length. They walked on, the deer in tow. On level ground now, the pulling was easier. They crossed a set of footprints in a patch of snow that apparently Aingeal did not see. With concern for Aingeal's anger toward him pulling at his mind, Mikael thought nothing of the tracks, other than they must be those of another hunter from Hitara.

He weighed what he wanted to know against the risk of revealing his and Esras' mission, and then he factored in his need to redeem himself with Aingeal.

Demon snorted at their approach. Mikael sat down on the deer to give his horse a moment or two to become used to the smell of the carcass before attempting to hoist it across Demon's back. Aingeal seated herself on a fallen tree.

"I don't know how to explain it, really," he began. "I left Fallon to find my brother, to tell him about our mother's death. He's at Sogg."

Aingeal said nothing. In that, Mikael understood that she knew there was more.

"And Esras believes a coven of witches intend to…" He stopped. How could he tell her about the Fallon? About its magic, and his need for the river. She'd not understand. She couldn't. He tried another approach.

"Esras believes Elkana witches would do battle with our people. One witch in particular. Hulda. At Sogg, we'll attempt to gain assistance from King Alsandair to stop her."

Still, only silence from Aingeal. She sat gazing down upon the wet and decaying leaves.

"The arrows," he said. "They are thousands of years old, yet ageless. They have a certain magic in them, if you can believe that. Whatever I shoot at with them, I will surely slay. I know that to be true."

"And you shot a deer with one," she said without looking up.

"Yes. It was as you said, to impress. I regret it."

She lifted her head then, and he saw that the light had returned to her eyes.

"I believe you, Mikael. Something of the arrows' power touched me when you donned the quiver this morning. I felt their magic, and I understood then, as I do now, that whatever magic they hold is for you alone, and that there is a definite purpose for them. But more than that, I felt your uniqueness. You have been chosen."

"You felt these things? How?"

"My father taught me. I started studying under him before his death, and still, he teaches me. Do not look at me so, Mikael. It is your turn to believe. My father comes to me, or rather, his spirit does, and he teaches. In life, he was a wizard of great knowledge. Eventually, I shall posses that knowledge."

Mikael thought of the spirits guarding the holy place where the Fallon River fell away into the earth. He wanted to ask Aingeal if every mortal had a spirit that would walk the earth after the body died, but he held back, afraid that the question might seem like disbelief of what the girl was telling him. Anyway, he could ask Esras later, or better yet, Oriana.

"And what will you do with that knowledge?" he asked.

Aingeal smiled at him, pleasing him more than a little. "Perhaps no more than my father did," she said. "Perhaps more."

80

seven

There are truths and lies under the sun. Priests I have appointed to
discern.
—Book of Morrigan

Mikael and Esras lingered in Hitara another day, despite Esras' urging to
be away. On the morning of their departure, Johanna packed venison and
biscuits inside an old apron that she had tied up in a knot. Mikael and Aingeal
left her and Esras in the hut, and walked to the barn to ready the horses. The
continued warming trend had taken all but the most stubborn snow patches
from the soft and greening ground. Today would be cloudless, Mikael
concluded. A perfect day for one more ride with Aingeal, but he knew not to
depress himself further by lingering with that thought. Perhaps he and Esras
would stop here on the way back to Fallon. He said as much to Aingeal.

Inside the barn now, she stepped between Mikael and the horses and faced
him directly, effectively forcing his attention upon her. "Mikael," she said,
and took both of his hands into her own. She wore a long linen dress, pleated,
and the color of rust. Across her shoulders, she had draped a green shawl
against the morning chill. Even in the musty stable, he caught her scent; she
was that close. She had not perfumed herself, and she smelled not of soap, but
of unsullied feminine youth, natural and real.

She kissed him then, on his mouth, and he accepted it without returning it.
Such was his inexperience, and his momentary bliss. As she pulled away, he
stood as in a stupor, grasping her hands now not only in affection, but for
support.

"Mikael," she said again, "we are alike, you and I, in that we're both still maturing. You have been chosen, but you've not fully accepted that. I have been taught, but I'm still a student. Perhaps we'll mature together, even if apart. I will remember you."

And then she left him with the horses and his confusion. He saw her through the still-open door as she ran across the sunlit meadow, not to the hut, but toward the woods. "Goodbye, Aingeal," he said, knowing he had waited too long.

Olafia of Hitara, although acquainted with Aingeal, was not her friend. She had attempted to be that at one time, but she soon saw that Aingeal was too quiet and standoffish. And then when her father died, Aingeal became even more distant to the young people living in or near Hitara. And so, Olafia's dislike of the uppity Aingeal increased, and she made an effort to speak derogatorily of Aingeal and her mother to those who would stand and listen.

Partly, she did it out of boredom. But the driving force was Aingeal's attentive nature to Johanna since Zane's death. Olafia despised seeing or hearing about Aingeal's poor mother who had lost all hope with her husband's death. Olafia's own mother was the village slut. For too long, Olafia did more than ignore her mother's escapades with the married and unmarried men of the piteous little hamlet; she denied it outright. But in the glaring light of the truth, the filth of her home was proven to be even filthier by the lewd and unrestrained acts of her mother.

Someday, she told herself, she would do lasting harm to Aingeal. The little high-minded bitch deserved it. It would be Aingeal's fault, really. Aingeal and she could have been friends. They could have been coven members together. But Aingeal had spurned her, and Olafia knew in her heart that it was because Aingeal held herself above the likes of the village slut's daughter. And because of that, Olafia had not approached Aingeal with an invitation to that first meeting. Probably, Aingeal didn't even know about the coven. She kept herself so aloof from the town's concerns, she likely had no opportunity to hear the rumors of a secret coven.

If Olafia had to move from Hitara to be a permanent part of Hulda's coven, so be it, but she would return. By then, she would have learned what the queen witch could teach, and then Aingeal would have something to worry about other than a lazy mother. If her suspicions about Hulda's ultimate goals were correct, it would be worth the two-day walk to the next meeting to tell Hulda what she had overheard between Aingeal and the boy from Fallon.

The only road out of Hitara was little more than a wide footpath, too narrow even for a cart to be pulled through, especially after the summer growth arrived. Johanna had said that if they kept to the road, they would see a cottage overgrown with vines before they hit the main road to Sogg. The cottage resident would welcome them and feed them, she said. Not that Johanna had been there, but her husband told her of the many meals he had taken there.

"Watch for it," she said to Esras as they rode away from the hut, "and refresh yourselves." The sad woman was still talking as they rode out of hearing into the warming day.

Demon and Elsa picked their way around rocks and fallen branches as Esras chattered on about finding Aingeal in the blizzard, and about Johanna's hospitality. He rode in front, and occasionally he turned to look back at Mikael and grin through his gray beard. He seemed in unusually high spirits, which Mikael attributed to a full belly and newly sewn pants. But Mikael wanted none of his cheer. What he wanted was to turn Demon around and go back to Aingeal. That being out of the question, he would just as soon ride in silence and brood. Eventually, Esras realized the conversation was one-sided.

"Son of Svein," he called back. "You think of the girl, do you not? Well, never mind her. There'll be girls aplenty in Sogg, and you can take your pick when business is finished."

"Let's not talk about Aingeal, Esras." Esras was too old to understand his feelings about Aingeal. Talking about her while he was leaving her would just depress him further. "How far to the main road?" he asked quickly, to change the subject.

"Who knows? Johanna's not been there, and Oriana's not talking."

"What do you mean?"

"I mean I've been unable to reach her since she showed us the way out of the storm. I think maybe it tires her, or uses some part of her, to contact me. It seems she's only there when we need her most. Sometimes I wonder if Morrigan should have given that kind of power to a woman."

"All magic doesn't come from Morrigan, you know." Mikael was thinking of Aingeal's wizardry, and the statement was out before he could stop it.

Esras took an interest in that, and slowed Elsa to a stop. Mikael rode up beside him.

"You mean like Hulda's power?" Esras asked.

"She's a witch," Mikael replied, "and I don't think the Goddess Morrigan gave her anything." He hoped he had covered his real meaning sufficiently, but apparently he had not.

"Aingeal told you, didn't she?"

How could the old man be so sharp? Nothing got by him. "Yes," Mikael answered.

"Do you believe that about her father coming to her?"

"Shouldn't I? Have you yourself not seen the spirits where the Fallon enters the earth?"

"I have surely seen them, Mikael, but there are those who say they see what they do not. Consider that the young people in Hitara are bored with their lives in such a secluded town, away from everything except what's right there. Do you think perhaps those children make up stories to brighten their existence a little?"

Mikael clinched his jaws in anger. Aingeal was no child. Neither had she lied. He couldn't check the words he would immediately regret. "She knew about the arrows before I killed the deer. How could she know that, if not a wizard?"

"The ash arrows? You fool! How many? Did you recover them?" Esras' eyes went to the quiver.

Mikael kicked his heels into Demon's flanks, spurring the horse forward, away from Esras and his overbearing self-righteousness. He spurred the horse again as if he might outdistance the facts that proved him to be the fool Esras had called him. Demon, delighted, reached for the ground ahead, digging in for the speed he craved. An evergreen branch slapped Mikael in the face, increasing his anger, and he rode on. He ignored Esras' call to wait. As he rounded the next turn at a gallop, he found himself looking into the open front door of a dilapidated house, probably the cottage Johanna mentioned. Mikael pulled hard on the reins, changing Demon's exuberance to confusion.

Esras caught up. They sat mounted, side-by-side, emotions draining and being replaced by caution and curiosity. Dead vines, like ghosts of snakes, crawled across the entire front and the one side Mikael and Esras could see. Decaying moss-covered logs and badly deteriorated rough-sawn boards whispered of age and neglect. Scrub growth, not yet budded, had taken over the yard, and the yellow contrast of daffodils at the front step spoke of days when someone cared.

"Looks deserted," Esras said. "The home of some spirit, perhaps."

Mikael recognized Esras' vague attempt to neutralize his earlier statements about Angeal's dead father.

Just then, the silhouette of a small human figure appeared in the doorway, backlit by a rear window. The living thing was emaciated, a skin-covered skeleton, but clothed. The lean face, oblong and a little pointed at the chin, seemed not to go with the large ears and crooked little nose. The top of the doorway was several feet higher than the bald man's head, and Mikael surmised that the little stick-like man, or spirit, was not the tenant the builder had in mind. He wore no shoes. His pants came to just below his knees—the kind of pants that middle and upper class men might wear with hose. His russet canvas shirt, many times too large, spilled about him like a muddy waterfall. He beckoned with a bony hand that protruded from the full-sleeved shirt. His other hand held a bottle, which dangled at his side, like the weight of it was too great to lift higher.

Mikael's unfinished anger reduced his caution and prevented him from conferring further with Elias about accepting the strange invitation. He urged Demon forward a few steps and dismounted. Without turning to see what Esras would do, he led the horse straight toward the little man who grinned at him now out of a toothless mouth. Elderly, he was, but no spirit. Mikael tied Demon's reins to a stunted bush and stepped briskly toward the door. The old eyes looked past him and widened, as did the grin, and in that Mikael knew that Esras followed. Their host stepped to the side and motioned them inside with the hand that held the bottle. Mikael heard its contents sloshing as he instinctively bent low at the entry to protect the arrows in his quiver. He was inside before realizing he held his longbow.

Floorboards creaked beneath Mikael's weight. Musty and mingled odors of staleness and decay met him immediately and saturated his senses. A half-darkness had taken up residence in the room Mikael had entered. The one vine-seized window on the east side gave little access to the daylight outside. Esras entered behind him, forcing Mikael one step further into uncertainty. As his eyes adjusted, Mikael found the one table in the center of the room and the four straight-back chairs that surrounded it. He saw a washstand whereupon sat an oil lantern that housed a tiny flame, drab clothing hanging by the window, and a door that apparently led to another room. A crumbling fireplace occupied most of the west wall, and sticks and sections of tree limbs lay piled in an adjacent corner.

The little man made a grunting sound and motioned for them to be seated at the table. He left the door they had entered open, to Mikael's relief, and he pulled out a chair for himself, looking from Esras to Mikael now, still grinning. The three of them sat down. The bottle was placed in the center of the table, carefully, as if either the bottle or the table might break. No sooner was this done than a look of concern crossed the wrinkled features of the old man's face, and he pushed his chair back and took three rickety steps to the washstand. He returned with three wooden cups. His grin returned as he distributed the vessels.

As yet, nothing had been said. Mikael became uncomfortable with that, and looked at Esras, who received the intent of his communication.

"We travel to Sogg, sir," Esras said. "Do you know how far we've yet to go?"

The crooked little nose twitched, but there was no audible response. Both of his shaking old hands hoisted the bottle, and he poured a pale pink wine into the cups. He lifted his, and politely waited. Esras took up his cup, and Mikael followed his example. The three of them sipped together. A mild and weak wine, Mikael found. With this drink, he thought, one might be able to extinguish his thirst without becoming addled. He sipped again and found that he was able to smile at the strange little man's hospitality.

"Three days," the ghost of a man croaked.

Due to its timing, his statement was not immediately understood.

"Excuse me?" Esras said.

"Three days to Sogg."

"So near?" Mikael asked, taking yet another sip.

"Do you wish to know your future?" The question came from his thin, quivering lips, meekly, directed at no one, yet to both of them, and effectively closing the subject of Sogg's location.

Esras responded. "We wish to thank you for the wine, sir, and to learn your name."

"I've no name that I can remember. I believe I had one, though." His frail voice broke. "Your future?"

"Yes. Please," Mikael said, feeling sorry for the old man and his sad and solitary existence. He unconsciously touched his coat that covered his coin bag, assuring himself that he could leave something for services rendered.

The nameless man rose and crossed the dingy room to fetch the oil lantern. Seated again, he turned the wick higher, spilling light the color of old gold across the dusty table. From somewhere in the many folds of his shirt, he produced a dirty canvas bag. He pushed the wine bottle away and sat the bag directly in front of him. It was tied at the top with a drawstring at which he worked with trembling, crooked fingers. He seemed to be getting nowhere.

"Might I help you?" Mikael asked.

No response.

Mikael swallowed the last of his wine and noticed that Esras' glass was empty also. They waited while the fingers trembled, failing time and again to grasp the string correctly. Finally, the bag was open. He pushed it to the center of the table and inverted it.

"Our futures are arranged by color," he said.

The expected small bits of bone and other totems did not appear. Instead, gemstones of every color rattled across the tabletop. There were rubies, opals, amethysts, beryl, amber, sapphires, sunstones, white jade, wine-yellow topaz, and garnets of orange, green, and pink. No gewgaws or baubles of any kind sparkled among the unpolished and obviously genuine jewels.

"By the apples of Idin," Esras swore.

Golden heliodor beryl, sunstones, a yellow garnet, and the wine-yellow topaz came to rest together. Adjacent to those were the blues—the sapphires and aquamarine beryl. There seemed to be no order among the reds and greens.

The ancient eyes studied what the hands had thrown. Twitches of concentration crossed his visage, and finally, after several minutes, lantern-lit tears fell among the shining stones.

His eyes met Esras'. "Do not go to Sogg."

"Why not?"

"Do not go to Sogg," he said again. "Believe the yellow stones. And then his gnarled fingers touched the sapphires. "Blue is hope, but together with yellow, it is slight."

"What about the yellow?" Esras asked.

"Goodbye, friends," he whispered, and Esras and Mikael had no reason to think the words were anything but a dismissal. Mikael laid several farthings on the table, but the man who was unexplainably wealthy with jewels took no notice of the coins.

Outside, Mikael turned to look. The nameless and ancient human was retrieving the gems from the table, one at a time, and placing them back into the canvas bag. He didn't look up from his work.

The coven met tonight on the extreme southern end of the swamp. A

87

quarter moon sporadically revealed itself through scudding dark clouds driven by a reckless western breeze. Hulda knew an anxiousness that she could not account for. The girls had returned. She had enough, and she should be able to begin their training with a sense of purpose that would keep her steady. But something pulled at her, some doubt that refused to make itself clear, and it kept her mind uneasy. She hadn't felt it before the girls were assembled, so maybe some treachery lay among them.

Kattrin came to her in the shadows created by the huge fire she had ordered built before the last of the day's light was gone. "My queen," she said, as if addressing her in public, "have I offended in someway? I sense that you are restless."

Hulda needed to pull sweet Kattrin to her, to feel her warmth, to partake of the calm assurance she offered, but such would not do in the coven's presence. "No, Kattrin, you've not offended. You could not. 'Tis something else, I know not what. I shall address the coven. The training must begin."

She stepped between the fire and the eager young minds. Directly in front of her sat Olafia. Their eyes met. Hulda remembered her as the dirty human who would have helped the snake-bitten weakling. In that meeting of eyes, Hulda knew the girl held the answer to the uncertainty that plagued her this night.

"Olafia, is it not?"

"Yes, Queen."

Hulda decided not to ask what secrets Olafia had brought with her to the meeting. That must be done in private, and quickly.

"Are you well, Olafia?" Hulda asked in her most pleasant voice. The sweet notes rose and hovered over the group, like a warm swamp fog. Like music, it was.

"Yes, Queen. I have…"

Hulda stopped her. "I know, Olafia. You have come a great distance. From Hitara, I believe. You will need refreshment before we begin. Go with Kattrin."

"But Queen, allow me to…"

"A useful coven member is quick to obey. Go."

Olafia got to her feet and went toward Kattrin, who stood behind and off to one side of Hulda. Hulda turned just enough for Kattrin to see her expression of concern. Turning back, she addressed the assemblage, the kindness in her tone now dead.

"I have access to all that has ever happened, or ever will," she said. "I can recreate events, or bring forth events that have never occurred. Through you, I will be as powerful as myself multiplied by your number. But not yet. You must be taught." With the images she brought within range of her mental vision, Hulda's uncertainty evaporated. She spoke now with assurance.

"From this night forward you will not leave the swamp until you are witches. I alone can make you such, for I alone hold all the elements of the craft. I lack none. Through me, you will meditate, fast, dance, endure pain, inhale the smoke of burning flesh, and you will become mine. I am your queen, and no one or nothing will you put before me. It is I you serve, and no other. The powers of magic that you will attain can come only from me, and although those powers will be upon you individually, they are mine collectively. My purpose will be served through the joining of our powers, and afterwards, you may chose to stay with me or to return from whence you came, keeping the status you will have achieved."

Hulda saw in each face that they believed. "I hold the secrets and the incantations that can forever scar the world. These I will teach you, and the demons of hell will respond when we recite them together. Death and destruction will be widespread, and you, my children, will be responsible." She smiled at them then, that they might accept her as queen teacher, mother.

"Whatever you were in the villages you have abandoned is now dead. You are a new creation. My creation, and you owe me your undying faithfulness. This you must engrave on your hearts, for all of your remaining moments of life are mine. If I never call you before me again after we have accomplished my purpose, you are still mine, and subject to my will. Are you prepared to begin?"

Their girlish voices were one. "Yes, Queen."

"Then I shall consult with Princess Kattrin. Meditate now on what you have entered into."

Hulda turned her back on the coven and walked into the darkness. She found Kattrin standing over a trembling Olafia, who was on her knees in the swamp dampness, her face wet and swollen from crying.

"This human bitch has information for you, Queen," Kattrin said. Her composure was intact despite the trouble she had obviously had in convincing Olafia to tell her what secrets she carried.

Hulda's first inclination was to vent her instant rage upon Olafia, who was the originator of her anxiety that night. But she fought that impulse, needing the detail that would only surface from a mind at ease, without fear.

"Don't you know, dear one, that Kattrin is your princess, that she is privy to all I would hear. Thank you for your loyalty to me, but perhaps you will remember, if you are to be one of mine, that Kattrin is here for you, as I am. Now what message do you bear for me, child?"

Olafia stood and ran a hand through her matted hair, as if that simple act could straighten it. The tears that tracked her face had cleansed the surface dirt, leaving dingy white streaks. She straightened herself to perfect posture, her pride returning. She glared at Kattrin. At that, Hulda became unsure that she would be able to keep herself from killing Olafia before she divulged what she knew.

"My queen," Olafia said, and bowed. Her voice was too loud; she spoke as if she were play-acting. "A boy of Fallon stopped at my village. He possesses certain knowledge that I overheard him share with a peasant girl who is a plague among our people. The boy, Mikael is his name, spoke of the coven."

Olafia stopped flat, waiting for the flattery and praise she expected, and waiting for Hulda to ask her for more. She stared directly into Hulda's eyes, infuriating the queen witch even further.

"Continue, child," Hulda managed to say.

"He travels to Sogg with one he calls Esras, to inform King Alsandair of the coven's intention to go against the humans at Fallon. He will seek the king's assistance in stopping you."

Hulda closed her eyes against the blasphemous creature before her. How dare the wretch speak in such an assuming manner of stopping the queen witch? She tried to calm and console herself with the certain knowledge that Olafia had only moments to live. "Did the lad say how he knew of the coven?" she asked.

"No, but he has some authority over his arrows. They strike as he intends. Aingeal, the witless girl to whom he spoke, told him that he had been chosen. She admitted to him that she learns wizardry from the ghost of her father."

"Is that all, child? Do you know her father's name?"

Olafia's distress was obvious. Her moment was almost gone. Would Hulda toss her back into the coven as an equal to the others, or would she somehow reward her, as she deserved?

"Zane was his name. Married to Johanna, a useless and wasted woman. And I remember that this Mikael has a brother at Sogg," she said. "That is all."

"You are less than the dung you excrete," Hulda said, her voice steady with intent. She delved into her vast reservoir of past murders for something appropriate.

"Might I have her?" Kattrin asked.

Never before had Hulda wanted more to kill, but she could refuse Kattrin nothing. "Yes, my sweet, take her. But tie her for now. The training of the others is paramount."

More urgent was the training than even Kattrin knew, Hulda thought, although Kattrin had probably connected the youth from Fallon with the all but forgotten prophesy of Zienna. But Kattrin didn't know about Zane, the wizard of Hitara. If any part of what Olafia said was true, Hulda must proceed quickly. The last thing she wanted was Alsandair's interference, or for word to spread to her coven that Zienna's warning might hold some merit.

For the first time since the spy was burned, Hulda experienced concern over what Zienna had said. Perhaps this youth from Fallon would prove to be an obstacle. A trivial matter, really. She would simply adjust her schedule.

eight

*In those places where strangers gather and tribes mingle, the increase
of death and rot shall not be contained, except through wisdom.*
—Book of Morrigan

Oriana lay on her pallet in the small and unadorned room adjacent to the
temple. She shivered under the four woolen blankets that did little against the
chill that came not from the spring air, but from within. The fever had taken
her suddenly last night, without the vague warnings that usually accompany
an illness. She hadn't felt tired, or even listless. There had been no uneasiness
in her chest or throat. But before the sanctuary received the full light of day,
a restlessness and foreboding had seized her and flung her into a chilled
despair. An evil of some sort, it was, and she recognized it, although she could
not identify it.

She attempted through the morning hours to warn Esras, but of what she
did not know. Certainly, the lack of specific knowledge of what dangers Esras
might encounter could prevent communication, but still she tried. Now she
had ceased, doubting her own conclusion that her malady was not physical.
The ominous presage remained, as real as the symptoms it manifested. She
turned under the blankets from her back to her side, and slept, albeit fitfully,
and dreamt of a dry riverbed and dying undines.

Johanna's venison and biscuits were several hours gone, as were the two
rabbits Mikael had taken with his bow and hickory arrows. Hunger forced

92

him off the road and into the wildwood, leaving Esras to care for the horses and to set up what they both figured would be their last camp for some time to come. If the strange little nameless hermit had been correct in his three-day estimate, he and Esras would be in Sogg by this time tomorrow. They would sit at a tavern table for supper, and sleep on straw beds that were intended for sleeping, so unlike the hard or sodden earth that had tortured them since leaving Fallon.

Esras had convinced Mikael that the hermit's vague warning about Sogg was not worth consideration. If trouble of any serious nature loomed ahead, Oriana would have let him know, and she had not. Upon arrival at Sogg, they would go directly to the castle and seek entry. Oriana had assured Esras the prince would receive anyone from Fallon. And the fifteen remaining ash arrows would prove that Mikael and Esras were Fallonese.

Mikael had checked his quiver often since his last encounter with Esras' wrath. Esras had lectured him almost nonstop since they had left the hermit's cottage. He was adamant that no more of the ash arrows be used before they arrived at the castle. If Alsandair knew the Book as well as Oriana had implied, he would know there were twenty arrows saved for the chosen one of Fallon. It would be difficult enough to explain the loss of the five not in Mikael's quiver now.

A rustling in the dry leaves ahead prompted him to nock one of his hickory arrows to his bowstring. No sooner was that accomplished than a yearling deer stepped into a small grassy glade lit by the dying sun. His shot was true, and he was back with Esras in time to prepare a hindquarter for roasting before darkness settled in. Much of the meat would go to waste, and Mikael hated that. The killing was bad enough, but to not use all of what he had slain left a bitter taste that would linger long after the meal was done.

Esras handled the clean-up chores, allowing Mikael time to prepare himself mentally for Sogg. Esras told him that meditation before arriving was necessary as there may be little opportunity for that upon entering the bustle of the city.

"We can ill afford a mistake," Esras said. "Fix your demeanor and confidence in your mind. Should entry into the castle be denied us upon our first approach, it will be that much more difficult on the second and subsequent attempts."

Mikael lay awake that night contemplating the clear sky that covered him here and his beloved Fallon River back in the valley. His river. Could it really be in danger? Were Esras' concerns founded in something that Mikael should feel stronger about? He had disappointed Esras in so many ways since leaving Fallon, and he was loath to do it again. He had come to love the old man, actually, in spite of this forced journey, and in spite of the fact that he had difficulty in accepting the reality of the dangers Esras feared. Certainly, Mikael was a child in the eyes of Esras and Oriana, and he understood that a lack of maturity might keep him from seeing what they saw, but still, how could he really believe that the strength of the Fallon could be harnessed by evil, or diverted to another's use?

He closed eyes and imagined himself lying on her grassy banks, listening to her soothing flow and the splash of the undines. Someday, he thought, as sleep began to take him, he would show his river to Aingeal. She would understand.

As he expected, Esras had him awake the next morning even before there was sufficient light to efficiently break camp. By the time sunlight broke across the tops of the oaks and evergreens of the eastern ridges, they were a mile from where they had slept, chewing cold venison as they rode. The track they followed became a road, rutted by the wheels of carts and wagons. Now and again they passed cleared fields and stacks of hay. Small areas fenced in by rails of oak held muddy pigs and sleepy-eyed cattle. By early afternoon, they were passing houses. Fully above ground they were, and so very different from the sunken huts of Fallon. Landowners and serfs worked behind oxen turning thawed ground that was finally free of winter's icy hold. Mikael saw maidens, young and old, moving about the greening yards of the homes, working at the various chores that keep farms alive.

How good it was to see some semblance of ordered human society after his travels. "Sogg?" he asked Esras.

"Not yet, Son of Svein, but soon, I think."

The distant between homes and farms decreased as they neared the city. Mikael had begun to think that King Alsandair had a firm grip on ruling the population, because the people appeared healthy and productive. *They're happy*, he thought—*happy under a ruler that cared about them and knew how to administer that care.*

But as the furlongs fell behind the hooves of Demon and Elsa, Mikael saw less and less of the clean and ordered countryside. Now he saw the huts and longhouses of Sogg, and the slums of the common churls and rag-pickers.

"I believe we have arrived," Esras said.

A stench arose, gradually, and then it covered the riders like a fog that would not be moved except by the strongest of winds, and even then it would return, for it was, he realized, a permanent part of the human condition at Sogg. Open sewers he smelled, and the uncleanness of too many humans packed together in one place. The smoke from a hundred cooking fires mingled with the foul odors of poverty. The deeper they rode into the city, the dirtier it appeared. No few of the people Mikael saw stared at him as if he might in some way relieve their piteous lives, or perhaps he thought, they saw him as something to prey upon. Unconsciously, he reached behind his right shoulder to check the arrows in his quiver.

"Easy, lad," Esras said. "You've seen poverty before. These wretches are not your enemy."

Mikael relaxed somewhat at that, glad that Esras was here. He began to take in the details of individuals who caught his eye, to wonder at their station in life, and whether or not they had a way to make improvements in their own and their families' conditions. But overall, the solemn citizenship projected a downtrodden, humbled appearance. If he could put a color to the slums, it was brown. The huts were brown, the dirt and mud, and the threadbare rags they all wore were brown. The children wore what their parents wore— canvas and flannel, except that the adults had shoes while the children did not.

Looking closer at the faces near enough to study, Mikael noted another difference between children and adults—the eyes. Those of the adults were lusterless, brimming with despair, and in some, sickness. But the children's hungry eyes were wide, brimming with curiosity, anticipation, and hope. Obviously, they didn't know what their parents had long ago accepted.

He heard a long and mournful wail from one of the huts as he passed. A woman in agony for some reason, he thought. His first inclination was to dismount and seek the source of the cry, to help, but he felt Esras' hand on his arm, and he steadied himself. An elderly man, bent and seemingly nearly lifeless, flung a pan of reddish liquid from the hut's entryway.

They rode on.

Out of the housing sectors now, they entered a complex of narrow and littered streets packed on every side with merchants displaying their wares, and sellers of services who cried above the din about the quality of their offerings. The marketplace of Sogg. Mikael was surprised to see several Elkana, male and female, not only selling, but shopping as well. The shops and businesses were separated by nothing more than sheets of canvas or blankets hung from frames of rough lumber and sawn tree branches. Mikael wondered how one protected his goods from his neighbors in such a setting.

As he and Esras rode by, a dyer of cloth argued vehemently with two young girls dressed in bright silken robes—dancers probably. The repugnant odor of fish assailed Mikael as he passed a fishmonger's place of business. Fortune-tellers stepped into the street, warning him he must know his future before it was too late. A beggar grabbed at his pants with one hand while holding the other out for whatever it might receive. An Elkana woman's voice could be heard shouting through the tumultuous throng of activity.

"Kralene and scandeele," she yelled, at everyone and no one. Mikael was reminded of the Elkana meal given to him by Hannes on the day he stole—no, took—the horses he and Esras now rode. How long ago that seemed.

"Pick up your pace, Mikael," Esras said. "Surely, this place abounds with thieves and cutthroats."

Mikael was all too glad to comply, and they proceeded deeper into the city, now almost at a gallop. The racket of the market faded behind them, and they slowed. Where the city was less busy it was also less dirty. Well within the older parts now, the riders found themselves on wider streets lined with structures built mostly from stone. Some were two levels high.

A solitary peddler pushed his cart toward them, but he seemed more intent on getting somewhere than selling the clanging metal wares that hung from every part of his cart. From somewhere up ahead, Mikael heard music, and upon riding closer to the sound, he saw a crowd of people gathered around a flute-playing jongleur. The throng faced away from the approaching riders.

Most of the peasants here appeared to be middle class, probably residents of the old stone houses. Other than being cleaner, their clothing was no different than that of the slum dwellers Mikael and Esras had only recently passed among. Some of the girls wore pale-yellow flowers in their hair, and some had made an attempt to adorn themselves with brightly colored scarves. Both the men and the women seemed entranced by the music. Almost all of them held goblets of red wine. Two soldiers, probably from the castle, perhaps assigned to duty as constables, stood a little back from the group of merrymakers, smiling, obviously enjoying themselves on such a fine afternoon. Must be some kind of celebration, Mikael thought. Looking closer, he saw the young jongleur played a double flute, a pan-like instrument made of reeds. He had cymbalums affixed to one foot that he shook to achieve harmony with the flute.

The jongleur noticed the approaching strangers and smiled at Mikael as they started by. At that gesture, a lovely dark-skinned girl dressed in flowing scarlet silk turned to see to whom it was the player gave his smile. She met

Mikael's eyes, and she nodded in greeting, and then faced again to the front. Desperate for another look, Mikael's mind raced for something to say before Demon had taken him too far.

"The king's castle, maiden. Do you know where it is?"

She turned a second time and the warm wind caught a strand of her black hair and dropped it in front of her eyes. She brushed it away and curtsied before she spoke. Now she smiled, more with her dark eyes than with her wine-stained lips. "Look for the towers, my lord," and she pointed in the direction he was already headed.

And then Demon took him by, and she was lost to him in the crowd. Perhaps she had mistaken him for visiting nobility, he mused. Maybe she thought Esras was his servant. He smiled broadly at that thought, and rode on, the cheerful flute fading to nothing. He resigned himself to reality and the purpose at hand.

"The castle," Esras said. He was pointing ahead.

Mikael saw the towers, plainly visible now above the leafless and budding trees, and he marveled at their height. Higher still were the banners of the realm's colors that fluttered on flagstaffs above the towers. The gold, silver and blue attested to the nobility, purity and justice of Alsandair's rule.

Mikael had expected the castle to be situated on higher ground, but as he and Esras rode closer, it became obvious that the huge stone and timber construction was only slightly elevated. Now he saw that the two towers stood in two corners of the castle yard, and that there were two more on the far corners. Massive, the castle was, and it gleamed in the afternoon sun with a majesty one might expect of a king's abode and fortress.

Only now did Mikael realize they were no longer among houses. He and Esras rode through greening grass that stretched in front of them and to the sides for almost as far as they could see, uninterrupted by structures or trees. They, or an advancing attacker, would have been spotted by now by the castle guard, and the reason for the open fields became clear.

Close enough now to see the arrow slits in the windows above ground, anxiety invaded his mind, and he knew not why. Was he not Fallonese? Was he not here at Oriana's bidding, and did he not have Esras' assurance that they would be received? But still, the enormity of the castle put him in the presence of something much more than himself, and he thought of the ancient glacier that the Book said had made the Fallon River.

The battlement, high on the front wall, was alive with soldiers, whether as a matter of routine or for the sake of the two riders coming in. However, the drawbridge was down, a strong indication that trouble was unexpected. The timbers of the huge bridge spanned the width of a wide moat, a necessary measure against invasion in the absence of the advantage of elevation.

A squad of soldiers and their sergeant stood on the bridge talking among themselves and paying little attention to the approaching riders. The soldiers, probably line units, carried crossbows, but the sergeant only a sword. They all wore chain mail, shoulder plates, and coifs, but were otherwise unprotected by their dress. The sergeant stepped to the end of the bridge to meet Mikael and Esras as they neared.

"Greetings, friend," Esras said in a voice unnecessarily loud. "We would see the prince."

"State your business." The sergeant's tone held no warmth.

"We are Esras Aronson and Mikael Sveinson, from Fallon, representing Priestess Oriana."

"What proof have ye?"

Reluctant to reveal what proof they had to a common soldier, Esras asked, "Since when does a Fallonese need to prove himself?"

The sergeant studied Esras' face momentarily. Then, "Dismount and cross over. Wait at the stables, but go no farther. I will relay your request." And with that, he turned and walked back to his men where he paused to turn and look at the two visitors before proceeding into the castle yard.

They followed, Mikael and Esras, leading their mounts. As they passed the soldiers, one of them spoke up. "A bit grubby for Fallonese, methinks. Serfs or rag-pickers, most like."

The other men laughed heartily, feeling somewhat free to do so, Mikael thought, out of the presence of their sergeant.

At the stables, a curly-haired fellow took the reins of both horses into one ample hand.

"My lords," he said, "I am Matthias, keeper of the royal stables. Are your mounts in need of feed and water? Shall I brush them while you're about your business in the castle?"

Fully expecting to be with the prince for a while, Esras said, "We're to wait here for the sergeant. And yes, some oats and water would be appreciated."

As Matthias led Demon and Elsa away, Mikael scolded Esras. "I don't think that'll be a courtesy service, old man. I hope you're carrying shillings enough to pay him."

Before Esras could answer, the sergeant was back. "Prince Andres is engaged at present," he said to Esras. "Come back in the fall."

Esras looked as if he had been struck by lightning. Mikael answered for him. "No, no, Sergeant, you don't understand. We're from Fallon. I have proof of that." He pulled an ash arrow from his quiver.

The sergeant backed away one step. "Careful there, knave. I've killed younger boys than you for less threat than that."

Undeterred, Mikael continued. "These are of the Goddess Morrigan. Know you nothing of their power? How only one from Fallon might posses them?"

"Your threat is vague, rogue, but not lost upon me. Be gone from here at once, or be skewered where you stand." He drew his sword.

Mikael could only stare at him with his mouth open. He felt Esras' hand on his arm.

"Come, Mikael. We go."

"But..."

"Now." Then, "Matthias, bring our horses," he shouted.

The sergeant stood his ground, his sword still unsheathed. Out of the stable the horses were led, not by Matthias, but a younger man, taller than Matthias.

"Bairre!" Esras screamed. "By the Aesir gods, I would be no more surprised to see Thor himself!"

Mikael stood transfixed. Could it be? He searched the face of the stableman for some physical proof that this might be his brother, but the years had changed the older Sveinson, and dulled the younger's memory.

"Old Esras," Bairre said, in his easy way of speaking. "I thought your spirit would have gone back to the ice fields by now. What in the name of the Nine Worlds are you doing here?"

Then Bairre's eyes locked on Mikael's. "Brother Mikael," Bairre said, his voice nearly a whisper.

"Tell this man, Bairre," Esras said, "that we are Fallonese."

"Ye've had your warning, rogues," the sergeant announced. He stepped toward them, raising the sword. "Your friend Bairre tried the same thing once, some years ago, and you can see that he's not advanced past the stables. Shall I call my squad?"

Esras mounted then, as did Mikael. Just before Demon bolted toward the yard exit, Mikael thought he saw a glint of moisture in Bairre's eyes. Then he and Esras were riding back across the drawbridge and hearing the jeers of the squad of soldiers that stepped leisurely out of their way.

The meadow grass seemed less green now as Mikael and Esras shrank away from the lengthening shadows of Alsandair's Castle. The middleclass streets they entered were now void of music, and even the light was failing due to the late-day sun, which had settled in behind the two-story buildings. The sun-warmed breeze that had earlier frolicked along the festive streets was now a chilling misery, reminding Mikael that he and Esras had nowhere to sleep and nothing to eat. He pulled his coat tighter around his neck. A dismal place indeed was the city of Sogg.

Hulda was pleased. Her new recruits caught on quickly, and were not repulsed at the thick mixture of herbs and dog blood they were required to ingest. The sixteen witches stood on the frost-covered leaves of the marshy forest floor with their arms interlocked, forming a circle around their queen and princess. The quiet scene, illuminated only by star and candlelight, suffered no disturbance other than the mild westerly breeze that the candle flames fought against. A wooden bowl of salt positioned between Hulda and Kattrin represented the elements of the earth upon which the coven would call.

The original nine witches, including Kattrin, much respected by the newcomers, drank first, and the goblets were passed, one to another, right to left. Only Hulda and Kattrin knew that a small portion of Olafia's bile had been stirred into the syrupy potion. This, Hulda told Kattrin as she accepted the pewter cup of greenish-brown liquid from her child lover, would be added assurance that the spirits would respond.

The Elkana ghosts she needed were unnumbered, and the bodies they had used were long ago decayed to dust. Even the forces that moved time had forgotten those men who died during those bitter years following the migration of the Fallonese from the north lands. But the spirits remembered, for the death of their host bodies was a direct result of the human takeover of the fertile Artinus lands. It would be difficult to prod them awake, certainly, but possible because of the unrest that accompanied the deaths. Not just the ancient warriors, but all the Elkana who had died during that time were uneasy with leaving their world to the human intruders. And that unrest was a potential awakening of souls in the earth's belly, where they waited, albeit unknowingly, to be vomited to the surface.

Necromancy, it would be termed by Hulda's enemies, and she hated that, because she no longer considered herself a necromancer, and she now held in contempt those who practiced raising the dead for their own purposes. And in reality, she told herself, she was not actually disturbing the ghosts to the point that they would surface, but only to the extent they would be bothered enough to create the undulations of the earth that were needed. In that regard, she must be careful.

She had practiced the art before, in years past—years that were now as dead and gone as the men whose spirits she conjured. Never had it been easy, nor pleasant, either for the dead or for herself. And never had she attempted to wake more than one individual spirit at one time. This time, however, she would need many, and thus many conjurers.

The last time, more than fifty winters ago, she had sworn to never again attempt to raise the dead. Almost, she had lost control of the spirit, an Elkana male, and almost it had escaped into the night on the eternal wind that mourned above the grave. How pitiful the specter appeared, hovering over the engraved stone, its filmy substance in torment there. Ripped from its rest, the only possession a spirit has, and confronted suddenly with the life it had lost, the ghost unleashed a wailing more sorrowful than death. A young man in life, dead before gaining his part of life's sweetness, but at peace with eternity until Hulda called him forth from the dark depths of time to give her...what? A confirmation of her power? Could she not have confirmed herself to be a witch by other means?

Now, she was at it again. But this time, there was no other way. By no other device could the queen of witches even approach, much less harness, the enormous energy that was required. And this would be the last time. So, no, she was not a necromancer, not really, and those who would remember her as such were simply incorrect. So be it. Her reputation in that regard would certainly be overshadowed by the land and power she would give back to the Elkana before Mother Sun set again.

As dusk became darkness, and somewhere before Mikael and Esras fully entered the slum area of Sogg, they found a stable for the horses. The proprietor was a haggard woman of advanced age who spoke more in grunts than words. She offered them lodging in a vacant room of her apartment above the barn, and led them there by lantern light. They could pay in the morning, she said. Mikael removed his quiver to duck beneath the low doorway that led into a spacious room entirely without furnishings. The old woman grunted something unintelligible and was gone.

"Go down and get the blankets from the horses," Esras said. His voice betrayed his fatigue.

Too tired to argue, Mikael placed his bow and quiver on the rough floorboards beside Esras' pack and started down the narrow stairway in total darkness. He heard whispers below him and then footsteps ascending. The two men that seized him were anything but gentle. One pinned his arms to his sides in a crushing hug. He smelled the sourness of the man's breath and the foulness of unwashed skin and clothing. Then the other man struck his head with something blunt. Through the wash of pain and confusion that flooded him, Mikael felt the hot rush of blood on his face, and tasted it on his lips. He could not form his thoughts sufficiently to cry out. He was dragged into the stable where someone stood holding a lantern. The light played across that individual's face, but he could not focus his blood-soaked vision to identify particular features.

"Have you killed him?" the face grunted, and Mikael knew who it was.

"I ain't sure. Who cares? Where's his stuff?" The voice was gravely.

"The old man has it upstairs. Get his coins."

The same stench hovered over him, and he felt hands inside his coat.

"Ain't much here. A few shillings. Maybe the old man's got more."

The voices, the light, and consciousness left him.

When next Mikael woke, it was to the glare of morning sunlight stabbing at his eyes from the open stable door. Nausea and pain gripped him when he attempted to raise his head. Confusion about his circumstances and whereabouts added to his misery. He sat up, bringing further agony to the left side of his head. He felt with his hand, and pulled blood-matted stable debris from his hair.

Suddenly he remembered. Esras! He stood too quickly and nausea pulled at his gut. Even in his rush to get to his feet and up to the rented room, he realized the horses were gone. The rotten board of one step broke under his weight as he bounded up the stairs. He saw spattered and dried blood on every step, and on the doorpost. The door was open. Esras lay on his back, his eyes open, staring at nothing. His splintered staff protruded from a chest that no longer moved in rhythm to life. The face was battered, and the gray beard caked with dried blood. The odd angle of his right arm indicated a break below the elbow.

Beside Esras was the filthy corpse of a middle-aged man. A swollen tongue protruded out of a scarred face that was frozen in rage. Esras had resisted until the end, protecting the arrows, no doubt. But the arrows were nowhere to be seen. Neither was Mikael's bow or Esras' pack.

Mikael fell to his knees, and then across the pitiful remains, weeping, his head on Esras' silent chest. The sobs came, and the tears, until there were no more of either to release. He stood and looked down on the man he had learned to love. A nameless fury entered into Mikael Sveinson then, and he shuddered. He backed toward the doorway.

"You!" he screamed, pointing at Esras' unhearing corpse. "You fool! You forced me here. For what? It's your fault, not mine. Yours and Oriana's. I'm going home."

But even as he descended the stairs, treading across the blood of Esras' murderers, he knew he would not go home. He knew deep within himself that Esras had died for Fallon. And not until this moment did he fully understand the necessity of putting himself between Fallon and the evil that threatened her.

For Fallon, and for Esras, he would stay in Sogg. He would complete what Esras had attempted for Fallon.

He stepped into the sunlit street, realizing he had no idea where to start. But full upon his stricken heart was the knowledge that Fallon's protection would have to wait until Esras' killers were dead. He turned right, toward the slums, to look for the grunting old woman. Peasants and peddlers stared at him as he passed, and he cared not that his soiled and bloodied appearance gave them cause to gawk.

A soldier accosted him before he had crossed the second intersection of streets.

"A rough night, churl?" The tone was anything but respectful.

Ignoring that, Mikael asked, "Do you know of an old gray-haired woman that grunts when she speaks, possibly accompanied by two thieving rogues?" Even in his anguish, he knew better than to mention the murder. He would be the first suspect, a bloodied stranger without means of support.

"Sounds and looks like ye've encountered Greta and her two rat-eatin' boys. What'd they rob you of? What's a churl like you got that's worth taking?" He laughed at his own wit.

The street trembled then, and lay still. The soldier asked, "What was that?"

Before Mikael could respond, the earthquake was full upon the city of Sogg. It came in waves, each longer and stronger than the one before, felt firstly by a gentle trembling and rising of the ground. The next rise was higher, and it split the street crosswise leaving a narrow crevice between Mikael and the soldier.

Mikael turned to run, knowing exactly what was coming, but having no idea to where he might run, or what would happen to him. His long strides took him up a crumbling hill that had not been there seconds earlier. Now the old abandoned stable was in view. And then it wasn't. It rose, then fell as a mass of dust-spewing rubble, not just to street level, but down through a widening fissure that swallowed the demolished structure as well as Esras and his killer.

The unearthly bellow of the quake drowned the screams of the people as they poured into the streets from their homes to meet the crashing violence that assailed them on every side. Mikael saw houses teeter and fall, or tremble and crumble. Many cooking fires were extinguished under fallen debris, but as many more sprang out of the destruction to become a thousand times their intended size, feeding on housing timbers and anything at all that a city of humans might store inside or outside their homes. The smoke of the fires that boiled forth from that hell mingled with the dust of crushed stone and earth, and the light waned. Darker still the day became, and Mikael ran through it, gasping for air, and choking on his own confusion. Such was the violence of the quake that it created its own snarling wind, spreading ash, smoke and dust throughout the chaos that was Sogg.

How many turns Mikael made to avoid fallen and falling debris, he did not know. His direction had no certainty to it, and he cared not at all about that, except that running somewhere was all he could do in his frantic attempt to escape from Hulda's murderous hate.

Something shaken loose, perhaps a building stone, struck him hard on his back between the shoulders, slamming him face down onto the ground. Stunned, he rolled onto his back to see broken timbers and stones falling toward him through a ceiling of brown dust. Before he fully gained his feet, he was beaten down again. Blood flooded his face, and he wondered if it came from the injury inflicted by Greta's son, or if he had some new wound that Hulda's earthquake was responsible for. *Too many enemies*, he thought, as stone and darkness covered him.

part two

blood and water

níne

Within the passing of ages lies the folly of men, buried at forgotten
depths, never to be resurrected, except by fools.
—Book of Morrigan

Within the dateless regions of eternity, hours and years fall away in mere
droplets of time, like the successive and insignificant tears of a glacier that
held too long to one state of existence. Whether the change wrought by time
relates to a glacier or to a living thing, whether measured in melted ice or
wasted years, that change is often so gradual that the affected entity, or the
observer thereof, cannot recognize it until the losses come too close together,
and by then the change is permanent. Whether the transition be one of
impairment or improvement, decadence or edification, forward movement is
halted, slowed, or accelerated, depending on, in the case of humans, the
mind-set the individual might achieve. For each individual, that mind-set
differs with past experiences that were not lost to eternity as the years fell
away.

Mikael had seventeen such years to look back upon. Reasons and
motivations for his mind-set were countless—not countless in numbers, but
in emotions and subconscious levels of hurts and losses that he could not now
articulate, even though he knew the events were recent in terms of his life. He
understood that the beginning of his coming of age was Bairre's departure
from Fallon. Not that he recognized any part of his change then, but the pain
of that had been the first impression to scar his mind significantly. That scar
was still unhealed when his mother died. Then there was Esras, who was to

the boy Mikael only an old man of Fallon, and Oriana's confidant; but to the man Mikael, Esras was truth, vision and wisdom.

Since his own departure from Fallon, Mikael had learned through Esras what it was to have faith, and to have foresight that permitted one to see beyond the here and now, even into the generations of Fallonese unborn. Through Esras, he had learned to kill when necessary in the course of pursuing values higher than individual lives.

Now he must consider the possibility that he was the chosen one of Morrigan, and the hope of Fallon—the people, the town, the valley, and the river. He would proceed henceforth as if he were, in fact, the One. And if it turned out he was not, he could be grateful to Esras that he had grown into the knowledge that nothing mattered beyond Fallon's welfare.

He fully understood now his connection to the river. He and she were one. He could not have peace until she had it. He heard the Fallonese spirits sometimes now at night, when Sogg was quiet and resting from the day's toil of rebuilding.

Tonight he had awakened, whether from dreams or to reality he did not know, but he had heard the wailing of the ghosts of Old Fallon bemoaning the losses the Fallonese now suffered through the pollution and dilution of the water's purity and power. But by the spirits' presence, whether they were in his mind or in his room, Mikael was comforted. He threw back his sweat-soaked blanket and arose in the dark from his pallet in the castle's keep, and without a shirt he limped into the summer night, letting the cooling breeze take his too-deep thoughts from him for a little while. On the battlement's catwalk, he encountered Sergeant Barnes, who stood like stone at his post, watching the moon-lit meadows below. Mikael didn't speak, hoping to have the night to himself.

"Evenin', my lord."

Their eyes met, and Mikael regretted his selfishness. "Good evening, Barnes. Why don't you go to the kitchen for some mulled wine? I'll watch until you're refreshed."

"No, thankee, Captain. Corporal Silvey will be along directly to relieve me."

"Very well," Mikael said, and walked on.

"Captain?"

"Yes?" Mikael turned.

"Will you be leaving the castle, sir?" Shall I tell Silvey to watch for yours and the ladies' return?"

"The lady?" And then he saw her. Aingeal, coming to him, a blanket wrapped around her.

Recovering himself, Mikael said, "Uh, no, Sergeant, we'll not be leaving. Just taking a breath of fresh air."

"Where goest thou at this hour, my lord?" Aingeal teased as she approached and opened the blanket to receive him. "To the city trollops when I am but a breath away?"

He accepted hers and the blanket's warmth, but his thoughts were not of Aingeal as he gazed into the predawn city, lit now only by the few lanterns of those houses where wives were helping husbands prepare for the coming day.

Through the darkness, Mikael rode in his mind with Esras, months earlier, across the meadows, rejected by the castle guard and then attacked in the night by a vileness so extreme that it took Esras to the next world.

Again he saw Esras' bloodied and broken body, the splintered staff, and again he was on the street, feeling the upheaval of the ground and hearing the screams of the quake's victims.

He pulled Aingeal closer, fighting the memories, but they came screaming at him from the city, across the dewy fields, climbing up from the moat to the castle's battlement, and assaulting him again.

He lay once more under the rubble that had fallen from a heaven his soul had almost entered by way of his mortal body being crushed. But his senses remained intact, and he knew the pain of broken bones, the agony of moving his cracked ribs to breath in the dust, and the torture of sharp-edged stones upon his face. He felt the fear leave him, flowing out in waves of hot blood from uncounted injuries, giving him the strength to die, as Esras had died. He didn't know that the fingers of one bloody hand protruded above the carnage, and that they grasped at nothing but fouled air.

He lay like death until the quake subsided. And still he lay, unable to move, watching a crevice of light that told him the morning was past, and later, that afternoon was fading into dusk. This was the twilight of the day and of his life, he was thinking, when someone took hold of the nearly lifeless hand.

The stones and timbers were pulled away, and his first sight of freedom was the soiled and sweat-streaked face of Bairre. As he stepped out of his grave, Mikael saw the street alive with soldiers and citizen workers who were digging for survivors. A few of the trapped were saved; most were lost.

Bairre took him to the castle, or what was left of it. Mikael's first thought upon seeing the fallen kingdom was that Bairre had taken him elsewhere, for this could not be Alsandair's castle. Where were the towers? Amazingly, the drawbridge was undamaged, and Mikael gazed down into the muddy waters as he was carried across. He thought it remarkable that the moat still held water—that one of the thousands of fissures opened by the quake hadn't drained it.

The main gate was ruined and almost impassable. The metal grillwork of the portcullis was twisted as if by the strength of gods, and the huge winch was crushed almost flat. Mikael felt every jolt and misstep as Bairre carried him over the debris into the castle yard.

Mikael was put to bed in the stable. He wakened in the dark, that night or the next, and Bairre was not there. Mikael wondered if he had really seen him at all.

"You must be Mikael." The nearby voice was feeble, barely audible.

Mikael sat up, but the scraping of bones forced him back. His right leg hurt him horribly. If he could light a lantern, perhaps he could tend to his injuries, or at least see their extent.

"Who's there?" he asked.

"It is only I, Matthias, the stable master."

"Are you injured, Matthias?"

"I am wounded grievously, I'm afraid. And you?"

"To some extent," Mikael replied. "Where is Bairre?"

"Gone to fetch a physician, if there be one alive."

A long paused ensued, and Mikael listened to Matthias' labored breathing.

Then, "Bairre left the castle soon after you and your friend rode away, to find you. He must have been in the city when the quake struck. I didn't expect to see him again, but he brought you here."

"How badly is the castle damaged?" Mikael asked. "How many casualties?"

No response. Mikael closed his eyes against the pain, and dozed momentarily, only to be aroused by Bairre's return. He carried a lantern in one hand and a bulging sack in the other. The lantern light bounced and swayed in the darkness as Bairre approached. He was alone. He walked straight to Matthias and held the lantern high to check on his friend's condition.

"No help anywhere tonight, I'm afraid," he said to Matthias. Then, "Where was your goddess today, Mikael, and where is she now?" His voice had turned as cold as the night.

"What?"

110

"Matthias is dead, as is most of Sogg."

"Bairre, I'm sorry. I was just talking to him."

Displaying no emotion whatsoever, Bairre came to Mikael. "Let's see about that leg, little brother. I'll have to set it myself. I think the knee is ruined."

He was like that, Mikael remembered. Bairre had always changed the subject when someone looked to him for an emotional response, whether the matter was serious or not.

You'll need some sewing, too," Bairre said. And he began.

Mikael endured the pain of Bairre's ministrations, and remembering Esras and the fight he made before his death, he didn't cry out. He would take what came to him from this night until his death. And he judged that for the tasks that lay ahead, his conviction would be tried many times over.

Bairre straightened Mikael's leg and tied strips of splintered timbers to each side, immobilizing it. He washed Mikael then, and checked each cut before suturing the ones that had to be closed. There would be scars, Bairre said, on his face, his back, both arms, and his chest. The leg may or may not heal properly; the knee was probably ruined.

Bairre nourished him with cheese and wine until Mikael could take no more of either. He saw that the items came from the sack Bairre had arrived with.

"You'll need the wine, brother, or you'll not sleep."

"I've had enough to sleep for a week. Now tell me about the castle and the city. How bad is it?"

"Not tonight," Bairre said. "Sleep now. I must see to Matthias."

So Mikael slept, even through the pain, for he was mentally and physically spent.

He awoke at dawn to find himself alone. His attempt to stand took his breath, and then his consciousness. His next awareness was Bairre helping him back to the pallet. Bairre knelt to ease Mikael's head back on a straw-stuffed canvas pillow.

"You might have broken the stitches with such foolery," Bairre scolded. "Mother always said you couldn't be still."

Suddenly, Mikael remembered one of his reasons for being at Sogg. "Bairre, I came to tell you." He hesitated, trying to form the words that would prepare a son for the news of his mother's death.

"Mother?" Bairre asked.

"Yes. How did you know?"

"I saw it in your eyes, brother. Did she go easily?"

"She did. I was with her." Instantly, he regretted the lie.

Turning his back, Bairre changed the subject. "Sogg is in ruins. Already the stench of death hangs over the streets. So many dead, but they were fortunate. I'm amazed we can't hear the wails even from here. The cries come from underneath the fallen stones. I expect that'll continue for another day or two." He turned back to face Mikael. "Only a few areas of the castle escaped damage. Parts of it are missing entirely. Most of the soldiers died. The king is…" He stopped, as if saying it would confirm the truth.

"Dead?"

"Yes. As is the prince."

"Who's next in line?" Mikael asked, and then suddenly realized how coarse the question must have sounded to one who had lived here as long as Bairre.

"I don't know. Andres had a sister—Elaine. I suppose she would reign, if she survived. I've not heard."

Mikael only now thought of the ash arrows he and Esras had tried to get to the prince. Now there were no arrows, no prince, no king, and no one that he knew of that would have knowledge of the arrows' origin. Even if he found such a believer in the royal family, even if he had the arrows, there were insufficient soldiers now to go against Hulda. What soldiers that survived the quake would be needed for months in the city and at the castle. Their duty now was to protect the citizens from looting, starvation and disease, and to rebuild. Years it would take. Years that Mikael didn't have. Already, the Fallon might be spoiled.

He tried not to think of the result of losing the river, but the images came to him like a procession of nightmares. The water level lowered, the undines dying, the village people aging at twice or three times their normal rate, crops failing, disease and death. He saw the end of all he had ever known of home coming to Fallon Valley.

"A soldier on the street," he said, "told me of a corrupt old woman, Greta by name. She's got, or had, two ruffian sons. Have you heard of her?"

"Who hasn't?" Bairre asked.

"They killed Esras, Bairre. Stole my arrows, the horses, all of our coins."

"Ah, the arrows. I heard you telling the sergeant of the guard that they were from your goddess. How did you expect such a statement to get you in to see the prince?"

Mikael's temper flared instantly against the man who had saved his life, brought him here to safety, and put his broken body back together. Bairre should have expressed sympathy regarding Esras' death, and he should not have spoken of Morrigan as if she were something he and Esras had dreamed up. He did not answer Bairre, not trusting himself to answer civilly.

Bairre apparently recognized the change. "Tell me what happened."

"Greta led us to an abandoned apartment over a barn, offering to let us stay there for a price, like the place was hers. Her sons knocked me senseless and killed Esras. Took everything we had. Esras killed one of them. I must get the arrows back."

"That's not likely. They and the horses were probably killed in the quake and the arrows buried in the rubble. I'm sorry about your friend." Bairre stood. "I'll get you something to eat."

"Wait. There's more," Mikael said. He might as well tell him the rest, even knowing Bairre wouldn't believe him. "The earthquake was unnatural. A group of witches caused it. They're led by one called Hulda." He spoke quickly now, to get it out before Bairre interrupted him with another remark of contempt. "Esras and I were to seek the assistance of Alsandair to stop her, but we were too late."

"I see," Bairre said, and he turned away.

To please her mother, Aingeal took as much of the boiled barley water as Johanna offered. The fever must run its course, and no amount of nourishment would expedite the matter. She needed to be outside, she told her mother, to stand in the frozen night stillness and let the cold take the fever. No, Johanna said, such a thing would not do. She would surely contract the lung sickness and die if she were to go out. More barley water would heal her, nothing else. Aingeal drank and then dozed.

In her dream, Mikael's white flint arrowhead that she had worn since his departure scorched her breast and radiated heat to her innermost tissues. The flint, her dream told her, was the source of her discomfort, not an illness. Try as she might, she could not reach through the heated haze of her dream to untie the leather cord that held the flint in place. She struggled against the unreasonable constraint, her arms heavy, too heavy to lift, but still she fought. As her frustration reached its apex, Zane laid a cool hand upon her brow. She looked into the tenderness of his gaze.

"Be thou still, child," he said. "You have all that I can give you."

He faded then, or nearly so, leaving Aingeal to wonder if the calming visage was real. Fully awake now, she was certain of her discomfort and the lingering vapor above her.

As the filmy substance of her father's form evaporated, she heard, "Every occurrence has meaning, daughter." The voice was less than a whisper, like a breath through fog. "Find the meaning while it's still before you."

Aingeal turned her head toward her mother's pallet, and in the almost nonexistent light of the dimmed lantern, mother and daughter's eyes met. An easy smile lay upon Johanna's features. She had seen Zane, the first time since his death, and finally, she was at peace. Aingeal watched her mother's eyes close and her face relax, leaving only a hint of the smile as she drifted off into an untroubled repose.

Aingeal considered her father's words, and the fire that held her. A meaning in her illness? Was that what he meant? Unconsciously, her hand went to the arrowhead. Even through the smock, she felt its heat, hotter than her fevered skin. She rose, a fully educated but untried wizard, understanding the message that only she could receive.

She dressed then in two layers of thick canvas, woolen socks, woolen scarf, fur-lined boots, and her father's coat. Neither Johanna nor Setanta stirred as Aingeal opened the door and stepped into the calm but forbidden cold. She heard Rose's soft whinny from the barn, but she would leave the horse here, for her mother. A half-moon and a sky sprinkled with specks of fire showed her the tree line to the south, but it was the white flint that directed her steps.

Away from the borders of the swamp, Hulda and Kattrin stood together on a knoll above their den watching the rising water. Were she not responsible for the flood, Hulda would be puzzled by the clear waters washing across the land, as there had been no rain. She reveled in her power and pulled the child closer, not for warmth against the harsh spring wind, but to comfort Kattrin. Her quiet sobs seemed out of place to Hulda, for they had succeeded, and the loss of their den to the flood was of little consequence. But such was childhood, she considered.

"Hush, love," Hulda said. A den is nothing. We'll want to move to Sogg anyway. Surely, the castle has crumbled, and all within have died with it. Now it's ours to take."

"You might have destroyed us all, Queen. I was sore afraid of the noise, the great pits of nothingness, the screams. And now this." Kattrin pulled away from Hulda sufficiently to look into her face. "Will you care for me, Queen? Will you keep me with you always?"

Hulda was suddenly aware of the moist and glistening green of Kattrin's eyes. "You know I will. I love you more than what we've gained, and more than my own life. Never will we be apart. You are mine."

Kattrin took Hulda's face into her cold and clawed hands, and pulled the smooth snout toward her own, and kissed her fully on the mouth, thrilling Hulda more than Kattrin could know. "Thank you, Queen. Thank you. I love you."

Never had Kattrin uttered those words, or any words at all that assured Hulda that her love was returned. The surprise of it now, and the rapture, kept Hulda silent.

"That much I can give you, Queen, and little else. I do love you."

The witch queen pulled her close again, accepting without question the gift she had lived for. Perhaps she should have studied Kattrin's eyes, but she did not, because Elkana were that much like humans, trusting as true the thing they desire most.

"What of the coven, Queen? May I have them?"

Hulda considered the options, weighing them as always against what Kattrin wanted. Then, "Not all of them, dearest, at least not yet. We'll need staff at Sogg, and someone to rule over the little matters that plague any kingdom." She took Kattrin's arm to lead her back to the coven in the swamp, which waited on their queen's next directive. "Tell me, princess, why do you hate them so?"

Kattrin let her green eyes stray toward the swamp and the coven before answering, as if she had never posed that question to herself. "It's not hate," she said. "I've no reason to hate, especially not Elkana. "It's the killing, I think. No, not the killing. It's death itself. Have you never wondered about that thin potion within something alive that holds it in such a state, and how fragile that thing is? What is it, Queen, that causes one to be dead, or not dead? And more wondrous and puzzling even than that, what sensations do the dying have?"

They were walking, and Hulda kept silent, seeing a side of Kattrin she hadn't known existed. Never had the child said as much at once than she was saying now. Hulda, even knowing the hardness of her own heart, was slightly repulsed by Kattrin's mind-set concerning murder. Repulsed, but also intrigued.

"Fear, certainly," Kattrin said. I've seen that in them. They cannot hide it.

MICHAEL A. GIBBS

But what else do they feel? When you gave the one called Olafia to me, I tied her as you told me. But later, after I took the bile from her, I butchered her. I couldn't stop myself. Did you not hear the screams? She died slowly, and in that slowness I thought I might find some answers concerning death by cutting into the most inward parts while she yet lived."

Hulda wondered what others her lover had seen die, and how many of those deaths were by Kattrin's own hand.

"Someday, I will have the answer in my own passing," Kattrin mumbled, as if talking to herself. "But that's no good because I won't have the knowledge long, because death will take it. I want it now."

And then they were in sight of the camp, if one could call it that. Elkana and humans alike moved about the place like confused ants, working at something. Closer now, and Hulda saw that they had begun to clear the more elevated areas. Working without instruction, the witches apparently believed they were to stay here. Dens had been started and abandoned, and other diggings were in progress. Fools, Hulda thought. How can they expect to den here where the ground is almost even with the water level? The human girls were breaking off tree limbs and saplings, as if they might build the shelters their race was accustomed to.

"Call them to order, Kattrin. I will speak to them now."

Kattrin moved among the young girls, touching them, whispering, giving them reason to stop their work and assemble before their queen. When all was quiet, Hulda addressed them.

"My children, why do you toil? Is toil not for the commoners of the villages you abandoned? Are you commoners?"

Her tone was gentle and the young women perceived that they were not being scolded.

"Would royalty live in a swamp? You are royalty, beloved, make no mistake, and all of you are members and inheritors of your queen's realm at Sogg. We'll rule there together. The peasants and upper class of Sogg that may have survived our power will need guidance. Your guidance. They will toil for you to rebuild the city, and it will be yours. So, stop your work, children, and sit with me now. We've much to discuss, and we've plans to construct." She smiled at them. "But first, I need to know your individual skills, so that assignments can be made, and your training fine tuned, so that when we take the city, no losses will occur, except to those foolish enough to oppose us."

And so, the day passed, with Kattrin trying each girl. The original witches

116

of the group understood the testing to be a mockery—that those of the coven who were ill-trained, immature, or lacking loyalty would be gone before the cold winds were slain by Mother Sun.

Two of the Elkana girls, Trella and Myronica, had become adept at moving from one point to another instantaneously, although the distances involved were short. Donella could create fire at will and fling it with the accuracy of a bowman. These three witches and several of the others were proficient in tampering with a victim's thought process, and this through mental ability alone, without the enhancements provided by potions. And all of the original nine, acting as one, had the physical strength of a royal regiment, and more. That unity would provide the needed strength for their final thrust at Sogg and the castle.

Mikael awakened to Bairre's gentle urging. He grudgingly became aware that dawn had seeped into the stable.

"I'm going to assess the damage," Bairre was saying. "I've left food and wine within reach. I've talked to some of the soldiers working to clear the debris. They tell me Elaine is well, yet sorely grieved. She's made her quarters above the kitchen. She needs to know you're here."

Mikael understood then that although Bairre had been given nothing by the kingdom above his position as a stableman, and even though he obviously didn't believe that witches has caused the quake, he was loyal, and loyalty required that his queen be told that another from Fallon was here. "Wait," Mikael said as his brother turned away. "I'm coming with you."

"You get up, brother, and I'll knock you back down. You know you can't stand on that leg."

"Let me try. It's been three days."

And with that, he threw the blanket back and tried to stand. Bairre grabbed him, and surprisingly did not force him back onto the straw mattress. Mikael stood on his good leg and leaned on his brother. Slowly he transferred some of his weight to the other side. Pain flared from his knee into his hip, but it was bearable. Maybe the knee was not as damaged as Bairre thought.

"Is there a staff of some sort?" Mikael asked. "Anything at all I can use to help me along."

Bairre retrieved one of the smaller diameter wooden rails that secured one of the stall gates and brought it to him. Then he fumbled around at Matthias' bed place and came up with a sheathed sword. It was short, perhaps two feet in length. He handed it to Mikael.

"Attach this to yourself. You mustn't appear as a ruffian. A sword will give you perhaps a small amount of credibility. I'll wear mine as well."

Mikael unsheathed the weapon. The blade had been forged from soft bronze, but it was wide and thick, giving it the strength the maker envisioned it would need in battle.

"This belonged to Matthias?" Mikael asked.

"Yes. He stole it from a soldier some years ago."

Together they left the stables, and entered what had been forbidden to Bairre since his arrival. They walked directly toward the kitchen and entered upon the quadrangle of that complex. The working soldiers ask nothing of them, and barely even noticed their passing.

"They've been carrying bodies out for two days, but you wouldn't know that by the remaining stench," Bairre said. "I think the foulest of the odors are coming from beneath." He waved his arm to indicate the several piles of rubble that were once parts of the castle the king had believed to be indestructible.

At the kitchen entrance, Mikael and Bairre encountered two guards, one armed with a crossbow, the other a sword.

"Bairre and Mikael, Sons of Svein, of Fallon, to see the queen," Bairre announced, as if that were sufficient.

"Off with you, rogues. The queen sees no one." The replying guard had barely even looked at them.

"Did you not understand me, Sergeant?" Bairre's tone was calm. "Stand aside or Her Majesty will be advised. Perhaps you'd rather be digging graves than standing guard."

Both guards looked at Bairre, and then at each other.

"How do I know you're of Fallon?" the talkative one asked. Have you proof? And even if you do, I have Her Majesty's orders that she's not to be disturbed except under the gravest of circumstances. Know you not that she's in mourning?"

"That's precisely why we're here, Sergeant. Stand aside, for we bring Her Majesty consolation in the form of information. A revelation that she will most assuredly welcome."

"Be gone from here at once, or be skewered." The sergeant rested his hand on the hilt of his sword.

"I'll withhold punishment, at least for now, for such offensive insolence," Bairre said, "because in your ignorance you've misinterpreted my words. I speak of the earthquake, and who caused it, and how I, as a Fallonese, can guide Her Majesty in the means of retribution. Or would you rather she not have that information? That's fine with me, Sergeant. Perhaps you have more authority in such decisions that I realize. Good day."

Bairre turned away as if to leave, and took Mikael by the arm. Three steps away, the guard called.

"I will announce you, but that's no guarantee she'll see you." The sergeant disappeared in the kitchen vestibule, but not before grunting something at the other guard, who eyed Bairre with renewed interest.

Mikael saw the smile that crossed his brother's visage. "What are you up to, Bairre?" he whispered.

"Nothing, except the queen should hear about why you came, and since you're here, you can tell her yourself. Maybe it'll make more sense to her coming from someone who believes it."

Immediately, Mikael recognized the need to get himself before Queen Elaine. The urgency of it coming so suddenly upon him momentarily took the pain from his leg. This would be the first step toward setting the world right again. He would learn from Elaine what he needed to know immediately— what position the royal government would take on all the vileness that had soiled the name of Fallon, and the blatant disregard of Morrigan's wish for her people.

The sergeant was back almost immediately. "Her Majesty will see no one today, as I told you earlier. Now don't make me..."

"You asked her directly, did you Sergeant?"

A growing impatience darkened the sergeant's eyes. "I spoke with her lady in waiting. But I've no need to explain that to you." He drew his sword.

Mikael thought of the forced removal of he and Esras from the castle not five days ago. Perhaps if he had taken action then, Esras would still be alive. He drew Matthias's sword, dropped the staff, and took two deliberate steps toward the guards.

Bairre's voice came to him through a dream-like haze. "Mikael, don't."

The bronze blade flashed in the yellow light of the early sun and fell heavily toward its intended target, but the sergeant was quick, and prevented his demise by blocking with his own sword. The clang of bronze on steel rang out twice more before the laboring soldiers took notice. By then, Bairre was into it, holding off the other queen's guard.

As if stupefied by the unexpected occurrence, the army of laborers stood their ground and simply stared, apparently awaiting someone's order. Only when blood appeared on the sergeant's face did they move forward, but before they could add their number to the explosive fight, Queen Elaine appeared from the kitchen, accompanied by four women.

Her mere presence brought instantaneous peace to the castle yard. Mikael, though he had never met Elaine, immediately recognized her as royalty. Her nobility was apparent, but not in her mode of dress. She wore a plain hooded robe of calico, open at the front, revealing a blue flannel gown underneath. Even though the hood and her hair concealed most of her face, a sufficient number of yellow curls were trapped by the fabric that Mikael caught the pink glow of her complexion. Young, she was, perhaps twenty.

She stood erect, her dignity fully intact, except perhaps for the hidden face, which Mikael assumed bore the lingering tracks of grief. As he stepped back from the offended guard, lowering his sword, he somehow felt sullied and unworthy, like part of the rubble that was now the environs of Queen Elaine, sovereign of all Artinus. But in spite of his feelings, his purpose took precedence.

He fell to his good knee, taking the pain of bending the bad one, and laid the sword on the ground. "Your Majesty, forgive my attack upon your guard, but he forbade my seeing you, a necessity, I humbly assure you, for I bear news from Fallon, from Priestess Oriana, indeed, from Morrigan herself."

Elaine turned her head slightly, and instantly one of the maidens was at her side to hear the whispered message. That maiden, not hooded, overly plump and of plain looks, spoke directly to Mikael.

"Identify yourself."

"I am Mikael, Son of Svein, and of Fallon. This is my brother, Bairre."

More whispers. Then, again from the pudgy maiden, "That one," pointing at Bairre, "seems familiar to us."

Mikael hesitated, hating that he did so, but he knew that in explaining Bairre's long service as a stableman would lessen his own credibility. "Bairre was denied entrance into the castle some time ago, because it was not believed he was Fallonese. He has worked in the stables since then."

Perhaps the simplicity of the truth would count for something. The maiden spoke briefly with Elaine. The queen then reentered the kitchen, followed by three of her servants. The one remained.

She said, "Mikael, Son of Svein, Queen Elaine will receive you in ten minutes," and then looking at Bairre, "but not the stable boy."

Mikael opened his mouth to object, but felt Bairre's grip on his arm, a sure signal to push the matter no further.

The girl stood facing them, her hands folded in front of her, almost concealed by the folds of her russet dress. Only then did Mikael take notice of her eyes. For such a plain face, the deep blue of her eyes seemed out of place. After what she obviously thought was the appropriate interval of time, she turned, and with a haughty look over her shoulder, she checked to see that Mikael was following.

She led him through the entrance, into the vestibule, and then surprisingly, they were outside again, stepping over and around what remained of the roof. The girl was agile for her size, and after she had cleared the obstacles and was walking across a short space of ground less littered, the sway of her ample hips reminded him how long it had been since he had been close to a girl. He thought of the dark-skinned girl in the street who had given him directions to the castle, but his thoughts were interrupted as the servant led him again into an unspoiled part of the castle, the kitchen's storage area, Mikael presumed.

The smell of rotted vegetables and spoiling meat saturated the large room. Two shirtless workman, soldiers by the look of their pants and boots, worked among the numerous crates, sorting by degree of spoilage. Apparently, this area of the castle had not completely escaped disturbance by the earthquake, for nothing seemed to be in order.

As one of the workers heaved a crate toward what was apparently the pile of goods to be thrown out, the other, apparently his superior, scolded him.

"Ye selfish lout. Are you so accustomed to Her Majesty's finery that you waste what might keep someone else from starving? Retrieve that and set it where it can be spiced."

Meat of some kind, Mikael surmised, remembering his mother spicing venison, pork, mutton, and even swans and starlings to cover the taste of deterioration. In that, Fallon was like most any other hamlet on the continent, for the river could do little in the way of providing fresh meat, other than fish. Too often, he had eaten questionable meat that had been heavily spiced with pepper, vinegar and cloves. Even the excessive salting would not keep meat fresh for long during the warm months.

Leaving the soldiers to their work, Mikael followed the girl into yet another chamber, this one even larger than the storage room. Elaine was there, the essence of dignity, seated in the light of a small window on the opposite side of the room, at a writing table. The three other women Mikael had seen outside now stood around her, as if waiting for instructions. Elaine was busy with parchments spread before her on the large hardwood table, her slender and unadorned fingers pushing some aside and placing others in front of her.

Elaine's was the only chair at the table, but the high-ceilinged room was amply furnished with items that could have come from anywhere. Mismatched didn't describe the odd array of chairs, pallets, tables and lounges. Mikael's first impression was that this undamaged room had been servant's quarters before the quake. Now, unknown to the citizens of Sogg and Artinus, the last remaining member of the royal family ruled from this inelegant and improvised throne.

The chubby girl announced him. "Mikael, of Fallon," she said it somewhat contemptuously, but just barely so, but there was enough of a smirk in the short introduction that Mikael heard her disbelief that he was anything but a street rogue. She left the room. Had he not been in the queen's presence, Mikael would have adjusted her demeanor.

The queen did not so much as lift an eyebrow, but continued to study the materials in front of her. Mikael stood in the doorway, unsure as to what he should do or say. So he simply stood, and waited.

Eventually, she waved a pale hand, and her three servants disappeared through a doorway Mikael had not known was there.

"Find a chair, sir, and bring it here." She nodded at the far side of the table at which she was seated.

Mikael had only to reach to the side to pick up a three-legged stool. He sat, and it wobbled beneath him.

"What do you suppose I examine here?" she asked, still not looking at him. "Forgive me, but what is your name?"

"Mikael Sveinson, your highness."

"These are the names and stations of all who lived within the protection of the castle." She pointed to what appeared to be several parchments. "Over four hundred names. A dozen were of royal blood. I say 'were,' because I am the only surviving royalty here at Sogg."

She wept then, suddenly, lowering her head. Yellow curls blazed like sunrise in the light from the window. Mikael turned his head, knowing he had no right to look upon such a private royal matter.

"I'm sorry," was all he could say.

Queen Elaine raised her young eyes to him, and Mikael turned back. She wiped at the tears.

"I have spoiled the ink," she croaked. From her lap, she retrieved a single piece of parchment. "These eighty-four are now all that remain to directly serve me." She seemed to compose herself, and her voice steadied. "Of that number, thirty-one are soldiers. The highest rank among them is sergeant, of which I have four. One of those is he whom you assaulted in the quadrangle."

"Your Majesty, as I have stated,…"

"Allow me to tell you how matters stand. If you are indeed of Fallon blood, I've no reservations about revealing private matters of the sovereign. If you're lying about your heritage, not even the gods can save you." Her cold gaze lingered upon him until he knew exactly what she meant. "But before that, you will provide me with the information you fought my guard to convey."

Mikael did that, touching on the major points, trying to keep his own beliefs out of it by giving her only facts. He told her of the assignment given to Esras and him by Fallon's priestess, and how that she believed the Fallon Valley was in danger. He described the early tremors, and his contact with the witches who caused them. And then he told Elaine that the earthquake was unnatural, that it was an attack on Fallon Valley, and on Sogg, and that the river was now likely altered from its original course, polluted from downstream of the valley. Although he doubted she would believe him about the disturbed Fallon spirits, he spoke of them. He explained that he had seen them at the place where the Fallon entered the earth.

Nothing in Elaine's expression spoke of her acceptance or rejection of his statement. "Tell me why your priestess selected you to come to the kingdom with this information."

"Two reasons, Your Majesty. I was to inform my brother of our mother's death, and…" He hesitated, not knowing how to put it.

"And what?"

"Oriana believes I have a connection to the Fallon."

"A connection?"

"Yes."

"And do you?"

"Yes. I can't explain it. I'm sorry. The river is inside me." He had likely destroyed his credibility with that.

"You're uncomfortable, Mikael. I didn't intend that. Perhaps when we're better acquainted, we can talk further of your attachment to your river. But for now, I shall provide you with an overview of my predicament."

Obviously, Mikael thought, she didn't consider him a fraud if she were willing to take him into confidence.

"Bluntly stated, the long-standing realm of King Alsandair is all but fallen. His other holdings are few, as you know. The Duke and Duchess of Olfusa to the north have no army, only guards. The same is true of Count

Axel, who watches over our western lands. They don't even know as yet that they serve me, and not the king." She sniffled. "I can expect no help from them, even if they survived the earth's trembling. My reduced military is capable of almost nothing. Not only are the city and the castle basically indefensible, I have far too few soldiers to police the streets. The looting and crime occurring there as I speak cannot be arrested, unless the citizens themselves are able to organize some kind of protective unit, and I seriously doubt that will occur." She was looking straight at him now. "The city will turn to me for help. When they learn of the realm's ruined condition, the castle itself will be a target of looters. "I have one hope, and I hardly dare to put my faith therein."

She stared at him, her lips pressed tightly together, as if to imply she would not speak until he made some gesture of understanding. But he could not, because he did not. So he asked, "What hope is that, Your Majesty?"

"Since childhood, my father and my brother, your king and your prince, have spoken of Fallon Valley, the river and the people. I know some of the old names there. I would test you."

"Test me, Your Majesty?"

"Who is the Priestess of Fallon?"

"Oriana. But I don't see…"

"And whom does she serve? What deity?"

"The Goddess Morrigan." Mikael then understood that she wanted proof of his identity.

"Where are Morrigan's prophecies recorded?"

"In the Book."

"Two more questions, sir." She stood and leaned across the table toward him. "From where does Morrigan say that Fallon's savior shall arise?"

"From childhood."

"Lastly, what weapon was saved for him from ancient Fallon?"

"The twenty ash arrows."

Queen Elaine stepped around the table, and bent to kiss Mikael on each cheek. The yellow curls fell around his face as she did so, and as she pulled back, he saw the tears, but the grief displayed in her earlier weeping was absent. She was smiling.

"We have much to talk about, Mikael Sveinson."

ten

What creatures under the sun foresee their death? Only man.
—Book of Morrigan

"No. I won't do it." Bairre squinted into the early sunrays. I've been here over six years, and not once was I invited inside. Now, as soon as they've got trouble, suddenly I'm one of them. Well, to hell with that. I'll stay in the stable."

Mikael slowed his pace to navigate around the fissure in the street that Bairre had just jumped. "Think about it Bairre. Before the king's death, no one knew who you were, but now they do. Those wasted six years are no one's fault."

"Not wasted, Mikael. I knew Matthias."

"Of course. I'm sorry. But circumstances have changed. It's not just that Elaine needs you, but it's your responsibility to her and to Fallon."

"I've no responsibility to Fallon. Elaine may be deceived in that regard, but..."

"All right." Mikael took his arm and stopped him. "I'll not force beliefs upon you. Mother tried that years ago, and it caused you to leave us. But surely, you've enough loyalty to the government that you'll support Her Majesty's order."

"Why me? Why now?"

"You know why, brother. You're Fallonese."

A looter broke from the rubble of a collapsed building and darted across the street in front of them, disappearing in the low shadows of houses that

125

once stood much taller.

"And what is it that she wants me to be?"

Mikael heard the submission in his voice. "Special advisor to Her Majesty, answerable to no one but her."

"Not to you?"

"No." Mikael wondered if Bairre's question had to do with jealousy over his own appointment to Captain over the military. "But we'll work closely together. I'll need your help and your council in reestablishing control. What say you?"

"I'll do nothing in the name of your goddess, or for her sake, not even for the queen."

"I understand that," Mikael replied. "I hope your views on that will change eventually, but in the mean time, I wouldn't advise you to be proclaiming your position on the matter either here in the city or inside the castle walls." Mikael smiled. "I take it then, that you've accepted. Come then, Advisor, let's complete our assessment."

A wine-colored sunset welcomed Mikael and Bairre back to the castle meadows, now guarded by bowman who stood watch around the perimeter of the royal holdings. The captain and the advisor strode across the grass with eyes lowered, both with fresh memories of the sunlit sadness and devastation they had seen in the city of Sogg. The few homes and taverns that escaped damage had been abandoned to the wants of looters and the needs of the starving. Those honest citizens who had survived the earthquake intact had lost everything now to thieves and scavengers. Mikael saw numerous corpses that were too fresh in death to have died on the day the city fell, citizens who were murdered for what they owned or they themselves had stolen.

From inside the broken homes of the city, an infinite variety of pitiable sounds of human and Elkana suffering flowed into the streets like a great tide of blood and sewage, where the individual agonies lost their identities and melded with the death and misery outside, and no part of it was distinguishable from another.

Mikael and Bairre sought the queen's presence as soon as they were inside the crumbled castle walls. They stood in front of her and reported what they had seen, each knowing that the full depth of the loss and despoilment could never be comprehended by one merely hearing about it. The pudgy maiden stood close by, apparently privy to all of Elaine's affairs.

"Your city is dying, my lady," Mikael said, after having described the conditions and circumstances in Sogg. "And her wounds fester, hastening her demise. Many have fled to the countryside, taking nothing but their bleeding lives. I fear that only Morrigan's intervention will save her."

Bairre groaned at that, and then the kitchen throne was silent until Elaine addressed them.

"Ask Morrigan, then, Mikael. "You must ask her. I think that only one from Fallon will achieve a response, for Morrigan is Fallon's goddess, not Sogg's. For Fallon, she may intervene. That, I believe."

Mikael accepted that responsibility, and almost he told Elaine that he believed he was the One, that Morrigan would indeed hear him, but he refrained, knowing the time wasn't right, and Bairre was too close. And no matter that he did not speak up, he told himself, for no good thing could come of it now, except perhaps the comforting of Queen Elaine. When he had some sort of confirmation that he was in fact Morrigan's chosen, when he knew and felt the certainty of it, then he would advise her. To tell her now and be proven wrong sometime later would destroy the faith Elaine had in Fallon. If Oriana and Esras' conclusions about him were wrong, if the arrows had been nothing more than some wizard's spell, if he was not the One, then what was he? No one. Simply a Fallonese student of war who had abandoned his studies to come to Sogg.

"But for now," Elaine was saying, 'it falls to me to rule, and rule I shall, starting with these orders to the commander of my army and the advisor to the realm."

She walked to the table of parchments that were spread across its surface. The maiden followed, turning her head towards Mikael in an unspoken summons. He and Bairre joined them.

"Bairre," Elaine spoke his name with sufficient volume that it might have been an introduction at a royal ball. "you will keep me advised of the people's progress toward restoration of the city, if such a thing can be observed and measured."

She paused, Mikael observed, perhaps to let that statement sink in—to make it clear that she fully expected some sort of progress to be made, and to establish her position that the city and the realm would survive. He admired her for that, and he recognized the particular traits of leadership that coursed the veins of royalty. In Queen Elaine's acceptance of her responsibility, Mikael drew strength, and hope for his river and Fallon Valley.

"You will monitor the crime, and I expect you to know by name the major offenders. As of now, it's your responsibility to notify the citizens that murder and looting in the name of survival will not be tolerated, that death is the punishment."

She looked at Mikael. "The administering of punishment will be the duty of the military, and because the city's life is at stake, the executions will occur without the usual legal delays and distractions. Do you understand that, Mikael?"

"I must say I do not." Did she mean for him to order executions? "There are means less harsh at your disposal, Your Majesty, such as banishment or imprisonment."

Her tone remained steady. "Banishment to where? Imprisonment where? Do I have the means to house and feed the offenders? You err to believe I don't grasp the severity of this plague. A plague it is, and it will spread until Sogg is dead. You yourself said she is dying. Is there time for tribunals and inquires? I tell you there is not." She picked up a single document. "Here is your authority. All it lacks is my signature." She leaned in toward the table to sign it, and her yellow ringlets fell about her face. "You shall have a duplicate, Son of Svein. Keep it with you."

Mikael was still unsure of her meaning. "Authority, my lady?"

"Authority to protect my city. To kill without question any who oppose my efforts to restore it to its former glory. The executions will fit the severity of the crimes, but be sure you understand that the mode of death is the only variable." Elaine paused to moisten her lips, obviously despising the words that fell from them. "Executions will be public displays, whether hanging, boiling, disemboweling, beheading, garroting, impaling, or drawn and quartered. Make it known, Mikael, and perhaps some will take heed." Her countenance darkened, not from determination, but sadness. "Never in the history of Artinus has such a decree gone out to our own. There is no other way."

Silence filled the wide chamber, and was deafening. Surely, none here had the birthright or credentials to look upon the private emotions of a queen.

Mikael spoke, both to terminate the mood and to broach a subject Her Majesty might not as yet considered. "Queen Elaine."

She looked directly into his eyes, jostling his confidence.

"The demons that conjured the destruction, what of them?"

"What of them, Mikael?"

"Should we not prepare for the possibility that Hulda will attempt to take the castle? To rule Artinus?"

"Hulda? You know our adversary by name?" She glanced at Bairre.

The fact that Bairre didn't believe that the earthquake was anything but a natural disaster was not a reason for Mikael to lie to the Queen of Artinus. Should she ask him where Bairre stood on the matter, he would tell her, but she did not.

"Yes," Mikael replied. "I know for a certainty, as Esras did and Oriana does, that Hulda and her coven of Elkana and human witches are responsible for Sogg's destruction. Hulda's purpose was to take the sacred properties of the Fallon River for herself, but I cannot believe she would stop at that, knowing the vulnerable position the realm has fallen into. I only suggest that we take precautions."

"That's a military matter, Captain. You'll have to deal with that as well as several other pressing issues, like how to go about recruiting enough Artinus citizen to replace those soldiers we've lost."

She stressed the word "recruiting," and Mikael assumed she spoke of pressing citizens into service.

"I leave all of that to you," she said, effectively opening further questions about himself and what he might be capable of, even under royal protection.

"The queen's advisor sharing quarters with a common military man? Preposterous, sir. I shan't have it." Bairre fell onto the bed, laughing.

He and Mikael had taken up residence in an undamaged corner of the great hall. Having entered in the dark, following along behind the pudgy maiden, Mikael was surprised with what he saw after she lit a lantern. The north wall had already been replaced and the debris removed. Two beds, two chairs and a writing desk had been provided. Clean breeches and tunics lay on the bed from which Bairre now watched the swaying of Petrina's hindquarters. The name had been revealed through nothing short of a direct question from Bairre.

She turned and met Bairre's eyes, a knowing look on her face. "Her Majesty has less private space than this, you know." The statement was an accusation.

Bairre's mood was not so easily broken. "Then perhaps we've room for another tenant." He winked at her.

Mikael saw the tension in her face. Torn between pride in her position as the queen's first maiden, and the temptation so blatantly put before her by Bairre, she failed to commit herself either way.

"Breakfast is at dawn. You are expected to attend, unless duty takes you from the castle before then." And with that, she headed for the exit, perhaps exaggerating the sway she must have realized was noticed earlier.

"That one would be easy enough, brother," Bairre said after she had departed.

Mikael painfully removed his soiled and tattered breeches, limped to the unoccupied bed, and laid his lean frame across it, face down. Exhausted, he expected sleep to take him immediately, but Elaine's tears, her smile, her grief and her determination became a confused tangle of thoughts that merged with his fresh memory of the dreary and wretched ruins of the city.

Bairre extinguished the lantern, and they lay in total dark, but still Mikael saw Elaine's face plainly. It faded, only to be replaced by Oriana's, then Aingeal's. It would be nice to have Aingeal here now, and her wisdom. If nothing else, perhaps she could simply give him a starting point, some reference that he could return to occasionally to see where he was among the many tasks and dangers that confronted him.

Tomorrow. Early tomorrow, he would consider what to do first. Mikael turned onto his back, leaving his problems on the bed's coverlet, and thought of home, and the river. What had she suffered since the quake? And her people, how were they affected? It occurred to him that he may not know until after Elaine's requirements of him were fulfilled. If he were still alive then, he would go home.

Bairre's easy breathing said that he was asleep. Why shouldn't his brother sleep? Bairre didn't have a goddess pulling him one way, and a queen another. Bairre didn't need the river to be a complete person. Bairre wasn't the One.

Mikael got up and put his dirty breeches back on. He walked out into the quadrangle where a soldier eyed him suspiciously, knowing he was quartered here, but having no idea that he was looking at his captain. The entire castle would know by tomorrow.

He walked, and subsequently found himself at the base of a pile of stone and timber that had been the forebuilding of the keep. He sat on a sharp-angled stone, and for a fleeting moment, he wished he were anywhere but here. That's when Oriana got through.

Mikael saw her in his mind as clearly as if she stood before him. He felt her warmth and her sincerity, but stronger than that was his sudden understanding the she grieved for the recent Fallon dead. He saw the ground open in a hundred places across the valley. Crevices became yawning chasms that swallowed Fallonese farmers who had tilled and tended the same land that now digested their remains.

Mikael was shown a dying river, dying from within, polluted downstream by the touch of witchcraft.

In Oriana's message, Mikael saw the flimsy substance of the spirits that guarded the place where the Fallon, up until recently, had entered the earth. The distress of the ghosts sent them aloft, above that sacred place, where they became no more than wisps of mist, indistinguishable from the wind-torn clouds.

The undines had disappeared, Oriana was saying. They had either died, or were simply absent. Deep in his consciousness, Mikael heard the priestess weeping.

Now as plain as speech, she told him that he was the chosen one of Morrigan, and in his hands lay Fallon's destiny.

The confirmation of his responsibility and identity did not disturb him as he had thought it would. Perhaps he had already arrived at the same conclusion, and Oriana's announcement came as no surprise. Or perhaps Oriana held his attention now with such controlled authority that surprise couldn't register.

Still, she held him, and in another part of his mind, he saw Oriana turning the pages of the Book. Then, "The arrows, Mikael. Where are your arrows?"

A royal page, a lad of about twelve years, woke Mikael to inform him that breakfast would be served in the kitchen within the hour. Mikael and Bairre hurried to prepare themselves, but still, they were the last to arrive. A long table had been brought in and the queen's maidens scurried around it like bees around their own queen, making sure everything was as it should be. Elaine and the four sergeants were seated before the uncovered pewter dishes of salted meats, pastries, dark bread, cheeses, stewed apples and prunes, wafers and jelly. Elaine sat at the head of the table amidst the emerald-green billows of a brocade gown that fell below her feet. The uniformed sergeants were seated on one side of the table, so Mikael and Bairre took the other.

Petrina directed the serving, but she herself served the queen. As Bairre's plate was filled, Mikael saw the nod from Petrina to one of her subordinates. That gesture caused an extra piece of meat to be added to Bairre's meal.

As he ate, Mikael thought of the starving population of Sogg. He was startled by Elaine's sudden question.

"Mikael, have you asked Morrigan for help?"

What simple faith this woman had in the Fallonese. It was childlike, really. To stake one's very existence on a prayer to a Goddess seemed ludicrous, even to him—the One.

"Queen Elaine, might I speak to you of that in private? Perhaps later?"

She was only partially deterred. "Then you have? Well, I suppose you have your reasons for not sharing that here and now. Come to me at your leisure."

From there, the queen addressed her sergeants, calling each by name, having them stand to introduce themselves to their captain. Mikael responded politely, but was unable to keep his thoughts from escaping the noisy kitchen to Oriana's temple. Oriana knew about Esras, surely, or she would not have made the mental contact. She had probably tried long enough to reach Esras that she came to the obvious conclusion. But why would she ask about the arrows? Did she simply see that they were absent, or did she know more?

And what of Hulda? Would Oriana not have warned him if Hulda were an immediate threat? That led to another thought. If Hulda did come against the castle, how would he defeat her without the ash arrows and such a pitifully small army? Elaine would have to be told everything, and immediately.

Coming out of his thoughts, Mikael didn't realize he was interrupting Elaine's instructions to the sergeants. "Queen, I am the One."

"Pardon?"

All eyes were on him now, breakfast forgotten.

"Don't do this," Bairre whispered.

Bairre was right of course, but for a different reason. Bairre wanted him to keep his mental fantasies to himself, and in that, Mikael was reminded of the difficulty he would encounter if he tried to convince Elaine of the truth in such a setting.

"I'm sorry, my lady. I was thinking out loud, I suppose. Might we speak soon?"

"You confuse me, Captain. First you put me off until later, then you start to speak, but follow that with a second request, putting me off once again."

Mikael detected a trace of venom in her words, a mild tremor that poisoned the kitchen air with tension.

"I wouldn't hesitate to say your behavior borders on disrespectful rudeness," she said, "but I shall forgive that on this occasion, considering the stress of your current station and the tasks awaiting you that I'm sure occupy your thoughts, even in my presence. I shall abandon my breakfast and speak with you at once in my chamber."

She stood, prompting everyone else to rise. "Petrina, you will do what you can to reestablish the appropriate atmosphere worthy of my other guests." The emerald billows swirled and rustled in agitation as she turned and glided toward an exit.

She had impaled him on a sword of shame in front of his sergeants and his brother. He hadn't deserved that. Was he not here of his own accord? He made no move to follow the queen until Petrina cleared her throat to get his attention.

"The queen awaits, sir."

Let her wait a little longer. Instead of following her steps directly, Mikael moved the other way around the table until he stood before the sergeants.

"Meet me outside the chapel in ten minutes." Mikael knew the chapel to still be standing. In his first order to anyone in his life, he regained some of the self-esteem cut away by Elaine's reproach. The sergeants would see his delay in running after the queen as a mark of confidence in himself, and the ten-minute requirement would tell them that he, not the queen, would dictate not only how long his conference with Her Majesty would last, but would also establish in his subordinates' minds to whom they would answer from this day forth.

Petrina could not contain herself. "Sir, the queen..."

"Silence, wench! See that my brother and my men are fed properly." And in thus saying, he told himself, he had cleared the girl's head concerning who he was, and where she stood with him. He made himself walk slowly toward the exit, his hands clasped behind his back, wondering if the sergeants could hear the hammer blows of his heart.

Mikael's timing in speaking with Queen Elaine was so very out of line with logic that he wondered about his reasoning ability. Why could he not have waited until breakfast was finished, thereby leaving Elaine's dignity intact? But he hadn't, and so he resigned himself to deal with circumstances as they lay. He knew he had little on his side to start with in terms of evidence of his true identity and purpose. Actually, he had nothing. And it would be necessary to calm Elaine before he could begin. That in itself would probably prove impossible, and the truth of that hit him hard and suddenly as he entered her chamber, a large room above the kitchen, empty except for Elaine and her throne. Being here was evidence that she still trusted him enough to reveal this place to him.

Elaine's usual angelic complexion now blazed with hell's passion, and

Mikael realized her anger had festered and increased because of his delay in coming to her. She seethed, it seemed, refraining from speaking as if she might inadvertently breathe fire upon him.

She sat in a high-backed chair padded with cushions bearing the realm's colors. Her legs were crossed, her arms folded, her hands buried somewhere in the depths of her gown, and her lips pressed together. An eastern window lit her darkened countenance with a dust-filled ray of sunlight that competed with the glow of her hair. Her eyes burned into his like hot daggers as he entered and walked to where he knew he should kneel.

As he went painfully to one knee, he said, "Your Majesty, I was tactless. The responsibilities of being appointed captain of the royal army came to me suddenly at breakfast upon meeting the sergeants, and certainly, I spoke too soon, and inappropriately. I beg your indulgence, and a few minutes of your time."

There, that ought to have done it, or at least softened her sufficiently to hear him. The legs were uncrossing and he could see her hands.

"Tactless? Inappropriate? You might apply those terms to the seduction of one of my maidens, but I'm not one to be trifled with, Captain. I thought I made that clear when I gave you the authority to protect my sovereignty and my city." The hands disappeared. "I am the Queen of Artinus. How dare you speak in riddles to me? In private would have been bad enough, but you have the manners of a pig, sir, to do so at my own table." Her tone softened, but only slightly. "Now speak to me plainly, and make it quick. You've wasted quite enough of my morning."

Mikael knew anger then, enough to rise without permission before this girl who was scarcely old enough to be an adult, much less a queen. He unsuccessfully attempted a submissive tone. "I shan't prolong my statement, Your Majesty. I see no way now to convince you of the truth of what I'm about to say. And finding myself in such a predicament, I'll simply state the facts as they are, thereby ridding myself of guilt should the kingdom fall in your disbelief—a disbelief prejudiced by your resentment of my earlier conduct, which shall prove a small matter indeed compared to what Artinus has and will suffer."

Her mouth fell open. "You dare speak…" She stopped, and then, "Say what it is you've come to say."

"Your Majesty has already established that I am of Fallon. Because of my birthplace, you've granted me an appointment within these walls. I would now be remiss not to advise you that I am not merely the captain of your military."

"Merely? Your insolence astounds me, sir. But go on."

Mikael hesitated, understanding fully that should he not be believed, the punishment implemented would be harsh indeed. But he had come too far to quit.

"I was sent from Fallon against my will, on the pretext of finding my brother in Sogg to inform him of our mother's death. Only after leaving, was I told by Esras, who is now dead, that I am the One chosen from the birth of Fallon to wield the ash arrows against intrusion."

Surprisingly, she didn't stop him at that point, but neither did she encourage him to proceed. He took that duty upon himself.

"At first I didn't believe it, nor did I want the responsibility of it. Even after the arrows were presented to me, I rebelled against the acceptance of something I had no choice in."

Still, Elaine sat quietly.

"I had occasion to use the arrows, and certainly their magic is real, but still I doubted that I was the One. I imagined that Esras and Oriana were mistaken. Subsequently, there were events that seemed to confirm that I had been chosen, and after the death of Esras and the theft of the arrows, I came to accept and understood who and what I am."

"So, you have no proof at all?" Elaine asked.

"None, my lady. That is, I have no proof at this moment. The arrows were stolen before the earthquake, but I cannot believe that the Goddess Morrigan would permit their destruction. Oriana has asked about them, and they must be found. By your leave, I'll take a few of the soldiers and search those areas of the city immediately surrounding the place the arrows were taken. I can identify the robbers." He decided against bringing the matter of Oriana's recent contact to Elaine's attention; that would probably prove to be too much.

Queen Elaine smiled, purposely. Her white, even teeth gleamed between thin lips that were naturally red with the substance of youth. "Am I to believe then, that I sit before one chosen by Morrigan, when I myself am queen only by mortal inheritance? Would that not place you above me? Should I not bow before the One chosen even before Artinus was named?"

"My intent is not to..."

"Your intent, sir, is unclear. From one perspective, you may be truthful. Indeed, you are of Fallon, and it's true that you are only now passing childhood. If the earthquake has hurt your valley, then surely this would seem an appropriate time for the One to make his appearance. However, from another perspective, you have no proof, only a tale of how your proof was taken from you, and further, you ask permission to use your own soldiers, when I have already instructed you to do what you will, militarily, for the good of the realm. So, what am I to believe? You are dismissed."

He had gone as far as he dare for now. He bowed, and turned.

Nearly to the door, she stopped him. "Wait."

She was standing. "Come with me."

He followed her to the stone wall behind the chair she had just vacated. A delicate hand pushed against a stone that owned no distinction from those around it, and a section of the wall moved inward leaving an opening large enough to permit passage into another chamber lit by wall torches and lanterns. The lighting meant that someone else was privy to this secret, or else the queen herself tended to the illumination.

"The royal armory," she said. "Undisturbed by the quake."

And so it was. Sconce light reflected dimly through the smoky chamber from scores of steel blades, bronze armor, and polished shields, all of which hung against the four walls from the timbered ceiling to the stone floor. Mikael, already tense over the uncertainty of what Elaine had in mind, hesitated before entering fully. Either she had decided to trust him, or she had brought him here to have him killed. The acrid air filled his lungs and he coughed, glad for the opportunity to conceal his concern.

"The smoke and heat keeps the air dry," Elaine said. "Otherwise, your soldiers would present less than a professional image going into battle."

Mikael relaxed somewhat at her reference to *his* soldiers. He stepped inside, but glanced back at the passageway to make sure it remained open. Elaine walked ahead, allowing her eyes to scan the bristling walls, as if she were a shopper trying to find just the right device for her next murder.

Mikael attempted to make a mental inventory of the armory's contents, but there was simply too much to see. The room had been unevenly constructed, perhaps purposely in order to conceal its existence from the outside. Not one of the walls was the same length as the other three. Overall, he decided, the chamber had the shape of a warped rectangle. He reached to touch the thin steel blade of a rapier, to test its readiness for service. He found it honed to a keen edge without the slightest mark of rust anywhere along its length.

Other long swords he saw, too numerous to count, some obviously of better construction than others, but all suitable for their intended purpose. There were daggers, lances, javelins, broadswords, shortswords, two-handed swords, axes, crossbows, longbows, and barrels filled with arrows. More arrows, perhaps several hundred, hung in quivers crested with the queen's silver, gold and blue. He lingered at the arrows a moment, long enough to draw Her Majesty's attention.

"Some are ash," she said, "but none are of Morrigan."

She believed him. Relief replaced the smoke in his eyes and lungs.

She stepped quickly then to the far end of the room to a rounded corner. Through the dimness Mikael saw her reach to draw a leather curtain aside. From where he stood, he made out the subdued outline of a two-handed sword, hung vertically away from any other piece of armament. She removed it from pegs set into the stonework, and he saw from her effort that it was heavy, but she managed the weight, keeping the tip from touching the floor.

He walked to her, to assist, not knowing her intention.

"It was the king's," she said, and stepped away from his reach. "It has not been touched by any but him, until now.

"Then forgive me. I only meant to…"

"He hung it here the day before the quake. He practiced with it, and with his long swords, faithfully, daily, even though he had an army to protect the realm."

Mikael heard the quaver in her voice as she remembered her brother.

"I thought perhaps I should have buried it with him. I'm glad now that I did not, for you will need it. But first, one question."

"Ask it, my lady."

"Priestess Oriana. Did you not say she was asking you something?"

The question was worded politely, coyly, to imply she wished to know the nature of Oriana's inquiry, but Mikael suspected that Elaine's real purpose was to have him confirm and explain the contact.

"She and Esras conferred occasionally, Your Majesty, and heretofore I could neither define nor guess the fabric of the medium that transported their thoughts. She spoke to me for the first time last night, and informed me that Fallon suffers greatly, and that the river is dying. She asked about the arrows."

Only then did she hold the five-foot weapon toward him. "My father named it 'Prejudice.'"

He accepted the sword, and upon detaching his eyes from hers, he examined it. The blade, of course, was steel, thick at the center but tapering to a finely honed edge, not what one would expect of a weapon intended for hacking. The maker had melded the blade into the handle in such a fashion that the completed work seemed that it was wrought from one piece. The bronze guard was broad, but not ornately decorated. The only departure from practicality was the precisely inlayed brass wire that adorned the silver guard. This was a weapon not intended for show or ceremony, but for fighting. In holding it, Mikael acquired some of the respect that Oriana and Fallon Valley held for their king.

He stepped away from Elaine, to heft the sword, to feel its weight and balance it at arms length. It seemed made for him. With one hand, he slashed and thrust, sensing the strength that it imparted. Forgetting the queen, he took the sword into both hands and cut down several imagined foes, the speed of his moves stirring the smoke and stale air of the chamber.

"You've used such implements of war before, I see," Elaine said, bringing him clear of the invisible battle.

"At Fallon I was a student of war, as all capable Fallonese men are." He moved toward the rounded corner, to replace the sword on the pegs.

"No, Mikael, it's yours. Take it with you today into the city. Find the arrows, and if you find the thieves alive, slay them. The Goddess would want it so. Take Bairre, that he might be about his queen's business. Arm your guard as you see fit, even from this room."

Aingeal fondled the hot stone at her breast. She stood on a knoll, overlooking the outskirts of what must have been at one time the City of Sogg. Even though the orange evening sun hung low in the sky, she saw few buildings high enough to cast a shadow. But the devastation caused her no concern, because two days ago she had shaded her emotions with wizardry so that she might not experience what could have otherwise delayed her arrival here. Fatigue and hunger, too, were eliminated long before they rose to slow her progress. Refreshed, she was, and unhindered by human needs and frailties.

She descended the long slope at an angle, letting the arrowhead take her to her destination by the shortest route. She had come to know that her mission was urgent—that time was a factor as critical as her arrival. The substance of that urgency concealed itself from her, and she wondered if that was a failing within herself, perhaps because of her inexperience.

The first few people approaching her simply stepped out of her way to let her pass. Aingeal saw the faded light in their eyes, and she took in the odors of their sickness and poverty, but she paused not at all to contemplate their plight.

Farther into the decimation she walked, not breaking stride even for the fetid, swollen and rat-gnawed corpses that lay in her path and accounted for the worst of the stench that emanated from the dying city.

With her purpose set, Aingeal didn't consider that her energetic step and erect posture were signals to Sogg's vermin that she was an outsider, perhaps carrying some item that would sustain their lives another day. She would not later remember how many times she was confronted by examples of Sogg's human and Elkana villainy. They approached with the darkness, accompanied by their closest kin, the rats that crave the filth of the night hours.

But no one touched her. None were capable of coming within arms reach after feeling her eyes upon their own, even in the darkness. And this was nothing for her, because she only had to reach into the shallowest reservoirs of her father's teachings to keep that kind of evil at bay.

On she walked, seeing through the blackness with vision that required no light. Gradually, the odor of rotting flesh diminished, and she entered that part of the city where shreds of hope moved among the rubble in the form of people working at restoring some part of what they once had. By lantern light they toiled, building walls, laying the timbers for roofs, and tending to the many injuries of those who refused to succumb while there was still a chance of their recovery and subsequent ability to aid their loved ones and neighbors.

The ugly and the beautiful of humanity Aingeal saw this night, but neither affected her. Time enough for that after her appointment with uncertainty was met, and her purpose, whatever it was, accomplished. Surely, she was close. The arrowhead glowed now, iridescently, the soft colors alive, prismatic in her hand. She slowed, searching the darkness for some indicator of the unknown thing she sought.

An easterly breeze pulled at her tunic and moved rattling leaves across her feet, and brought the aroma of wood smoke and cooking meat. She turned to face that direction, watching the stone in her hand, asking it for guidance. As if extinguished by the breeze, the arrowhead cooled against her palm, and its light faded, giving it back the cold properties of white flint. She had arrived.

Aingeal stood facing the side of a stone house, the rear half of which lay in an undignified heap in a narrow alley to her left. A gray smoke visible against the night sky failed in its attempt to spiral upwards to cleaner environs, but was shredded and swept away by the breeze, taking its odors back across the torn city. She walked around to the front, and only then saw the soft trickle of lantern or candle light seeping through the hostile bars of a

139

curtained upper-floor window. An arrangement of white quartz and slate served as steps to a wide door that was closed solidly against nighttime intrusion, and Aingeal felt within her bosom, behind the arrowhead, that the heavy oaken boards of the door and the iron bars of the windows were not meant to keep evil out, but secrets in.

She didn't knock, but paused to study the massive brass door handle, and behind that, the inner lock work she could not see, except in her mind. She concentrated on the task, simultaneously calling on the lessons of a summer night long ago in the barn at home, even before she had Rose. The latch moved, clicking softly, and she only had to push at the heavy door with her foot to swing it inward on its rusty iron hinges that reluctantly refused to make their squeaking complaints in the presence of a wizard.

She stepped from the breeze-tossed darkness of street air into the dank inner darkness of undiluted evil. Nothing good lived here, and any trace of former good had long been scoured from the filth and foulness of these floors and walls. Directly in front of her, a staircase curved up and away into elevations she couldn't sort out in her mind. She again caught the pungency of cooking meat, wafted to her on a draft that came from above, crawling like snakes down the rickety steps that were littered with animal bones and teeming with roaches. A rat darted away from her feet as she approached the steps, and she took in the smell of old urine and dried feces. But disgust was foreign to Aingeal in her present state. She ascended, soundless.

eleven

The blind conquer the dark while others stumble in the light.
—Book of Morrigan.

Hulda and Kattrin, alone in their new den near a new branch of the Fallon, discussed the best way to rid themselves of that part of the coven that had become unneeded. The queen witch and her princess could delay them a while longer with lies about going to Sogg, but soon they would begin to talk among themselves, questioning their queen's motives. Some would break away entirely if their speculations elevated to rumors that were believable. That could not be permitted. If just one of the girls made it home, the earthquake would be revealed for what it was, rather than the natural occurrence Hulda needed it to be in the eyes of the citizenship she would soon rule. She and Kattrin would establish sovereignty as the *saviors* of Artinus, not the destroyers. A handful of would-be witches trained by Hulda for one specific task, and having performed that task, would not prevent her total success by their incompetence in other matters during the days ahead.

Kattrin wiggled out of Hulda's arms and faced her directly. "Whom have you chosen to keep alive?"

"The ten of us that hold true power. No more than that. I needn't tell you that once we're established at Sogg, jealousies and bickering over rank and position could jeopardize everything. Trella, I want. She'll be of value later on. As for the other eight, love, I'll leave their disposal to you; however, I suggest a mass killing to lessen the likelihood that someone will escape."

Kattrin stroked the older Elkana's face with her clawed hand. "The stolen waters have done much for your complexion, Queen. You're even prettier than you were." Kattrin made the soft clucking sound of contentment that had become a habit with her when she was alone with Hulda.

Hulda nuzzled the child, pleased with the compliment that would have meant nothing from any other, even though Hulda had some days ago felt the forgotten strength of youth seeping back into her tissue and bones. She had more stamina now, and she realized only tonight in the dark den that her night vision had improved.

She looked at Kattrin now, studying the girl's face and naked form, searching for improvement to what she had always considered perfection. She found nothing different. "Have you been at the water, dearest? Have you quenched your thirst there?"

"Yes. We have the Fallonese secrets at last, do we not?"

Hulda searched Kattrin's eyes, finding them no greener, no brighter. "Secrets no longer. Artinus will thank us for taking from Fallon what the Fallonese should never have kept for themselves. We'll be praised for the gifts of nourishment and prosperity that we share with all. We will be remembered."

Kattrin laid her head on Hulda's stomach, and sighed. "Shall I go now to the coven, while it's still dark?"

"Would it not be better," Hulda asked, "to separate them first, so that those who remain will not see the others die? We wouldn't want the few we keep to be uncertain about their own positions."

Kattrin snuggled closer. "You are wise. Forgive my impetuousness."

Hulda closed her eyes. "Sleep now." She thought of Kattrin's fascination with death and killing, and wondered if the child's age accounted for it. Perhaps maturity and the responsibility of assisting in the administration of the new government would curb such an unusual appetite. They were inconsequential, really, Kattrin's fantasies.

By design, Bairre left the castle an hour ahead of Mikael and his soldiers. He was dressed in stableman clothes and had dirtied his face. He carried nothing to draw attention to himself or make it appear that he had anything worth stealing. Under his tunic within easy reach was a dagger that Mikael had insisted he keep with him. Bairre's instructions were to walk the streets of Sogg on this his first day of duty as Elaine's advisor. He would report to her all he observed that might assist in identifying the numerous criminals that continually stalked the innocent since the city's ruin. Additionally, he was to make discreet inquiries concerning the whereabouts of Greta.

Mikael, uniformed to befit his rank, led Sergeant Barnes, Corporal Silvey, and four soldiers openly into the midmorning streets. They were armed and armored. Mikael carried Prejudice in a leather sheath slung across his back. At his belted waist rested the largest dagger the armory offered—an open display of intent. The sergeants carried crossbows and long swords; the soldiers, longbows in their hands and axes at their belts.

Their one-day mission was to post the queen's broadsides regarding her intolerance of crime, to set examples by enforcing those laws they observed being violated, and to "recruit" young men into service. Only Mikael knew of the queen's authority for him to search for Greta and the ash arrows.

As Mikael stood by while a soldier tacked the first poster to the standing timber of a lamppost, he observed two men on the opposite side of the street exiting a partially ruined residence. One carried a bulging canvas sack. An elderly Elkana man stood in the doorway bleeding from a head wound and cursing the departing thieves who were apparently unarmed.

Trepidation closed in around Mikael like a dark fog. He wore the queen's uniform and colors. He carried the king's sword—a sword that represented justice. In his service were six men, also here on the queen's authority, doing the queen's bidding. He recalled Elaine's instructions and shivered inwardly. He had told himself after receiving those instructions that he was capable and willing to obey her, the last remnant of Artinus royalty. But now, reality faced him squarely.

"Captain?" It was Barnes.

"I see them, Sergeant." He was surprised at the steadiness of his voice. Seconds mattered. He turned the matter in his mind for a different view. Were there mitigating circumstances here? Starving humans stealing from Elkana. Would Elaine accept that as sufficient reason not to kill? He knew she would not.

"Stop them, Silvey." The pursuit would give him a few moments more.

The corporal moved to intercept the perpetrators, and at his sharp command to halt, they did. Mikael tensed. Why didn't they run? Silvey took possession of the sack and ushered the two men to Mikael. Upon stopping directly in front of his captain, Silvey opened the sack.

"Cheese, captain. And some kind of meat. A pair of breeches, too."

The odor of spoiled meat sprang from the open bag and accosted Mikael nostrils. He didn't want to look at the men's' faces, to know them at all, but he did. Both were young, perhaps thirty, one dark haired, the other nearly bald. Neither displayed fear or even anxiety, and were probably confident that their offense was minor in the eyes of soldiers who surely understood that they were simply surviving.

The dark-haired man had hazel eyes. His stance took on no semblance of pride or hostility. Before he dare think further, the two-handed sword was out. Mikael thrust it forward. The hazel eyes widened in surprise and pain. Before the bald man could even realize what was happening, Mikael drew the now bloody blade back and swiped sideways, and the bald head fell to the bricks even before the body. The eyes blinked once.

Mikael wiped the blade on the ragged coat worn by the torso, and sheathed it. "Tack a broadside to that one's chest."

He desperately needed to be sick, but dare not in front of his men. He turned to face Barnes and Silvey. Both were staring at him in disbelief. "A word with you, Corporal, if you please." He stepped beyond the hearing of the others.

"Was this not discussed?" Mikael asked. "Were you not given orders to call upon when so confronted?"

"Yes, Captain, but…"

"Do we need review those orders?"

"No, sir, it's just that…"

"In the future, carry out your orders, and don't bring your hesitation or squeamishness to me. You should have cut them down immediately. In refraining, you have offended the queen. You have placed her decree below your own morals." Mikael saw by Silvey's expression that the point was being solidly placed. "If you can't follow orders, you shouldn't be in a position to give them. Are we clear?"

"Yes, sir, I'm straight on the matter now. Thank ye, sir."

Thrice more that day, broadsides were attached to the bleeding corpses of two humans and one Elkana, all of whom were dispatched by Silvey, or at his order. By this time tomorrow, those citizens who couldn't read the posters would have either heard of its message, or seen for themselves what needn't be written to be understood.

With enough to report to Elaine, Mikael tried to establish his position in relation to where he and Esras had been attacked. He knew he had passed the general vicinity earlier, but now he was deep into the city. He asked Barnes.

"Does the name Greta mean anything to you?"

"Yes, sir. My aunt, rest her soul…"

"Anyone else?"

"Do ye mean the hag that bred those no-account, murdering boys? Yes, sir, I know her, as do all of my men. If the quake didn't get her, you'll likely find her on the south side in one of the taverns where she'll be spending stolen coins." He frowned. "I mean if there be any taverns left."

Twenty minutes later, the six men were entering the south side slums, refreshed with cheese and dark bread carried with them from the royal kitchen, and consumed while they walked. Mikael thought of Bairre. Having not seen him anywhere in the city, he wondered if he might have already returned to the castle. He hoped that was the case, as the broken city would be especially hazardous after the quickly approaching darkness enveloped the streets.

Twilight softened the ugliness of the slums, and painted the east sides of standing structures with a dying purple glow, but the stench remained, although it was not as strong here. The immediate area had been left mostly intact by Hulda's wicked assault. On one street, Mikael saw only two houses that the tilting earth had toppled and crushed. Every window in every home was dark, but the subdued voices and scuffing sounds behind those windows revealed occupancy by tenants who had valid reasons to let the night hide them.

However, one particular structure of board and stone threw its pale lantern light onto the packed dirt of the street with sufficient vigor to announce its presence boldly, as if the souls inside had divine protection against the evil outside. Laughter and quick-paced lute music spilled onto the low front porch and out into the street where it mingled with the yellow light.

"Idun's apples," Barnes said. "Methinks we've found an open tavern."

He licked dry lips, but a swift glance at his captain's face kept him from asking about the drink Mikael knew he wanted.

With his mind back on business, Barnes asked, "Should we inquire within, Captain?"

Closer now, Mikael saw the two armed men at the front, and he caught glimpses of movement in the shadows of the building's near side. Thus protected, a thirsty patron might live long enough to get inside.

Upon spotting the approaching uniforms, one of the tavern guards, a burly man in his mid twenties, rushed inside, probably to inform his employer. His sword clanked against the doorway as he entered, reminding Mikael that he had as yet failed to acquire even one "volunteer" to serve in the queen's army.

"Give me a broadside," Mikael ordered. He accepted it from the hand of a soldier, and tucked it inside his tunic. Turning to Barnes, "Only you and I will enter. Send one man around to the back in case there's an exit to watch. The other three will remain here." He spoke loud enough that all five could hear him. "No one is to leave or enter."

Barnes acknowledged the orders.

"And Sergeant," Mikael added, "remember the punishment for any who defy the queen's decree."

Mikael drew his sword and took the two steps from the street onto the wide porch. He stopped far enough from the remaining guard to leave room for maneuvering the twenty-pound weapon.

"State your business," the guard said.

"My business is the queen's. Get inside."

"Who the hell is the *queen*?"

Obviously, the man had not been informed of Alsandair's demise. The flat side of Mikael's sword struck the young man's temple and he crumpled.

"A volunteer," Mikael said to Barnes. "Bring him inside."

The spacious and odious room they found themselves in held several tables and about a dozen humans, two of whom were women, probably prostitutes. All turned to look at the uniforms. Voices and music fell silent.

At the far end of the room was the guard Mikael had earlier observed run inside. He stood with another man behind a thick oak plank that was supported on each end by a wooden barrel. Horn cups and earthen jugs were neatly arranged on the plank directly in front of the guard's companion, a small man with disheveled dark hair that fell about his face seemingly from everywhere. Two small black eyes peered out of that entanglement, and Mikael thought of a rat in a mound of rotted hay. The little man wore a dirty linen apron, the pocket of which bulged with what could only be coins. The tavern proprietor, no doubt.

Mikael retrieved the broadside from his tunic and handed it to Barnes. "Post it."

Barnes passed among the tables and tacked the parchment to a wall.

"What's it say?" the little man asked.

Mikael approached within arms reach. "It says that King Alsandair is dead." He heard a gasp from one of the tables. "It says that Queen Elaine is now sovereign. It says my orders are hers, and that those who disobey her orders, or who choose to ignore the laws of Artinus, will be put to death.

Lastly, it says that the citizens of Sogg will repair the city."

"Is that all?" the little man asked.

The tavern vibrated with laughter from the patrons, and Mikael heard the shrill voices of the whores. With the flat side of his sword, he raked the cups and jugs off the plank, and the laughter stopped even before the diluted wine spilled into the cracks between the floorboards.

"Where is Greta?" Mikael asked, knowing he would kill for the information, not for the queen, but because Fallon was at stake.

No response. He turned to face the bloodshot eyes of the tavern customers. One stood as if to leave, but Barnes stopped him.

"I shall rephrase," Mikael said, now looking at the tavern keeper. "I have it on royal authority that Greta and her murdering son frequent this place." He lifted Prejudice and pointed it at the poster. "I'm not asking now. In the queen's name, tell me where to find Greta."

The little man's eyes squinted at him. "You'll have to arrest me. I've a duty of my own. A duty to protect my customers. Go ahead, take me to your queen. I've a few things to say to the bitch. She might want to hear how your treating her loyal..."

His severed head bounced off the bar before hitting the floor. Half of the patrons bolted for the door, but were forced back inside by the waiting soldiers. Now Prejudice's tip rested easily against the chest of the tavern guard. The man's pale face and neck glistened with the blood of his dead employer.

"Greta," Mikael said to him.

"One street over, half way down. A two-story building, looks abandoned." The words tumbled out, pushed by breath stagnant with fear.

Mikael lowered the blade, and a sigh of relief escaped the guard's trembling lips, but his eyes widened when Mikael again raised the dripping steel. He lowered it gently, flat side first, and tapped the top of the man's head twice.

"You are now a soldier in the queen's army." Mikael walked among the tables, tapping heads until four more strong men volunteered.

He addressed his six new recruits. "You'll be housed, clothed, fed and trained." Then, pulling Barnes toward the front door, "Take them to the castle. Secure them and report to the queen. I'll be along later."

Odd, how the human and Elkana rats shied away from the mysterious girl.

147

Mikael watched her crossing the street at an angle, as if her destination were firmly fixed. She was slight of form, he noticed, and she walked with a straight back, her head up. She crossed his path, coming from a side street, not pausing or faltering as she was approached several times by those who surely intended harm, but turned away quickly at the last moment.

Mikael saw that occur several times as he followed her through the gloom. Now she approached a house that emitted faint scraps of light from a second story window. Was this not the very house the tavern guard spoke of? But it was not Greta that Mikael limped along behind, but a young girl, one with an agile step and a confidence he could not define.

Mikael stood not ten feet behind her as she stopped at the door, which opened for her after a short delay. She obviously had a key, although at no time did he see her hands about the lock. A trick of the night, perhaps. As the door swung silently inward, the girl's scent came to him on a draft. Familiar somehow, but before he could sort the matter out in his mind, his nostrils were assailed by the repugnant smell of roasting flesh.

As she started her ascent of the staircase just inside the door, Mikael made a quick decision. Logic had nothing to do with it; logically, he would know more about the girl's business here before revealing his presence. But he could not bring himself to associate the innocence of such youth with the sinister and ill-omened foulness of this place.

"My lady, one moment, please."

She hesitated for the smallest portion of a heartbeat, but then took another step upwards.

"Madam, please, in the queen's name."

She turned then, but the darkness of the stairs revealed nothing more.

"Might I inquire whose house this is?" he asked.

"Mikael?"

He knew then, and the sudden knowledge stunned him, and for the moment, he could neither move nor answer.

"Mikael," she said again.

He wouldn't later remember seeing her descend the stairs. She was simply in his arms and pulling him outside.

"Who's there?" asked a gravely voice from the head of the stairs. Mikael had heard that voice before.

Now they were on the street, six feet from the door, and still she tugged at his arm.

"Something wicked and dangerous here," she said.

"Aingeal, why are you here?"

"The arrowhead led me." She pulled back a little. "Why are you in uniform?"

His own questions of her went unasked, his concerns unuttered, taken from him by the sudden appearance of a large dagger-wielding man at the doorway. Greta's son, surely.

Reaching over his shoulder for Prejudice, Mikael lunged. The steel tip carved a deep groove in the closing door. Before the latch was set, he kicked hard against the oak boards that separated him from one of Esras' killers. The violently swinging door slammed against the big man's shoulder, knocking him to his knees at the base of the stairs. As he rose, he screamed, and Mikael knew it was not from fear, but to warn whoever occupied the upper rooms.

The man's size neither slowed him nor affected his athletic leap onto the fourth step of the staircase. He was halfway up before the thick blade sank into his right leg just below the knee. Mikael sensed the hardness of bone, and he heard the muffled crack as it broke. The ruffian fell and rolled onto his back to face his death, which came quickly, but mercilessly.

"Why?" Aingeal asked from the doorway, but Mikael had not the time for explanations.

At the top of the stairs, a choice of direction confronted him. To either side was a room, both closed to the world by canvas curtains. The room to his right emitted light where the canvas failed to stop it. He pushed the dusty curtain aside and stepped in. Greta sat on a stool on the far side of the room, poking a stick into the low flames of a crumbling fireplace. The flames hissed at the grease that fell in white globs from two large pieces of meat on a grate.

"You've killed my boy, haven't you?" she asked, glancing at him before returning her gaze to the fire.

"Yes."

"Do you have a writ? Has the king sent you here?"

"Don't you recognize me, Greta?" Dust swirled from behind him, and he knew Aingeal was there. "Not many days have passed since you rented me and my friend a room above the stable."

She didn't answer, but the focused gaze told him she remembered.

"You took some things from me, Greta. I've come for them."

"Too late," she said, her voice raspy but even, her eyes in the fire. "Unless you want some of the horse. I'm afraid the meat's a bit spoiled, but maybe I've cooked most of the sourness out."

The sword came up of its own accord.

"Mikael," Aingeal said.

He stopped, feeling the weight, wanting to drop it against her shriveled neck. Through his private rage, he saw Esras, his easy smile, and then his bloody corpse. Was that why he was here? For revenge? Or for the justice Elaine required? For neither, he realized. He was here tonight for the arrows—for Fallon. To kill Greta would be murder, nothing less. The punishments he had administered today were the justice Elaine had decreed for offenses committed after the decree. But Greta's crimes, at least the ones he knew of, as heinous as they were, and certainly punishable by death, were acts to be heard before a royal court according to the laws of Artinus as they existed before the earthquake.

Which brought him to another question. Had he murdered the son? Perhaps not, even under the old law, because the man was a murderer himself, armed and attempting to thwart apprehension.

So, maybe the army's captain had acted thus far within the boundaries of his authority. Why that was important to him, he didn't know, for nothing mattered except Fallon.

"You took weapons from me," he said, lowering the sword that she never saw him raise. "Where are they?"

"Oh, that. Probably still in the other room, unless we've sold them." She cut a piece of the horsemeat with a small knife and put it in her mouth.

Demon or Elsa, Mikael thought. "You're the queen's prisoner. Move from that spot before you're told and that'll be your last meal."

He turned then to speak to Aingeal, but she wasn't there. He took Greta's lantern and found Aingeal in the other room, bent over, rummaging through piles of clothing, small farming implements, sacks of grain, cooking utensils, and as varied a compilation of stolen goods as probably had ever been stored in the city of Sogg. He stood in the doorway, watching her, wanting her.

"Now I understand," Aingeal was saying. "*This* is what the arrowhead was leading me to." She came up with Mikael's bow and the quiver of arrows.

They rattled against each other in the quiver, as if complaining about the delayed rescue. She counted them as he watched her face, and in her bright eyes he saw more than was there when they parted at Hitara—a coming of age perhaps. No, something else. A completeness. Would she ever need more than she had? Would she need him?

"Fifteen," she said. Apparently, you've refrained from showing off for your girlfriends."

She smiled sweetly, and he debated within himself whether it was her or the arrows that he wanted most. As she stepped close, bringing the arrows, he had his answer. The quiver of sacred arrows was forgotten as he embraced her. How good it was to have her near again. Nestling his face into the auburn hair, he realized that in their time apart, his opportunities to miss her and hold her in his thoughts had been stolen by the events that had kept him occupied. In that, he had been selfish. She had left her home to come to him. She deserved more of him, if she wanted him. She deserved his thoughts and affection, and he resolved to not allow present or coming circumstances to interfere further. If he survived, and if he ever returned to Fallon, his victories would be incomplete without Aingeal.

Greta's death was not an easy thing to watch. Mikael, having assumed that Elaine would preside over the judicial proceedings, resented her absence at the hearing and the execution. Much to his displeasure, she had excused herself from the entire matter, appointing him to see that the sentence was carried out. Greta's two-day confinement after being convicted and sentenced had given her time to consider the upcoming beheading. In Mikael's opinion, those two days of anguish were cruel indeed. She had suffered greatly by the looks of her the morning she was lead into the sunlit castle meadow. She resisted not at all as the procession of soldiers accompanying her stopped at the block and basket that had been set up in advance. Mikael wished they had forgone the basket; its presence and position added to the cruelty.

Because Her Majesty's instruction had placed Mikael in charge, he stood near enough to see the wrinkled face before Greta knelt to receive the axe. He tried to think of Esras, and the justice that was being meted out here today, but such thoughts gave him no relief. Greta's eyes were sunk into her face and testified to the two sleepless nights of dread and fear.

As she knelt, her thin wrists tied behind her back, those eyes, although dark with foreboding, found Mikael's, and she smiled. It was faint, that smile, so very faint that no other observed it. The cracked lips parted, almost imperceptibly, and the tips of her few yellow teeth were visible to him. She did not mock him as her captor, nor did she hold him in contempt with her smile. She simply saw someone in the sea of strangers who was familiar. Mikael recognized that, he felt it deeply, and cursed himself for meeting her eyes and seeing such a pitiable gesture.

A soldier instructed her in whispers how she was to place her neck against the block. The hushed conversations in the assembled crowd ceased in expectation of what they had come to see.

Greta closed her eyes. Mikael would remember her clearing her throat a heartbeat before the axe fell. How odd, he thought, that she would attempt to rid herself of some minor irritation just then. Had she waited the smallest part of an instant, any concern over even the greatest of discomforts would have been eliminated forever.

He took some selfish comfort in that. Even though she had given birth to the bastard devil that killed Esras, and even though she had probably condoned the murder of countless others, there was a certain amount of relief, or grace, in knowing that Greta had been removed from the squalid conditions of her life.

Dawn stole into the stable and removed the blanket of darkness that covered the bed of Bairre and Petrina. She woke, not from the invading light, but instinctively, as she had every morning since Prince Andres had selected her from among the entire kitchen staff to attend to the whims and needs of Elaine. Since the day the royal family was reduced to one, Elaine had come to depend on Petrina, and in that dependence the queen had begun to confide in her. Petrina had gradually but surely learned Elaine's moods and desires. She knew when the queen needed a confidant and when she needed privacy, and since Elaine had been thrust into the never-expected position of Queen of Artinus, Petrina had paid particular attention to those royal matters she was not excluded from. Not for her own gain, at least not at first, but out of gratitude, Petrina studied and memorized Elaine's reactions to the daily demands placed upon her. And in that, Petrina was successful in becoming needed, which was a thing she'd never had, and now having it, she became leery of anything that posed the slightest threat to that which she had earned and would keep at any cost.

She lay now facing away from Bairre, her eyes open, conscious of his cool arms around her, and listening to his breathing. She wondered if he considered her an easy mark. Perhaps she was. Not many men had wanted her, but Bairre was not her first. And Bairre had approached her differently, and that difference had attracted her. He was bold, straightforward in what he wanted, and it was almost as nice to be wanted as it was to be needed.

She rolled in his arms, pushing her warm fleshiness against him, knowing he liked that, knowing her full body was not unpleasant to him like it was to some others she had known. She wondered if she loved him, hoping she did not, or would not, because he was the brother of one who had inserted himself between herself and Elaine. The queen seemed to believe in Mikael as something other than a drifter who blew in through the portcullis on the spring winds. Certainly, he was not what he represented himself to be. Elaine was blinded by the teachings of Alsandair, who most devoutly believed in Morrigan as the goddess of Fallon. It was that belief that caused her to give Mikael his appointment as captain. Ridiculous.

Bairre had made enough scoffing comments to let Petrina know that Mikael was at best, self-deluded. At worst, he was an enemy of the realm. No goddess had chosen him for anything, and there were no arrows with fantastic powers to be unleashed only at Mikael's command.

But Bairre would do nothing to disrupt the favor in which he had found himself. Neither would he do anything against his own brother. Perhaps it was best that Petrina have him believe she loved him, and nurture the relationship, but try not to love him at all, because his brother had to be stopped, or at least exposed, and when that happened, Bairre would have no further use of her, regardless of his spiritual beliefs or disbeliefs.

But for now, and until she devised the means, she would press Bairre gently but consistently for anything she might use to regain that part of the queen's attention that was being wasted on Mikael Sveinson.

The advance of spring was not ordinarily a welcome prospect for the Elkana, for they preferred the cooler months. But delightfully for Hulda, the continued fair weather hastened the decay of the eight corpses in the swamp, for she had worried that the coven would uncover Kattrin's butchery. She instructed the princess to have herself and the remaining eight witches ready to go at dawn before the sun-warmed remains began to announce their presence. Let the vultures and maggots dine in private, she told Kattrin, and let them keep the deaths as their own secret.

The mid-morning sun illuminated the path ahead and served as a constant reference point to guide the experienced witches toward Sogg. Kattrin walked with Hulda behind the group, leaving Trella, the most trusted, in the lead.

"There are rumblings, Queen," Kattrin said. "Discontent."

"Over what?"

"Trella, I think. Some are referring to her as the 'second princess.'

Nothing more than jealousy, it seems."

Hulda took the news more seriously than Kattrin could know. Petty jealousy within the coven was one of the troubles she hoped to avoid by eliminating the girls that had been left behind. Hulda trusted Trella almost completely. Her reasons for that trust lay deep inside Elkana culture, and could not be articulated, only felt and known. Much of the coven's strength rested in Trella, and she would be faithful. Perhaps one or more of the other girls had recognized Trella's energy and devotion to purpose, and were jealous of her, and the disease of jealousy, as contagious and virulent as ulcerated swamp cankers, would have to be cut out and destroyed.

"Keep me apprised, love," she said. "I must have the girls as one cohesive unit. We'll not arrive at Sogg divided among ourselves."

The morning after Greta's execution, Queen Elaine requested that Mikael and Bairre join her for breakfast. Mikael thought it time that Elaine meet Aingeal, so he brought her along. Although she had shared his quarters since her arrival, as far as Mikael knew, Elaine had not been told. Upon entering the kitchen, Mikael noted that the sergeants were either late or had not been invited. Elaine, already seated, had pushed her pewter plate out of her way to make room for documents she was studying. Petrina stood at her side, her eyes scanning the parchments as her queen examined one and then another. Mikael could not fathom why she trusted that particular servant with the affairs of state.

Elaine looked up, the studious frown replaced with her welcoming smile, which instantly vanished upon seeing Aingeal. Mikael saw the now all too familiar jutting of Elaine's chin, which meant that he had again violated protocol.

He bowed. "Your Majesty, may I present Aingeal Zanesdottir, of Hitara?"

Aingeal did not bow, but rather lowered her head momentarily. "Queen Elaine, I am honored. I hope you can excuse my intrusion. If so, I believe I can be of some service to you. Mikael…"

"Mikael can speak for himself," Elaine said. "And I'm certain he will. Please be seated. Petrina has prepared baked swan."

Mikael, uneasy now because of Elaine's unfriendly tone, took a seat at the opposite end of the table from Elaine, and Aingeal and Bairre sat to his left and right. "Your Majesty," he began, "I thought it prudent to introduce you to Aingeal, and explain her part in the recovery of the ash arrows. And I hope you'll learn to depend on her as you do Bairre and I, for she has certain uncommon abilities that may prove invaluable in our efforts to keep your subjects safe."

"Is that right?" Elaine's tone was unchanged.

If he didn't know Elaine as well as he did, he might have thought her demeanor was unintentionally colored with the palest hue of jealousy. "Might we speak in private, the three of us?" he asked.

"We *are* in private, Captain. Do you not trust your brother as much as I trust Petrina?"

Mikael had learned that when Elaine used his rank instead of his name, she was not pleased with the immediate circumstances. Petrina glared at him now, her contempt as perceptible as the aroma of the well-done swan. Torn between distrust of Petrina and his duty to the queen, he hesitated, his uncertainty speaking for itself.

"Come now, Captain. You've brought her here, now explain her presence."

It was not a request. "I met Aingeal on my way to Sogg. At that time, she was a student of... of her father." He glanced at Petrina, whose eyes were back on the documents. "She's a wizard, Your Majesty."

Petrina looked up, Bairre grunted, but Elaine's expression remained untouched.

"By wizardry and the inherent power of Morrigan's arrows, Aingeal found Greta's abode. We have her to thank for the justice that's been served in your name in that matter. Aingeal will know when immediate danger threatens us. What abilities she has beyond that, I know not."

"Are the arrows on your back the arrows you speak of?"

"Yes. I have fifteen," Mikael said.

"I see them, and I believe that they and you are of Morrigan, because I have been taught since childhood that they and you would come." Elaine's gaze shifted from him to Aingeal, and then back again. "But I'm not convinced of this girl's power or motive. However, I'm certain of you, Mikael, and that's enough." She stood. "Welcome, Aingeal of Hitara, to Sogg and my broken home. I accept you here as I did Mikael and Bairre. In return, you will do what you can in my protection and in restoration of my holdings."

Aingeal bowed, and as she rose, she took Mikael hand in her own. He felt her trembling.

"Petrina," Elaine said, "if you please, set another place for breakfast."

Petrina's actions suggested no reluctance, but in the tightening of

Aingeal's fingers on his own, Mikael understood that Aingeal felt Petrina's hostility toward yet another partaker of Elaine's attention. And that truth was an oddity in itself, Mikael reasoned, because Petrina, as a loyal servant dedicated to the good of the realm, should welcome that which the queen saw as beneficial. But the subtle yet definite variations in Petrina's demeanor hinted at something undefined that left an almost invisible haze over the entire situation, causing relationships to appear out of focus and uncertain. Could Elaine not detect any trace of that?

As the meal progressed, Mikael let himself put aside the many problems that confronted him, and he began to relax. The swan was fresh, delicious and cooked to tender perfection with just enough cloves and cinnamon. As was the custom, it had been prepared with the feathers left intact. The spiced wine had been warmed, and went well with the waffles and jelly. His enjoyment came to an abrupt end before his hunger was satisfied, when Elaine spoke.

"Aingeal, you were a student of your father? Is he then a wizard also?"

Mikael set his wine aside and waited, somehow fearing Aingeal's response.

"My father is dead, Your Majesty. But he taught me well."

A perfect answer, Mikael thought. Too much information now might give Elaine cause to doubt.

"I'm sorry, child," the queen said. But I must ask—have you the power to tell us where this witch is that created the earthquake? Does she pose a further danger?"

"I know this, and this only—she has departed her home territory, but is stalled somewhere twixt there and here. The evil I felt on the day of the quake is not near."

This was news to Mikael.

"And what has stalled her?" the queen asked.

"I don't know."

"Mikael," Elaine said, "have you heard from Oriana?"

"No. My contact with her occurred only on that one occasion. I don't know if I've lost the ability to receive, or if she attempts communication only in time of need. The latter is true, I suspect."

"Keep me apprised, please."

With that, the queen returned to her meal, and Mikael thought the topic exhausted, until Petrina addressed Aingeal.

"And where is the witch's home? Perhaps Her Majesty would want to send the army to intercept, if in fact it's thought that the menace is headed here."

156

Even Elaine looked puzzled by Petrina's input.

Aingeal looked at Elaine, unsure whether or not to respond. Elaine nodded, effectively advising Aingeal to proceed.

"In the great swamp. From there she caused the destruction."

"I cannot spare the military at this time," Elaine said. "Restoration is paramount. Thank you, Petrina."

Elaine's gratitude seemed sincere, and Mikael relaxed again. The meal ended without further tension. However, that night, Mikael wondered if perhaps the queen got her first whiff of doubt when Petrina failed to bring her the warmed wine she was accustomed to at bedtime, nor could the girl be found anywhere within the castle walls.

Petrina knew no one would look for her in the stables, so she insisted that Bairre take her there.

"I don't see why we have to leave my perfectly clean and heated room to come out here," Bairre complained as they entered. The familiar smells of hay and horse dung assailed him as he followed her in. He had thought he was done with this place. "Our little fling is not exactly the realm's best kept secret."

"Little fling? Is that what it is?" In her sudden anger at Bairre's insensitive comment, Petrina momentarily forgot her purpose.

Bairre retrieved the lantern from its peg and lit it with the small torch he carried. "No, of course not. I only meant that we've been seen together quite often, and to others it may seem we're having a fling. Even Elaine's probably heard of it by now."

Never having had a real lover, she believed him, and the calm that resulted brought her back to what she needed. "I'm afraid for Elaine. Do you believe a witch caused the earthquake?"

He held the lantern near her face. "What? Are you afraid of something, Petrina?" Seeing her sincerity, he answered. "I don't know. I haven't really thought about *why* it happened. Mikael certainly believes Hulda caused it."

"What do you believe?"

Bairre considered that, maybe for the first time. Always, he had dealt with what he *didn't* believe. "I believe in myself, and I suppose that's all."

"Will you take me to the Great Swamp?"

"Petrina, what are you thinking? Are you in trouble?"

"No, not like you think. But I need to talk to this Hulda, if she exists."

"Why?"

She kissed him then and pushed herself against him, backing him toward the pile of hay. "Will you, Bairre? Will you do that for me?" Another kiss, this one wetter, longer. Pulling at him now, she attempted to get him down.

"Petrina, stop. You can't get what you want like that—not from me. If I take you to the swamp, it'll be because I want to, and I don't. Besides, Elaine wouldn't let us leave the castle that long, especially now."

She feigned anger and spat her words at him. "I thought you were different from your brother. I thought you understood that he's a fanatic, and that he's contaminated the queen with his insane notions of witches, magic arrows, wizards, and a river he thinks is his. You're stupid, Bairre, and if you'll not help me protect Elaine, I'll have nothing more to do with you." She took the lantern from him and turned away.

"Where are you going?"

"To the swamp." She stepped into the night and turned toward the main gate, having not the slightest idea where or how far the swamp was from Sogg, but understanding that she didn't need to know. Her steps were quick, determined, believable.

"Wait." Bairre's urgency was a half whisper. He went to her. "We'll leave when I say, not before. And not tonight. I've got to work out how to cover our absence."

Bairre lay awake in the dark, nestled into the most comfortable bed he'd ever known. He was warm and filled with hot nourishment from the kitchen, where the royal pastries and meats awaited his next whim. To risk his newfound treasures, especially now when the common people were starving, was unthinkable. Yet, he had thought about that and little else, and was now committed to the risk. And for what? A chubby kitchen maid. How many tavern wenches much prettier than Petrina had he used and discarded without caring or even looking back? What was it about Petrina that made it impossible not to want her again and again? Something indefinable and intangible that no woman had cursed him with before.

So, he would do this thing for her. He would take her to the swamp, and perhaps they would indeed find Hulda. And he would not tell Mikael, which amounted to a lie. That was the part that hurt the most. Having walked away from his family those years ago, expecting never to see or hear of them again, and now to have Mikael back, had improved his outlook on life many times more than his new position and its comforts.

He loved Mikael, and even though he could not believe in Morrigan nor accept any of the Book's teachings, he would not discourage those beliefs by Mikael. Every man to his own way was the creed he had lived by, and the creed that had given him the strength to leave Fallon. And other than this one deceptive act, he would do nothing to prevent Mikael from moving forward in his fight for the valley, even though nothing could be regained, because nothing had been lost. The Fallon River was a river, nothing more, and the Fallonese had suffered nothing in its divergence, except in their minds. The health and prosperity of the valley people were not evidence of divine assistance, but simply the evolvement of the fierce northern fighters and takers whose ancestry accounted for their longevity, and whose inherited determination and abilities accounted for their wealth.

Bairre thought of Oriana and turned onto his side beneath the woolen blankets, as if he could turn his face from the priestess. The people had listened to her babblings from the Book, as the old ones had listened to the religious leaders of Fallon since the beginning, and they were deceived, all of them. Ludicrous, it was, that such a strong culture could be weakened by a foolish fantasy, and even more ludicrous that the lies had persisted even after the glacier had moved the people south.

Bairre's anger at his abandoned kin, and at himself for letting Petrina penetrate an emotional barricade that had held for years, kept him awake an hour longer. If he had some reason to agree with her on the matter of finding Hulda, he'd be able to rationalize that he was doing this thing not because she controlled him, but because it was right. But he had no such comfort to give himself, because he saw no point at all in leaving Sogg. Surely, Petrina had facts that he did not.

Mikael had told him almost nothing, and until now, he was thankful for that, because Mikael was driven by a myth that Mikael knew was not shared by his brother. In respect for Bairre's non-belief, Mikael had avoided the subject, except to the queen in Bairre's presence.

But now Aingeal had arrived to reinforce in Elaine's mind the very things the queen already believed about Sogg's fall and the hope of its restoration through a Fallonese bearer of ash arrows, and a wizard. The fact that Aingeal supported Mikael's efforts—efforts based on faulty beliefs—was a strong indicator that she was a fake with perhaps no special talents at all, just another hamlet peasant girl with designs on something better.

"To hell with them all," Bairre said aloud. "I'll probably be better off in the swamp."

He slept then, albeit fitfully, amid visions of Hulda and Petrina.

Conclusions were arrived at among the staff at the castle concerning Petrina's absence. Some said she was off on some errand for the queen. Others thought she had been dismissed because of her amoral conduct with the royal advisor, and still others believed she had been abducted, for she had simply vanished from their midst. However, Elaine and Mikael finally agreed that there should be no search party sent out, nor would it be necessary to initiate an investigation through interviews of those in a position to have knowledge of the girl's departure. Bairre was also gone, and although he had business in the city, Mikael said, Her Majesty might want to delay inquiry until he returned, because of the likelihood that Petrina was with him. Upon her safe return, there would be ample time to reprimand her concerning the abandonment of her duties and her conduct with the advisor, which was intolerable given her station as the queen's first maiden.

These decisions and conclusions were unknown to Petrina, although her concern over the probable disciplinary measures being considered at the castle were a weight that added reluctance to the task she had set for herself. She and Bairre pushed through the new growth of the countryside with barely a pause to appreciate the freshness of the early summer air or the small wild creatures that flushed and scurried away from the intruding sound of heavy and hurried steps.

Bairre, strong with endurance from a lifetime of toil in and around the stables, was surprised at Petrina's agility and energy. Constantly on his heels, she would have taken the lead, urging him forward, if she had known the way toward the lowlands they sought. She seemed without affection now, her purpose fixed, and her attention set on nothing else. Even during the still, clear nights, she neither offered her warmth nor permitted his touch, and Bairre began to understand that Petrina's warmth would not be his again until the mission was completed.

Two days into the journey, they found it necessary to cross a shallow branch of a wide stream that had not existed when Bairre traveled from Fallon to Sogg all those years ago. The knee-deep water was cold, but not as cold as the clear waters of the Aine that Bairre played in as a child. Could this be one of the new branches of the Fallon that Mikael spoke of? Probably not, because it lacked the clarity and chill of glacier melt water.

Suddenly, he remembered the undines. His parents had told him they were real, a product of Morrigan's love of Fallon, and he had believed because he was a child, and children were easily deceived. On the lush summertime banks of the Aine, he thought he had actually seen an undine through the glow of twilight as something surfaced near where he sat. Surely, it had been nothing but a fish, although its grace and easy movements had remained a part of that memory even until now.

Having crossed the new stream, Bairre and Petrina found themselves away from the low ridges south of Sogg, and the terrain leveled out onto a grassy plain dotted with evergreens. The closer to the swamp they came, the more Bairre's thoughts went to Fallon, and home. It lay in peace on the other side of the Great Swamp, and even though the many years separated him from there, he would be able find it with ease. There were those that would remember him should he return. Perhaps some would even welcome him.

"My feet are wet," Petrina whined, effectively bringing him back to reality.

He realized then that they were very close, and peering ahead through the dying evening light, he could see the black trunks of dead trees extending upward into a haze of darkening fog. The leafless and inflexible branches reached up and out, as if warning he and Petrina to come no closer.

"We'll spend the night here," he said.

With his sword, Bairre felled a small pine and then placed one end into the notch of another tree, allowing the other end to rest on the moist ground. He cut several boughs from a standing tree and worked them into the branches of the tree he had cut down. With more bows placed on the ground inside that simple framework, he and Petrina would have a reasonably dry sleeping arrangement and protection against the night breezes.

At dawn, he left Petrina sleeping and stepped out of the crude shelter to relieve himself. The light of the eastern sky told him to expect a clear day. He shivered against the morning chill, but consoled himself with the certain knowledge that the temperature would rise quickly. As Bairre walked away from Petrina, a calm he hadn't know since leaving Fallon gently took hold of him. The marshy smell of mud and grass gave him a peace that he heard in the windless silence of the wilderness. Then, the faraway calls of waking crows broke the stillness, but reinforced the serenity that could not survive anyplace inhabited by people. The thought occurred to him that he and Petrina could make their home here, just the two of them, living off love and what the wilderness might provide.

Foolish, that thought. Perhaps he didn't actually love Petrina, and certainly, she would never abandon Elaine.

He walked on, headed toward the soggy swamp border, which was marked by the line of dead trees. How would he ever find anyone here, much less a particular witch? He stopped to silence his sloshing steps and to take in the peace again, and the vastness that surrounded him.

A distant high-pitched sound came to him from somewhere in the breaking day, but faint, so faint that its direction could not be determined. Crows, probably, their calls distorted by distance. He returned to Petrina and woke her, offering cheese and bread that he had carried from Sogg.

Her eyes still closed, she reached to pull him toward her, but stopped, waking fully and realizing where she was. Again, Bairre experienced her reluctance to touch him. She took the food and crawled out into the day, ready to go.

As they approached the scarecrow trees, Bairre said, "Fallon Valley lies on the far side of the swamp. I've no knowledge of what lies in the marshes, except mosquitoes and snakes. When I left Fallon for Sogg, I walked around that way." He pointed to the right.

Before Petrina could respond, he heard again what he had earlier thought was crows, but at this apparently closer location, he knew the cries were not those of birds. They were human, or perhaps Elkana.

"What was that?" Petrina asked.

"Stay with me," he said, and walked toward the voices.

Having gone less than a hundred yards, the voices became somewhat clearer. All were female, he was certain of that. Had he found the witches this easily? Even though he could not as yet tell what they were saying, he decided that they were arguing. The volume of the voices rose and fell, and those involved seemed to interrupt each other continually, but the swamp growth and the distance absorbed enough of the words that he could make no sense of them.

Turning to Petrina, he said, "Wait here, and keep quiet. I'll try to see who it is."

"See who it is?" Petrina's eyes flashed a message to him that he had said something stupid.

"It's Hulda, of course. We've found her. *You* wait here. You've done what I asked by bringing me here."

"You can't go to her alone, Petrina. She's a witch." He reached to take her arm. "Do you forget what she's done to Sogg?" He surprised himself with that statement. Why had he said that? He knew better. It was an earthquake, nothing more.

Petrina pulled free, making no attempt to conceal her annoyance. She stepped around him and walked deeper into the swamp, toward the voices.

Hulda's rage entered upon the black fringes of violence, and she felt that, and controlled herself. Three of the original nine had demonstrated disrespect in the extreme by their suggestion that Hulda had grieved the coven by giving Trella a supervisory position. One human and two Elkana girls, Theane (human, and beautiful by human standards), Myronica, and Cara, stood in front of the other four they represented. Cara had apparently been appointed to speak for the group, and speak she did, although numerous interruptions came from those in agreement who wished to be heard.

Trella stood behind Hulda with Kattrin. She had already informed her queen that the discontentment of the others was not known to her, and she apologized to Hulda for that, for as Kattrin's second, she should have been aware of unease within the coven. But now, since the matter had escalated into open argument, Trella said nothing, letting Hulda handle the revolt.

Cara was speaking to Hulda. "We'll not heed another instruction or piece of advice from Trella." Her face had flushed crimson with an ego that carried her onward. "We see plainly how it'll be once we've taken Sogg. We'll have to go through Trella to consult even Kattrin. We refuse…"

Hulda screamed, venting her anger in a screeching blast that silenced Cara immediately. The sound rose with the swamp's morning steam, and died. She could find no words to address the blatant disrespect. She had killed so many times for so much less, but even in her fury, Hulda's wisdom stayed her hand. She may lose if she attacked them all at once, for the girls behind Cara were well versed in witchcraft. Together, they may prove too much. And besides, she would need most of them once they reached Sogg.

But not all of them. She could afford to lose one, maybe two. Kattrin would expect it. And it was necessary, apparently. Simple logic would fail, as it almost always did when jealousy was the agitator.

In the silence, Hulda's eyes fell upon Cara's, and attached themselves there like a flame to a candlewick. The younger woman lost her color, apparently reading Hulda's intent. She turned to Myronica, then Theane, but they would not meet her eyes, as much as saying that Cara had gone too far, and they had no support to offer her.

Hulda recognized that weakness in the young witches, and confirmed yet again to herself the value of terror. Yes, she would kill one of them. Cara. She would kill Cara. A necessary price for the maintenance of cohesion.

"Kattrin," Hulda whispered while still staring at the girl she had condemned.

With that breath from Hulda, Cara knew. She took a faltering step backward and bumped into one of her own. "Queen," she said, "I have spoken for all of us, for the good of the coven. I felt it needful to bring the matter to your attention." Her voice quavered with fear, her confidence gone.

Kattrin stepped to Hulda's side, and Cara broke. She fell to her knees and dropped her eyes to the bright-green moss. Her black hair fell about her face, and in the early sunlight, Hulda saw the soft strands dancing from the tremors that had taken hold of Cara.

Cara looked up now, her complexion faded to the color of bones. "Queen Hulda, if I've shown disrespect, it was unintended. Now that the matter has been placed before you, we of course leave it to you. We will all abide by your ruling, as always." Again, she looked up into the faces of those beside and behind her, needing a supporting comment. "And if Trella is to be Kattrin's second, then so be it. We've only come to you today for a decision, that's all."

Cara's cowardly reversal was as nearly disgusting as her earlier display of disrespect. "Kattrin," Hulda said again. She heard the sudden intake of breath from Kattrin, and then her faint sigh, and Hulda shivered from the delight of giving her lover the kill she craved, even considering the loss of one of their own.

Kattrin took the one step to the kneeling Cara. "Stand up, child," she said, her voice low and kind.

Hulda smiled in spite of the corpse that she expected to be prostrate before her in the next moment. Kattrin was no more than a child herself, and yet she had used that term to address Cara. Hulda experienced a sudden warmth upon realizing Kattrin had probably heard her use that tone with others, and now copied it. A compliment, to be sure, but more. Kattrin respected her, Hulda thought, as well as loved her.

Cara stood, facing Kattrin. Hulda saw Cara's eyes focus on something in the morning forest, behind Hulda. And then the girl screamed.

"Intruder! Queen, an intruder—a spy!"

Cara was pointing now, and even in the urgency of a possible threat to the coven, Hulda saw the relief on the condemned girl's face that came from a possible stay of execution. Hulda turned then, as did the entire coven, to peer into the steam-enshrouded and limbless trees for that which Cara had seen. And Hulda saw the distant and dark silhouette of a human female moving steadily toward her, disturbing the black water, turning it with her steps to droplets of sunlit dark gold that rose and fell before the approaching stranger.

Hulda noted the confidence in the intruder's steps, and her powers of perception told her that the girl carried a purpose not harmful to the coven. She was overweight, this human, but she carried herself well. A volunteer perhaps, to replace the soon to be deceased Cara.

"Permit her to approach," Hulda said.

"Queen," Kattrin whined. "What of Cara?"

"That can wait."

Petrina walked into the midst of the witches as if she belonged there. She spotted Hulda and correctly identified her by the way the others stood around her. She walked directly to her across drier ground and stopped only inches from her.

"I seek Hulda," she said. "Are you she?"

"I am."

"I bear news for you from Sogg. Information that you need."

Hulda studied the girls face. "Your eyes are untypical in humans. Have you some special ability?"

"No. I am Queen Elaine's maiden, nothing more, and in that capacity I have learned certain things that will interest you."

Who upon Satan's world was Queen Elaine? But needing to prove that she needed nothing from Sogg, Hulda ignored Petrina's obvious impatience to impart whatever news it was that she had carried from the city. "I've not seen so deep a blue before. Can you see the future?"

"I can see yours, Hulda, queen of the witches, if you fail to receive what I've brought to you."

Such forwardness was a direct offense against Hulda, but she accepted it, understanding that an outsider, especially a human outsider, had no conception of the respect due to one of her power. And strangely, the girl's straightforward manner was refreshing. Hulda would liked to have seen such calm in Cara's aggression.

"Speak your mind, child," Hulda said. "Your name first, if you please."

"My name is Petrina, an unimportant fact, except that I'll ask you to remember it when you come to Sogg. Is that not your intention?"

"Say what you've come to say." Hulda's tone had lost its kindness.

"I have come about Mikael Sveinson, a mere boy from Fallon Valley. He testifies, and the queen believes, that he is chosen of the Goddess Morrigan, and that it is his destiny to return to his people the river that you despoiled. To that end, he will fight you."

"This is what you've come to report?"

"Have you not heard of the One who would come from childhood? I tell you this is he. He lives within the castle walls, accepted by Elaine, appointed captain of the royal army. He has certain magic." Petrina gazed steadily at Hulda in an attempt to appear believable.

"I've heard this lie before, Petrina of Sogg. I killed the liar. And she was only half human. You, child, are all human, as are those of Fallon. I've no use for any of you. Shall I kill you also?"

At that, Kattrin's breathing became audible.

Petrina's calm remained. "Perhaps you haven't been told of the arrows he carries. Perhaps you're ignorant of the wizard who has come to his aid."

Hulda tried to hide her curiosity. This was in truth the third warning that had come to her, and she was wise enough to ignore nothing. To learn all that this girl from Sogg knew of the matter, she would continue her bluff.

"Rumors persist among the human settlements, just like the rats. I've no time for weak-minded beliefs. What's your motive for coming here with lies? Do you seek my protection?"

Petrina hesitated at that, not having considered revealing her jealousy. But here, out of hearing of any from Sogg, she would speak her mind. To do otherwise would be folly, for Hulda would recognize the deception.

"I do not wish for this Mikael to remain at Sogg. He has convinced my queen that she needs his services, and whether that be true or not, I confess that I do not know. I merely wish him dead, or at least gone from the castle." She dropped her eyes. "Since being taken into the castle by Queen Elaine, I've not encountered a rival for her affection, and I see that in Mikael Sveinson. If there's any truth to what they say about him, I lay that before you, that you might either advise me on how to destroy him, or do it yourself."

"I'm inclined to believe you," Hulda said. "But still, I don't believe in gifts to humans from goddesses. I alone hold power over this land, and it is I who will rule Sogg. Even so, tell me now of the arrows and the wizard, and the one you call Elaine, but be warned; if I sense deception, you'll not leave this place except in spirit."

Petrina told her of those things she had observed and overheard. She spoke of what Bairre had told her, and of Aingeal. She went on to describe the damage and death the earthquake had brought to Sogg, how many of the royal family had died, and how the citizens and soldiers had begun to rebuild. She itemized the castle's defenses, both in weaponry and personnel.

Then, "I have betrayed Elaine. I care not for the people of Sogg, but only for her. And it is for her that I have betrayed her. If you have the power to create earthquakes, I know that Elaine's weakened defenses cannot stand against you. I ask only one thing in return, that you spare Elaine's life, and mine, and that you give her some station of dignity when all is accomplished."

"A little late for request, my dear," Hulda said. One of the coven giggled. "You have already relinquished the information, and only now do you ask. You're not much practiced at bargaining, I perceive." She smiled at Petrina. "But we shall see. Return now to Sogg. That's all I can give you. I've told you humans are useless to me, except those few behind me now. To grant a human anything is against my nature, but I will consider your sacrifice. Go now."

twelve

In that hour, the faithful will fail and the trusted shall betray, but who can judge such matters?
—Book of Morrigan

The relief of having confronted Hulda and survived, combined with the surprising acceptance of her own disloyalty, set Petrina's face aglow in the light of the small cooking fire she shared with Bairre that night. Although she had told him nothing, he recognized the change in her, and was glad. Petrina's recent hatefulness and aloofness had seemingly disappeared, taking with them Bairre's own questions about why he had agreed to lead her here.

He watched her now across the fire that illuminated their small sector of the wind-warmed wildwood. Petrina picked daintily at the boiled crayfish tails that a new branch of the Fallon had relinquished. The darkness hung back, granting the intruding fire just enough light to spark desire in its maker. Bairre moved around the breeze-buffeted flames and risked a kiss. It was returned, and in that meeting of souls, he sensed that she was content, that she had gained whatever it was she had come to get. The strangeness of wanting the plain Petrina was forgotten as he laid her back upon new ferns that softened his rough ways. She welcomed his eagerness, reveled in it, and afterwards, in that warm glow that loosens the ties of secrets, she told him what she had done. But she told him in her own way, and that was to push him off her, only to roll atop him and whisper the words that came sweetly and softly, a muddled breathing through lips that brushed his own.

At first, he accepted it, almost understanding her logic and emotions, but the more she talked, the more he came to realize that Petrina was wickedly unstable. If witches could take the city, Mikael would be in danger. Petrina's confessions tonight included the unsealed bargain between her and Hulda whereby Elaine and Petrina would be saved alive. What of the rest of Sogg?

Not that he believed Hulda or any other living entity had caused the devastation at Sogg, and certainly he was not convinced that a handful of human and Elkana women could overrun the city, but Petrina obviously believed those things, and she had made a direct effort to betray the throne by bowing before the evil she believed in. In that revelation, Bairre saw her plainness a little clearer.

He accepted a few more of her kisses and tugs of affection, and then turned away from her as if to sleep, but he slept not. What a position Petrina had placed him in. Covering their absence from the castle with a lie was bad enough—he had been prepared for that since leaving—but to further that lie with the deception Petrina had worked out, was too much. He was part of it now, a willing participant who none would excuse if the truth came out. All of the ugly facts fitted together to pose a question he couldn't answer. Should he betray the betrayer?

In the light of the alarming news from Sogg, Cara's insubordination was set aside. Much to Kattrin's displeasure, Hulda dismissed the offender with a heart-stopping warning to never again speak derogatorily either to or about another member of the coven. Cara's relief was evident as she bowed and backed away from Hulda to rejoin those who had pushed her so close to death's embrace.

For the remainder of the day after Petrina's visit, and long into the breezy and moonlit night, the coven talked of nothing but the one from Fallon. Hulda, who lay in the dark on the damp swamp floor with Kattrin, heard the witches' babble as they continually fed lengths of dead wood into flames that the queen and princess avoided. Their smooth bellies slid together, and the sensation gave Hulda comfort. She attempted in vain to allow Kattrin's caresses to keep her mind away from the coven's muffled conversation. Perhaps, Hulda thought, when considered from a strategist's view, it was good that they had reason to be careful in the coming assault. Maybe with this new concern, they would forget the petty rumblings of discontent that are always emitted from warriors with no battle to fight. Now they had something to make them cautious—something to give them a reason to prepare.

Something like magic arrows or one chosen from the beginning by a Fallon goddess.

Before today, Hulda had dismissed such talk as religious hype from a weak race. But she could not help but remember the words of the dying Zienna, and then later, Olafia.

"It's not me or my father you must defeat, but him," Zienna of Ranga had said. "From childhood, he will come among you."

And Olafia, who reported that the lad from Fallon had been "chosen," and that he possessed arrows that struck as he intended.

And now here it was again, this time from a stranger, a maiden from the castle at Sogg. Might there be some truth hidden among the religious teachings of the humans? More likely, this Mikael was simply some enterprising young man taking advantage of the humans' weakness of grasping for hope in a hopeless world, and he was probably even now making a place for himself within the castle. Yes, that must be it. He was proclaiming himself to be a savior of some sort, and based his testimony on what the humans were taught by their priests from childhood, and even the new queen had accepted him, if Petrina of Sogg could be believed.

Nevertheless, Hulda would take no chances. She would have what was rightfully hers, but perhaps she should delay her advance upon the city until she had more information. Maybe she would send someone in ahead of the coven—someone she could trust to obtain the truth and return it intact to her. But who?

Kattrin sighed and snuggled against her.

Mikael and Aingeal were with Elaine, seated at the dining table going over the latest reports of reconstruction when Bairre and Petrina entered the royal kitchen together. The queen was cordial and stood to greet her first maiden with a kiss. She nodded at Bairre before reseating herself.

"We've been worried, brother," Mikael said. "We were just discussing what might have extended your absence." In that, Mikael gave Bairre the opening he needed to tactfully explain himself, and in implying tardiness, Mikael served a warning to his brother not to lie. Mikael knew Elaine well enough by now to know she would not tolerate deception. It would go better for Bairre if he were straightforward about his affair with Petrina.

"Have you been attending to royal concerns, Advisor?" Elaine's bright tone was laced with sarcasm, but left room for the truth.

"Your Highness, I would speak to Mikael in private, if such could be arranged."

Elaine's back straightened. She looked at Mikael, not at Bairre, as if Mikael held the answer to his brother's blatant rudeness in disregarding her question. But Mikael had not a hint of understanding of Bairre's demeanor.

Seeing that, Elaine stood the second time.

"Bairre Sveinson," she said, "I appointed you advisor to the realm. Might I assume that you've been about your duties these last several days?" She glanced at Petrina, who stood with her gazed focused somewhere near the queen's feet. "If not, I suggest you tell me where you've been, and the purpose of your journey."

Elaine's face had reddened. Bairre's had paled. He cleared his throat, but didn't speak.

"Now, Bairre. I'll have the truth now, if you please."

Bairre's reluctance implied guilt, but Mikael sensed a conflict of some kind seething inside his brother, pulling him two ways at once. Likely, the truth would tarnish Petrina's honor. The grip of Aingeal's hand on Mikael's told him that she had already found some truth that was yet to be revealed to him.

"I have betrayed you, Your Highness." Bairre's head was up and his attention focused on Elaine. "I took Petrina to the Great Swamp, knowing she sought Hulda, the witch whom some say destroyed Sogg. We found her. Petrina will tell you the rest."

"Liar!" Petrina screamed. Her pudgy face was distorted with anger and unbelief.

Mikael suspected instantly that Bairre sought to rectify some great wrong that Petrina had caused him to commit.

"I've seen no witch, my queen," Petrina said. "Bairre is lying to you. He led me away from you, and intended to keep me from the castle. But he could not hold me, Your Majesty. I have returned to you." She dropped to her knees, and through artificial sobs, she continued. "I admit to following him, to wanting him as a lover, but he is our enemy, Your Majesty. I know that now."

Aingeal's grip tightened.

They had been standing together, Bairre and Petrina, almost touching, but now Bairre sidestepped away from her as she knelt before Elaine.

"An investigation, perhaps," Elaine said to Mikael. A tribunal. Surely there's more to learn in this matter. You will see to that, Mikael, as captain of my military, even though you are a brother to the defendant."

Mikael hesitated only momentarily. Elaine spoke of trying Bairre as a traitor to the realm, and *that* he was not. Perhaps he could bluff Elaine.

"Of course, my lady, but as your captain, I feel obligated to remind you that investigations and tribunals take time."

"Your point?"

"Bairre has spoken of betrayal and implied that Hulda may have gained some advantage. Do you not recall your own order that any who oppose your efforts to restore Sogg to its former glory will be put to death without legal delays?"

Elaine's eyebrows rose. "Are we speaking of that now? When the order was given, I referred to the looters and murderers preventing restoration. But I would be derelict to draw such fine lines for the sake of my own household. It shall be as you say."

She was quick of mind, the Queen of Artinus, Mikael thought. She had turned his attempt to avoid an investigation back on him, presenting even an uglier prospect, probably for no reason other than to prove her will was law. Or perhaps simply to have her way, being certain Mikael would concede rather than risk his brother's life.

"Execution decisions are not mine, Your Majesty, but yours. But if this is a military matter, there's more at stake than proper investigation and punishment. We have a confessor in front of us, possibly two, and the information they obviously have is paramount to procedures, for there may be facts to be acted upon immediately." He wondered at his ability to speak without emotion, for his mind was contorted with the several possibilities that may surface as fixed reality in the next few moments. "Might I suggest, Your Majesty, that you require those facts now? I suspect that not only will the best course of military action be revealed, but Your Majesty will also have a clearer understanding of the degree of betrayal we might be faced with." He bowed and stepped backward, signaling he had no more to say, but he added, "Your captain's suggestion, my lady, nothing more."

He thought her facial features relaxed somewhat; perhaps she had accepted his last statements as a concession.

To Petrina, she said, "Get off the floor." And to Bairre, "Out with it then, young sir. I've not dismissed you as advisor yet, so you will advise me fully."

Mikael could not but help watch Petrina's face as she stood. Her surprise and anger had turned to fear in the knowledge that Bairre was about to reveal the politically incorrect deeds that would probably bring her death.

Bairre's voice was steady as he began. If he were afraid, it didn't show. "I had hoped Petrina would be given an opportunity to explain her motives, for they are lost to me. I only know my own, which were bad indeed. I've told Your Highness that I led Petrina to the swamp, and so I did. That was at her request. I saw no real harm in it at the time, for I held no belief that Hulda or any other had assaulted the realm. I'm still not convinced that such is the case. Be that as it may, we found the coven of witches, and I stood back while Petrina conversed with one whom I can only assume was Hulda." Bairre paused to look at Mikael. "I've no direct knowledge of the content of their conversation. I only know what Petrina has told me was said. My confession is complete, Your Majesty."

"Not quite, sir. I find no indicators of deception in either your demeanor or your face. I cannot say the same for Petrina. You will tell me now exactly what Petrina told you."

Bairre didn't hesitate. "She told Hulda that the One from Fallon is here at the castle. She named him." He stole another glance at Mikael. "She reported that he has arrows of power. From what Petrina told me, Hulda was made aware of Sogg's condition and defenses. Petrina requested of Hulda that she leave you and herself alive when she comes."

Sunlight from the wide kitchen window placed tiny lights in the tears that formed in Elaine's eyes. "Oh, Petrina."

The maiden broke. Her garbled words fell out in a torrent of confessed emotions. "Queen, I am nothing without you. I was nothing before you took me in. Yes, I did these things Bairre has reported, from fear that I was losing you." She pointed at Mikael. "He has deceitfully gained your confidence, posing as one who can save the realm, but he cannot, for he is nothing but an intruder, an outsider who seeks to take advantage of the troubles that have befallen us."

Petrina went back to the floor and crawled to Elaine like a scolded pet. "Queen, have mercy. But if you cannot, do not cast me out, but slay me quickly, for I would rather be numbered among the dead peasants of Sogg than to live outside your grace."

"Stand up, Petrina," Elaine said.

Petrina stood.

"Questions. First, what evidence do you have that Mikael Sveinson is not what he appears?"

Petrina's words were venom. "Did he arrive here with honors befitting one sent by a goddess? Has he proven himself to be anything above a Fallon peasant? Could the Goddess he claims to represent not have given him the means to prevent the earthquake? I tell you he is a deceiver, here for one reason, and that's to take advantage of beliefs he himself does not hold."

"You make no sense, maiden. You find treachery in the heart of one from Fallon, but yet you turn to witches for support. And certainly you've offered no evidence of your accusations."

Petrina noted with distress that Elaine had not used her name—a certain indication that the queen had separated herself from one who had betrayed her.

"Must I believe in Fallon's goddess to believe witches have crushed the city?" Petrina asked. "To believe that they still yet will attack? I saw them, Your Majesty. I spoke with them. Even if I doubted before, I can no longer. Hulda will come, she and her coven, to rule, and the miserable remains of this place cannot stand against her. That's why I betrayed you—to save you."

"Bairre," Elaine said, "where was Hulda when you left her? How far from here?"

"Hulda will consider my words," Petrina said. "She will delay…"

"Silence, traitor. You've said all you'll ever say to me." Then, turning back to Bairre, "Advise me, Advisor."

"In the swamp, but at its near border, Your Highness. Not three days from here."

"Prepare as best you can, Captain. If the inner keep has been repaired, confine the traitor there. See to it that the advisor stays in his quarters. You'll have my decision on what's to become of them in due time."

Oriana walked alone across the dry and bitter ground that should be sprouting the year's first crops. Nothing grew here now but an occasional dandelion sprout or some unnamed weed that would not have been seen here before the earthquake. The gentle, dark soil of the valley, so lovingly turned in the fall by Fallonese spades, now lay pale, cracked and parched in brilliant sunlight that had heretofore illumined not excess and wasted bounties, but the sufficiency the children of Morrigan had enjoyed since She gave them the river.

Remembering the Fallon as it was before, Oriana stopped walking to silence the crusty sound of her moccasins brushing the hot earth. She listened. The river spoke now not at all. The gentle lapping of the silver clarity against grassy banks was absent. No fish broke the surface, no bird dove for minnows, and no undine created the slightest disturbance to the seemingly dead and barely flowing shallows of what had been the mighty Aine.

Turning into the morning sun, Oriana walked to the water. She stopped at a place she had often watched Mikael sitting in the emerald grass with his bare feet dangling in the icy flow. Now, the dead grass barely clung to the hard earth that formed the banks of the river. Not a trace of vegetation grew here, and the absent drone of insects left a void of silent misery.

Mikael's feet would never reach the water surface now. Indeed, he would have to approach the stream from somewhere else, for here the distance of the sharp drop from the bank was now too severe for man or animal. Oriana was glad in her own way that Mikael was not here to see the river die. But he knew, there could be no doubt of that. She had sensed that in their last contact.

Perhaps she would try to reach him again today. But then she really had nothing new to tell him. The witches were still a threat, of course, but Mikael would be aware of that. No, she would save her thought transfer energies for another time, perhaps a time when some small piece of hope broke from the desolation of Fallon Valley, and she could relay that to him, and in that way encourage him to continue in the fight she knew he had undertaken.

In the midst of a spoiled land and a dying race, Oriana's strong and faith-filled heart fluttered with hope, and in her own way she knew that the child Mikael had grown to maturity with the Fallon's decline. The hope of Fallon was Mikael Sveinson, and while he lived, she, as Morrigan's disciple, could ask for no more. The Book promised no more than his birth and growth. Even if he failed in the task she was certain he had accepted, prophecy was not undone. If the once-bright waters of the Fallon ended in stagnant ponds of scum-covered despair, if the Fallonese evolved into the den-digging creatures they had seized the land from, not one could say Morrigan's promises were lies. For the Goddess Morrigan had promised nothing in that regard except that Mikael would arrive.

Kattrin's one piece of earth-colored canvas fell in dirty wrinkles from her shoulders to beyond her knees. Elkana, due to their constant digging and their resulting home environments, were not overly concerned with hygiene. Perfectly evolved to be denizens of the subterranean, the thick skin of an Elkana prevailed against more than the cold and damp of Elkana dens. Rashes and skin disorders were unheard of. Even the smooth and relatively thin skin of faces and underbellies were, without exception, blemish free.

An Elkana, male or female, expected to see dirt on those of their own kind, and cleanliness bore not at all on how they perceived physical beauty, which was instead measured in body shape, posture, the slope of one's forehead, the curvature of the neck, and the starting and ending points of hair growth.

Kattrin knew she was pretty, even lovely, and it had been easy for her to be reassured by Hulda that she would fit in at Sogg. She simply had to determine her place in that established society, and make her observations from there. Find the Elkana of Sogg, Hulda had said, and become accepted among them. Learn from them about Sogg conditions, and what was being said about the government there.

But most importantly, substantiate or lay to rest the rumors about the boy from Fallon. Is he real? What powers do the people say he possesses? Has anyone observed him? How might he be identified? Who are his companions?

Kattrin resented to some extent having been chosen for this mission. Was she not a princess? Only Hulda's insistence had brought Kattrin here, to the city she would someday rule. Hulda had convinced Kattrin that her looks would get her into the confidence of Sogg citizens quicker than any other coven member could make the same progress. And the quicker the invasion could be accomplished, the more certain would be its success, because each day that passed, the ruling foundation of Sogg became stronger.

Ordinarily she would be preparing for sleep at this time of day. Unaccustomed to all-day traveling, she was tired. How many new branches of the river had she waded? Her legs were even now wet to the knees from the latest and shallowest of crossings that she had to make before climbing this last ridge of grass and wildflowers. Now she waited in the high grasses above the city as the trailing edge of twilight darkened the streets. One by one, windows were lit from within stone and wooden structures that housed human and those Elkana who had chosen to live above ground. She kept her back straight as she descended. A princess should never bend or bow, and she would not, even if it meant her silhouette were visible to the vermin below her.

As she approached, she saw the evidence of work halted for the day, and she felt a certain pride for having had a part in the wreckage that was being removed to make room for rebuilding. Let them build, for they were constructing nothing other than Hulda's city, a city that would eventually be Kattrin's.

Her first step onto a stone street caught her off guard, and at first she thought the city must have been built on a field of slate, but in the brightening glare from windows, she saw that her feet were upon flat rocks placed adjacent to one another. The newly placed stones had been fitted together by skilled workers or perhaps artists, for the cracks between the stones were all but invisible.

Having lived in the wildwood since birth, and never having ventured into a village, Kattrin wondered at the workmanship that she saw on every side. The stones of the homes fit together as well as those of the street, and the structures had been worked into perfect rows, horizontally and vertically. In that arrangement, the width of the street was kept constant its entire length, or at least that part of the street visible to the gawking Kattrin. For a fleeting moment, and counter to her previous flood of pride, she experienced a pang of regret that such painstaking artistry had been attacked and ruined. Kattrin saw the destruction as more of a tragedy than the deaths that had accompanied the tumbling of mortared stonework and the upheaval of perfect streets.

But the people of Sogg, in their ignorance of what had happened, were rebuilding, like ants after a hard rain. Could they not comprehend that the falling apart of stones could occur a second time as easily as it had the first? Stupid, the Sogg citizens must be, to build on nothing but faith and hope.

Kattrin walked the street, unafraid, gazing into open doors and meeting the eyes of the humans who lingered outside their homes attending to late-hour matters. Some stared, perhaps because an Elkana was not expected in this sector, but no one challenged her, and on she walked toward what she thought to be the center of the city.

She found her kind, the Elkana, but she didn't tarry to speak with them. On and on through the moon and lantern-lit night she walked, until she became convinced that the Elkana lived together with the humans, not in dens, and not in separate areas of their own. Some sort of understanding must exist here to allow that, for the two races had different needs, different ideals.

Satisfied that she now held a working knowledge of the layout of the city and its current state of repair, she stepped to the door of an Elkana home just as the new day suddenly dumped raw light into the street at her back. She knew it to be Elkana because of the strong odor of kralene emanating with the lantern light through the vertical boards of the house.

Facing a heavy oaken door, she knew not how to announce herself. The traditional Elkana approach to another's abode could not be accomplished here, for there was no soil to scratch with the claws of her feet, which would send the faint vibrations to den inhabitants. No den here, just wood and stone.

She scratched at the door, uncertain that the sound would be heard or correctly interpreted from within.

"Whose there?" came a gruff voice from on the other side.

"I'm lost, sir," Kattrin said in her loudest voice, which was not loud at all. "I'm in need of nourishment."

A male Elkana, middle-aged, dull-eyed, and hunched over, opened the door, which groaned on leather hinges and scraped against a splintered floor. He was thin, this citizen of Sogg. Kattrin noted immediately that the stale aroma of cooked greens clung to him like grease. She experienced her first ever revulsion of uncleanliness, for here was a kind of filth she had never before encountered—a foul sourness made permanent by the city. His complexion appeared less moist than it should, and Kattrin suspected malnutrition. Perhaps he had resorted to eating human food.

His dark eyes brightened somewhat upon falling into hers.

"What is it?" he asked in a voice that was vastly lighter than he had used before.

"I'm hungry and lost sir. I've wandered here, drawn by the aroma of kralene."

"Are you alone?"

"Quiet alone."

"Then come in, child, and partake of what little we have to offer. Kralene only, I'm afraid, some thin scandeele."

She stepped inside ahead of him and found herself in a large room that made up at least one-half of the entire home. Kattrin brought her hand to her face upon being assailed by the odor of raw sewage. But even stronger was the sickening smell of kralene that had apparently soaked into the heart of the building.

The room was well lit with candles and lanterns, an indication that her host had risen before the sun.

"You're up early, sir," she said. "You must have duties to attend to. Please don't let me interfere with your routine. If I might have but just a mouthful, I'll be on my way."

He began a response, stuttered, and fell silent. Kattrin had seen this before. He was girl-shy, and obviously stricken with her looks. The moment was shattered by a raspy female voice from the other room.

"Who is it, Krarl? Who are you talking to? Another beggar?"

The voice materialized in the doorway in the form of a haggard woman dressed in faded blue britches that appeared to be of human origin. Mats of thinning reddish hair fell about her face so very much out of keeping with

Elkana tradition. Hair should never be allowed to stray forward of the ears. Kattrin's earliest etiquette instruction mandated that a female's hair be either cut short or pinned back. To let it fall forward and conceal any portion of one's face amounted to nothing more than disregard of one's pride in herself as Elkana. Had these city dwellers lived so long among the humans that even the most basic teachings had been cast aside?

Krarl found his voice. "No, certainly not a beggar. A lost child, I think, nothing more. I've asked her to eat."

The woman approached, dragging a crushed foot. "We've barely enough to live on, child. Would you take that from us?"

"Lyra, we can spare a little, don't you think?" His meek tone implied that Lyra ran the household.

Lyra frowned, not at Kattrin, but at the situation. Silence reigned. Kattrin glanced around the room and found it almost bare of furnishings except for a wide sleeping pallet against the southern wall.

"What's your name, girl? Where are you from?" Lyra finally asked.

"Zienna," Kattrin said. "From Ranga."

"Ah, I know the place. Good people in Ranga." Lyra's face smiled now, revealing her rotting pointed teeth. "Come into the kitchen and eat with us before Krarl goes off to work. He's working at the castle, you know, and the queen pays him in meat. So we survive."

She entered and felt the light but hideous grip of Krarl's hand on her arm, guiding her to a chair. The kitchen made up the back half of the house. Small bunches of yellowing scandeele hung from the rafters, and Kattrin wondered where in the city it was grown. In the corner opposite where she sat, a rusting stove gave life to a kettle. Lyra dipped a horn cup into the kettle and came out with a steaming liquid Kattrin knew was scandeele. She stepped to Kattrin, dragging her foot.

"Here, child. Drink this and regain your strength. There, that's right, drink it down." Lyra's smile widened. "Now tell us, Zienna of Ranga, how do your people fare since the ground opened. Were there deaths?"

"Only one." Kattrin almost smiled at that, remembering Zienna's screams.

"Were the dens destroyed? Do your people still live there?"

"I don't know," Kattrin answered. "I was away at the time, and the land and waters were so changed, I could not find my way home. Now I find myself here. I know of the one death from the report of a queen's representative sent out to assess the damage." How easy it was to lie to these wretches, and how stupid they were for believing her.

"Well that's news indeed," Krarl said. I thought the queen had forbidden any of her people to leave Sogg, you know, because of the reconstruction. Everyone is needed."

Kattrin smiled her sweetest smile and allowed Krarl's gaze to linger on her green eyes long enough that she could have told him anything and he would have accepted it. "I know nothing of that, Krarl." She deliberately used his name. Now, she would get what she came for.

"Is the castle damaged greatly then? Are their no defenses?" Is there none to save us?"

"Have you not heard?" Krarl showed genuine surprise. "No, I don't suppose you would have. But even those who don't work close to the castle have seen him. Many have even spoken to his brother, the queen's advisor."

"Advisor?"

Krarl was standing erect now, feeling important that he had something of value to share with the beautiful intruder. "Yes, appointed by Elaine herself. The king is dead, you do know that?" He didn't wait for her answer. "Bairre is the advisor's name, and as I said, he is the brother of Mikael of Fallon?"

"Fallon, you say?" She kept her face up so that he might see her fully.

"It is said," continued Krarl, "that he has the powers of a god, and that he's here to protect us from further destruction. Did you not see all the progress the people have made since the earthquake? It's because of him, so they say."

"What powers does he have?" Kattrin suspected that Krarl had no knowledge of his own, but knew only what he had heard.

"Magic weapons some say. Others say he talks to Morrigan herself."

"What do you say, Krarl?"

"Me? I've seen him in the courtyard, and I've watched him instruct the soldiers, but I've not observed him in battle. I know that he's killed several insurrectionists shortly after being appointed captain of the military. Everyone knows about that." He looked at Lyra, who still stood at the little stove. "That's why we've been able to restore the city, because Mikael has made it known that thievery and looting are capital offenses. Because of him, wives and children are safe while the men work, and we're able to leave our tools at the work sights at night, without fear that they'll be stolen." Krarl saw that he had the girl's attention, and he pushed his chest out. "Mikael has recruited an army. Many young men joined him of their own accord after seeing how much he has accomplished. I believe he is all that the people say he is."

"He's nothing," Kattrin muttered. "A human whose heart will stop as quickly as your own."

"What?" Krarl asked. "What's that you say?" He stepped closer.

Kattrin struck like a serpent, springing from the stool quicker than Krarl could react. She ripped into his throat with her pointed teeth, and with a snap of her head to the side, she severed the main artery and removed enough of his larynx that his startled cry was hushed. As he sank toward the cold floor, Kattrin leaped at Lyra, who was too stunned to even remove the cup she had just dipped into the kettle. Such was the force of the young witch's assault, the elder woman was knocked to the floor. In her fall, the kettle was overturned to release its almost boiling contents onto both Lyra and Kattrin. Lyra screamed from pain and surprise, but Kattrin felt the scalding not at all; she was too much caught up in the killing to heed the dark splashes of wasted nourishment that washed over her face and breast like yellow poison.

Now she was atop the still screaming and thrashing Lyra, studying the visage of pain and fear that was fixed in the woman's face like death. Kattrin held her down, and found the task not difficult. Lyra was weak and soft, so unlike Elkana women of the same age who lived as they should in the valleys and on the sides of Artinus ridges.

With one hand, Kattrin grasped Lyra's throat and squeezed until the screaming lessened, then stopped. With her free hand, she raked her claws across Lyra's breast and watched the blood soak through the shredded linen garment. The witch shivered from raw ecstasy at the pending death. She unsheathed her dagger to slowly insert it into Lyra's ribs from the side, then withdrew it to hold it in front of terror-filled eyes.

"Lyra, Lyra, listen to me." She kept her fingers clamped to Lyra's throat as she spoke. "You are dying, Lyra. What do you feel?"

The thrashing began anew, and again the knife slipped through thick skin, except this time it entered a lung.

"What do you feel?"

Kattrin saw frothy blood oozing from Lyra's nose, then her mouth. Concerned that death would come too quickly, she let go of the throat.

"Talk to me, Lyra."

"What's happened here?"

The husky male voice was behind her. She turned to see two Elkana men standing in the doorway of the front room. They seemed loath to enter. Kattrin sprang. In two bounds, she was between the men, pushing them roughly aside, fearing their discovery of what she'd done, and hating them for spoiling Lyra's death. Then she was in the dawn street running as only an Elkana youth could run. The speed cooled her reddened and nearly scalded skin. She paid no heed to the waking neighborhood of workers who were off to whatever task they had been assigned. She changed direction often, dodging between buildings and taking the narrow alleys where the homeless lay as if dead. She heard the grunts as she stepped on and over them. She found a wide, bricked lane that led her away from the rising sun, and she picked up speed, glad for the straight shot that would take her somewhere away from the questions she knew she had raised.

The killings were unnecessary, she knew that. But so delightful, they were, and Hulda had denied her such pleasures lately. The death of two wretched Elkana who had adapted the ways of human living were not really worth mentioning to Hulda, and so she would not. Hulda would probably scold her for such diversions, for such was not part of the present assignment. Kattrin resigned to refrain from further killings until she was away from Sogg.

With the castle towers in view now, she slowed. The castle of Sogg? On a newly constructed battlement, she saw soldiers, too many to count.

Kattrin approached the largest group of people she had thus far seen, maybe thirty persons, and they were entering upon a flat open area of grass that led to the very walls of the castle. Human and Elkana, together, men and women, walking, chattering. Many carried sacks, which her sensitive nostrils reported were filled with cooked meat and bread. Workers, probably. She fell in behind them unnoticed, and then moved among them. Perhaps she would gain access to the castle.

But her hopes declined when she saw the guards that stood upon the already lowered drawbridge. She slinked back toward the rear of the procession that was now forming into a single line. The soldiers were checking each individual, examining documents that apparently held authority for the peasants to enter. Perhaps she might seize one of the passes from someone near her. No, that would create a disturbance that would surely be noticed.

At the last moment, she made a decision that would either get her past the guards or cause her arrest.

"Your pass, girl," a tall and quick-eyed guard said. "I've not seen you here before, have I?" Then, seeing her eyes, "No, I'm sure of it. Where's your pass?"

"I haven't one, sir. I'm here to see Mikael of Fallon."

"On what business? Here now, stand aside and let the others through." He pulled her to the side of the bridge, gently.

The remaining workers passed by, their claws and shoes scraping the ancient boards of the drawbridge.

"Now, girl, what is it you would be wanting with the captain. He's no time for small matters."

She did her best to look hurt. "Sir, the matter I bring is by no means small. But it is for Mikael's receipt only. I cannot divulge the nature of my business to any other. Will you fetch him for me, please?" Her smile was sweeter than the fresh warmth of the new sun.

"Uh, ordinarily I shouldn't... I mean to say, well... whom shall I say awaits him?"

"One with news of his homeland."

Her mind whirled as the guard left her at the raised portcullis. What would she say to Mikael? How might she deceive him into believing she actually knew of the present conditions in Fallon Valley, a place she'd never been? If she could only see him momentarily, to confirm his presence, and perhaps get an idea of his station here, she would at least have something to report to Hulda. For a fleeting moment, Kattrin thought of darting into the castle's courtyard and concealing herself where she might spy on the realm's proceedings, but the presence of the two other soldiers on the drawbridge and the many soldiers moving back and forth across the courtyard prevented her.

Before she could form an alternate plan, the guard returned, walking with a human man and woman.

"Captain, this is she," the soldier said.

"You are Elkana," was Mikael's greeting. How is it you have knowledge of Fallon?"

Mikael was taller than she had expected, but why she should have any expectation at all, she didn't know. He carried a stout bow, and the white fletching of arrows gleamed in the early light behind his shoulder. The magic arrows? The girl with him was pretty for a human, and Kattrin experienced a flash of jealousy.

Kattrin glanced at the guard before asking Mikael, "Might we speak privately, sir?"

"I've a strict policy concerning the admission of strangers within the castle; however, perhaps we might ascend to the gate tower. Please excuse me. This is Aingeal."

Kattrin bowed, and it was returned. Mikael, Aingeal and Kattrin entered the tower casing and climbed the stained stone steps. Pigeons whirled away into the warm morning air as the party came out upon the tower's platform. The height and position of the tower were well suited for defense. Archers could send their arrows into the ranks of an attacking force for hours here, with minimal danger to themselves, because the platform was protected on all sides by a wall just high enough for a bowman to shoot from.

Before Mikael could ask her to state her business, Kattrin said, "Sir Mikael, I asked for privacy." Only then did the idea come to her that she may gain an opportunity to kill him today, and thus remove Hulda's concern over the pending invasion.

"Aingeal is my constant companion. She knows Fallon through me, as well as if she were born there. Don't let her presence concern you."

He had a way about him, this Mikael of Fallon. He left no room for debate. He was confident of himself, and she could only hope that in his desire for information about his home, she would find a weakness.

"As you wish, my lord. Might I ask how long it's been since your last contact with someone from Fallon?"

"You may not. What you can do is identify yourself and state your business."

Kattrin flinched. Men didn't act that way toward her, not even human men.

"I only asked to know where to begin." She waited. Nothing. "Some died, sir. Did you know?"

Aingeal spoke for the first time in Kattrin presence. "She's a fraud, Mikael. She wants something."

Mikael's eyes stayed on Kattrin's, but he didn't speak.

"That's not true, my lord. Why else would I come to you? I've heard of your strengths, and I..."

"And you came to see for yourself," Aingeal said.

"No, I..."

"Barnes!" Mikael yelled.

Instantly a soldier stepped onto the tower's platform.

"Take her to the keep," Mikael ordered. "She's the green-eyed witch, Kattrin. Post two guards at the door."

The soldier identified by Mikael as Barnes, and two others, accompanied Kattrin to the keep. Gently, Barnes pushed her into a well-lit room accompanied by a young human maiden. The heavy door was no sooner closed than the scraping sound of the wooden timber being pushed through forged keepers announced that she was indeed a prisoner. By the grunts and orders being issued, she knew that two men were needed to set the bar. She heard only one set of retreating footsteps.

The furnishings of her new accommodations were eloquent, and Kattrin wondered why such a place would be used to house prisoners. Silk curtains adorned the one barred window, and scented candles burned on several maple tables that had been carved by an expert craftsman. Not less than three beds, all fringed with silk, occupied the large room. And there were lounging beds against the walls, a writing table under the window, and a dining area complete with fresh flowers.

As female of her race were prone to do, she looked almost frantically into each area of the room, searching with her eyes for the privy. Elkana women were far more than discreet in such matters.

"It's there," Petrina said, pointing to a wide curtain.

"I know you," Kattrin said.

"And I you. You were with Hulda. Why are you here?"

"Mikael Sveinson," was the witch's response.

Petrina smiled. "We've something in common."

"I'm not certain what she is," Aingeal said. "But I felt an evil akin to that which pervaded the home of Greta. I can tell you only that she's not what she seems."

Mikael sat with Aingeal in the kitchen waiting for Elaine. The queen had sent word that she had made a decision concerning Bairre and Petrina. Mikael ran a finger through the dust on the long table—dust that would never had been allowed to collect there if Petrina had been about her duties as first maiden.

"I've no doubt that she's Hulda's princess, the same girl Esras told me about. I expect that Elaine will order her immediate execution."

Elaine, wearing a full-length robe of blue linen, stepped in at that moment from the door leading to her chambers. Her just-brushed hair upon the deep blue of the robe gave her the appearance of true royalty, and brightened the large room. Two maidens escorted her. As the queen settled into a chair at the head of the table, the shifting air brought to Mikael her scent. She had just bathed in scented water, and the lingering effect was pleasant indeed. He couldn't turn the guilt that assailed him. Aingeal sat within touching distance, yet she smelled of only herself, which was pleasant enough, and certainly, it was no fault of hers that she had no access to perfumes. No vanity existed in the thoughts of the young wizard, and even though she had no use for artificial scents, still she could detect Elaine's, and surely she must feel some concern about the temptations of men, particularly himself, about the allure of women who primped in the fashion of the Queen of Artinus. Thus having allowed himself the enjoyment of Elaine's feminine vanity, he accepted the guilt.

"Captain, have you any advice for me regarding our prisoners? If not, I'm prepared to direct you in that matter."

"And another, Your Majesty, if you please." Mikael said. "I've recently ordered the arrest and confinement of an outsider, an Elkana, whom I believe is of Hulda's coven. She entered the castle with lies, no doubt as a spy. Evidence is minimal. Her description matches my knowledge of one called Kattrin."

"The first order of business is Petrina, but perhaps we can handle both matters at once."

She sounded annoyed that he had presented her with yet another problem. "I've little advice, Your Majesty, regarding Petrina," he said. "Except that I would ask you to consider that Bairre reported the matter upon learning that Petrina had betrayed us. I don't mean to offer an excuse for his taking the maiden to Hulda, but I do feel he did so in ignorance."

"Is that all?"

Mikael nodded.

"Petrina and the witch will be beheaded today."

Mikael's heart all but stopped in fear of her judgment concerning his brother. Her pause, and her steady blue gaze upon him were potential explosions.

"Bairre will suffer confinement to the castle unless he's about his business as advisor. Believe not that my hand is stayed for your sake, Captain. Know you not by now that I'll see justice done in all royal matters? I find no little excusable fault in Bairre. He was deceived by female prowess, by the lies of lovely, but lying, lashes over dark eyes that have bled the souls from mortal men since before Thor was conceived." She smiled. "A lesson learned for my advisor, I think."

Mikael was relieved and stunned. Elaine had said more about not punishing Bairre than condemning Petrina to death. As thankful as he was for not only keeping Bairre from the headsman's axe, not to mention Elaine keeping him as her advisor, Mikael could not help but feel that the queen had failed in her duty as queen to justly administer punishment. Bairre had assisted, although unwittingly, in betrayal of the realm. Common sense, or even a deeper sense of loyalty, should have kept him from the swamp. Removal from his position as the queen's advisor would have been appropriate even in peaceful times. But now, with an attack having all but crushed the realm, and with another attack likely, Bairre's childish errors would seem to call for execution, or at least removal from office. Admissions and confessions should never erase the crime. Had the perpetrator been any other, Mikael would not have questioned a death sentence. Somehow, he must show that to Bairre.

In the dark of her mind, within the core of that place where thoughts are born, Oriana fought to clear the impenetrable black fog that blocked her every attempt at communication with Mikael. She stood by her pallet in the room behind the temple, her eyes closed, her hair loose, and her head bowed. All she could manage was a fleeting glimpse of movement within the fog, and that was not Mikael, but something else, and not an enemy. Neither was it a messenger from Mikael, or even from Sogg. Something else. What?

She lay down on the sunlight-enshrouded pallet and attempted to start over, but the fog remained intact. Perhaps it was her exhaustion. Perhaps she was trying to hard. Sleep might revive her energies. She tried to ignore the pitiful pleas of hungry children outside her door; she could do nothing physical for them, and she needed quiet. In silence, she would find Mikael, and she would tell him of the conditions here. He would want to know.

Oriana slept, and in sleep, she saw them. The spirits of Old Fallon. Fallen warriors, those chosen by Odin's messengers to fall in battle or in service to Morrigan. They traversed the ice fields in Oriana's vision, sitting erect in translucent dignity astride white stallions of no firmer substance than themselves. Each carried the weapon he fell with, and each wore the same armor, still stained with the blood spilled from his last enemy.

In her vision, Oriana stood in the silent snow, unhooded, and they rode past her, each turning as if to look at her, but the forms were nearly faceless, and if they saw her, she could not tell.

Something in the indistinct substance of one rider reminded Oriana of Esras. As that spirit passed, and just before the link was broken, she heard, "Tell him we're coming, priestess." The voice was not unlike the tinkling of ice falling from the frozen branches of time shaken by the tremors of winter.

***

Petrina's last breath was to be taken late in the day, after sunset but before dark. Because she had lived within the castle walls these past years, the execution would not be a public affair. News of administered justice would be broadcast throughout the city because the citizens had a right and a need to know about matters of state, but only the essential personnel would attend. That included Bairre, because, according to Elaine, his attendance would further instill in his mind the result of betrayal.

Sergeant Barnes accompanied his captain to the keep. They found no guard posted at the door. After announcing the intrusion, Mikael assisted Barnes in removing the bolt. The sergeant swung the door inward on a room that was empty except for two dead guards. The barred and darkening window, high above the courtyard, was intact.

thirteen

*Shall your eyes turn from the truth toward vanity? Shall ye die in dark
pools of ignorance, having bled for naught?*
—Book of Morrigan

Captain Mikael Sveinson accompanied the royal advisor into Sogg, riding
mounts from the royal stable. A reconnaissance mission, Mikael had termed
the outing—an opportunity to survey the restructuring of a city that was alive
today with the energy of hope for that which the citizens had once taken for
granted. Mikael had declined to bring mounted guards, telling Sergeant
Barnes that the fires of terror kindled by the looters had been extinguished,
and that Barnes had done well in that regard. Barnes could not know that his
captain's real purpose today was to have some time away from the castle with
his brother.

The spring morning chirped to him and Bairre from among the new maple
leaves that quivered in the warm breeze. Mikael's gelding tossed its head and
pranced, anxious to break the restrictions of the slow pace its rider had set.

"Easy, Loki," Mikael said. "We'll not need to run today."

Bairre's unnamed mare seemed content with the dawdling gait, slowing
even more at times to turn its head toward the new greenery carpeting the
roadside.

As they entered upon a wide street lined with freshly repaired homes,
Mikael eased Bairre into conversation as tactfully as he could. He knew his
brother well enough not to jump too quickly into spiritual matters. "Without
recapturing our escapees, I doubt that we'll ever know how they did it. Maybe

189

Kattrin is a sorceress." He laughed. "Without someone opening the door to release them, and then replacing the bolt, it seems impossible that they got out."

"I was in my quarters, if you'll remember, brother. I had nothing to do with it."

Mikael privately reprimanded himself. He had broached the subject carelessly. "I didn't mean that. I was just thinking out loud about how it was accomplished. Do you believe in that kind of magic?"

"I don't know. Petrina apparently does. I'd wager my boots that she's gone back to the swamp with Kattrin."

"Petrina's gone back to the witches, you think?" Mikael asked. "Maybe so. There's magic there, if unusual powers can be termed as such." How was he going to keep Bairre on the subject; he seemed still disposed to brooding about losing the girl. "Powers like theirs come from somewhere, you know. They don't just happen."

"I suppose."

"These arrows, for example." He pulled one from his quiver and nocked it to his bowstring.

"Mikael, don't start."

"See the pigeons on the roof there?" He pointed to a dozen or so birds perched on the parapet of a sharply angled roof, two stories from the ground.

"Mikael, I don't want to…"

"Flush them for me, but keep your eye on the dark-colored one."

"What?"

"Humor me, brother."

Bairre clapped his hands several times, and the disturbed pigeons rose in the air and circled, not willing to exit the area. Mikael fixed his intent on the almost black pigeon and loosed a white arrow. As the fletching stopped in the breast of the bird, he heard a gasp from Bairre.

"Of all the luck. You'd not do that again, I dare say."

"The white one, then," Mikael said, and drew his bow a second time. His intended target vanished from view as the flock rounded the building, but Mikael released the arrow. When the white bird was next in sight, it had ceased its flapping and was falling, a red-stained tip extruding from its back. It fell to lie not far from the black one.

"It's not me," Mikael said, "but the arrows." He spurred Loki forward, and dismounted to retrieve the ash arrows, which he wiped clean on his jerkin.

"I don't understand. They're inanimate. Just wood, stone and feathers."

"They're from Morrigan, brother. What further proof do you need?"

***

That night, well into those late hours when most men of clean conscious were deep into whatever dreams they had chosen for themselves, Mikael and Bairre lay awake in two different rooms, with two different reasons for failing to find sleep, neither of which had to do with guilt.

Bairre stared into the protected dark and saw pierced and bloody pigeons falling from the sunlit sky of Sogg to an unstable earth that had never before been so much out of tilt. Again, he ran through the facts that gave support to the childhood teachings he had long ago cast into the Fallon's current.

His brother came to Sogg because of the valley's beliefs, and the earthquake followed his arrival. Aingeal, a human from outside the valley, was here now, professing to be a wizard. Hulda and her witches were at the swamp's edge, he had seen that for himself, and Petrina said those witches would attempt to take Sogg. Petrina had escaped the castle through apparent magic. And now the arrows. All explainable, logically, but when such facts were combined, logic lost much of its position within reality, leaving Bairre with reason enough to be concerned. He had left his home to be away from people driven by spirituality, only to now find himself teetering on the high edge dividing logic and that very same spirituality.

Where was the truth of the matter? Who held it?

Mikael's sleeplessness had come upon him accompanied by a mild but confusing pain behind his eyes. Dreamless rest had held him until Oriana's garbled message seized his peace and hid it from him. Spirits of Fallon, she said, were coming. They were mounted, they were an army, and they were still very far away, somewhere upon the northern ice fields. Old Fallon? Why would the ghosts of the ancient dead come here?

As little sense as the communication held, one part of it was as clear as the Aine used to be. It wasn't a warning, but an enlightenment that came with Oriana's love, as if the news were good. And then, as the link faded, Mikael saw Esras, which made even less sense.

Kattrin considered disposing of the fat and overbearing human while she had the chance. Hulda wouldn't even have to know. What good would it do

191

to take Petrina back to the coven? It was far too late to train her as a witch, even if Petrina had the aptitude, which she probably did not. Lazy, probably, after having dwelt for so long in the shelter of plenty.

Pretty, in her own way, though, here in the beams of a full moon. No, not pretty, really. Sensuous, perhaps. Affective. To let her live would be to take the chance Hulda would be attracted to her.

Kattrin, propped on an elbow, gazed at the sleeping girl beside her. How careless of the human girl to sleep so easily, so deeply, in the presence of an almost stranger. Petrina's sonorous breathing was revolting and vulgar, a graceless trait of humankind that reminded Kattrin of some dying animal gasping for its last breath. It would take little effort to claw her throat open now and stop the disgusting sound. But perhaps not just yet. First, she should learn why Petrina had been incarcerated. Their escape and flight had left little time for discussion. All that Kattrin knew now about the chubby human was that they shared a common enemy. Petrina's death could wait another day.

Unwittingly, Kattrin saved her own life by refraining. The grip that the unsleeping Petrina had on the dagger stolen from the castle whitened her knuckles, and would have prevented disarmament before she might severe the lizard-girl's ties to the mortal world with the slender blade.

Hulda displayed no hint of being perturbed by the appearance of Petrina a second time. Her relief of having Kattrin back unharmed was, however, obvious to the entire coven. The lovers embraced for an interval of time not consistent with merely a queen/princess relationship. The soft, cooing sounds from Hulda were clearly audible through the lacey night fog that lay over the swamp in thin patches. They walked away together, Hulda and Kattrin, leaving Petrina standing in the cold and caustic glare of coven hostility.

But Petrina had come too far, and she had lost too much, to be jostled by a few slit-eyed vermin. She raked them with her eyes, picking out the boldest, the weakest, the human.

"Do you have some directive from Hulda regarding me, witches? No, I think not. You'll wait as I do until we have her orders. Now be about your business."

There were some murmured slurs, a few Elkana grunts, but the girls dispersed singly and in couples. Petrina sat down with her back against a tree. A chill came upon her with the night breeze. The fog thickened. Is this what she had come to? To sit alone in the dark wildwood without purpose, without companionship of any kind? Had she lost everything in her failed attempts at trying to keep just one part of her life?

Elaine had ordered her death, probably. Not that a traitor shouldn't die, but how painful to be sentenced by the only being on the earth that she cared for.

Her thoughts went to Bairre, and in anger she remembered how he had given her up to Elaine for whatever punishment would come. What a farce his professed love had been. She was less to him than his loyalty to the realm, which meant simply that he loved her not at all. He had deceived her in that, and for that she hated him. But still, she shivered to remember his strength their last time together. Perhaps he would have loved her if she'd had more time.

Bairre would not come for her now. If any from Sogg came, it would be to arrest her. Again, Petrina wondered how she had come to this. In her loyalty to Elaine, in trying to save Elaine alive, she had gained nothing, and now found herself in a lower position than before Elaine took her from the streets. At least in those early days, she had a place that was home, but now even that was lost to her. If the witches didn't kill her, the depression would.

Hulda had prepared a new den in Kattrin's absence, and her endeavors to make it comfortable for Kattrin were apparent. Candlelit, roomy and even perfumed, the den interior diminished Kattrin's anxiousness about making her report. The warm wine that Hulda offered further relaxed her. Actually, other than killing the two Elkana, she'd not committed any offense that Hulda would see as unforgivable. And certainly, Hulda would understand about Petrina. The human girl had much to tell, maybe. If not, it would be easy and pleasant enough to dispose of her.

And so, with those items settled in her mind, she lay upon Hulda's breast and closed her eyes. She would sleep, unless the queen wanted otherwise.

If the queen wanted more than to simply hold her, Hulda's ever-deepening affection for the child overpowered her own desires, and she allowed Kattrin to rest. It was enough for now to have Kattrin close, to take in the lingering scents of wildwood travel, and to have her lover's breath at her neck. The night hours passed gently, sweetly, and with the dim hues of dawn and the low musical greetings of the waking songbirds, Kattrin stirred and half opened those green emeralds of light that Hulda lived for. She moved the child to lie among the layers of coverlets, and then the queen crawled toward the increasing light.

She found the new day too warm for Elkana comfort, and heavy with the aromas of wood smoke and cooking scandeele. A few feet from the den now, Hulda spotted Petrina, asleep under a dew-soaked maple. The human girl had slept in the open without a blanket. Hulda experienced a fleeting moment of guilt; she had completely forgotten Petrina was here. But rather than blame herself, she blamed the coven, all of whom surely saw the girl's circumstances. But no matter. The sun would warm the plump girl soon enough. Depending on Kattrin's report, Petrina may not have to worry about such small discomforts after today.

As if her thoughts had the power to bring Kattrin to her, she turned to find her standing at the den entrance.

"Princess, you might have rested another hour." Hulda found herself pleased that Kattrin had followed her out, rather than sleeping alone.

"I've a few matters of importance to discuss with you," Kattrin said. "Delay is dangerous."

"Tell me, child."

Kattrin hurried to get it all out, as if it were a chore to be quickly accomplished. Had the bright glare of untarnished affection not obscured Hulda's vision, she might have seen the dull edges of deception in Kattrin's childlike report. Kattrin reported Sogg's state of repair, what little she had seen of the military's strength, and the working unity of the citizens. Hulda frowned when she learned that her lover had been locked away in the castle, but then smiled at Kattrin's resourcefulness and perfected witchcraft that allowed her escape.

"The oaken bar was heavy," Kattrin bragged. "Two men were required to set it in place. But I moved it with only a light touch of my hand against the inside of the door, and it fell away. The guards died easily enough."

Kattrin explained that Petrina had also been imprisoned, but that the circumstances of her fall from grace were unknown. And then she spoke of Mikael.

"He is a leader of the royal army. His orders cause soldiers to move quickly, like loyal dogs. None question his authority. He carries a two-handed sword, a bow, and a quiver of white-fletched arrows."

Hulda turned her head and gazed through the black trees, and Kattrin hushed, knowing that Hulda was reaching into the depths of her mind and memory, analyzing what facts she had in an attempt to find the truth of the threat posed by Mikael of Fallon.

A minute later, "Did you see their queen?"

"No, but I met a wizard. She saw my motives plainly, and her report caused my arrest. I've no doubt she has such powers."

"Bring the girl to me," Hulda ordered. No trace of tenderness surfaced in her tone. "She'll be truthful immediately, or she'll die immediately."

The swamp had lost its morning mellowness, and the sun had reached its apex by the time Hulda's interrogation of Petrina was complete. At no time throughout the questioning did Petrina falter.

Petrina had nothing now—nothing but the hope that Elkana witches would take her in. And so they would. Petrina may prove valuable, Hulda concluded, when the coven entered the city.

Petrina was offered a station within the coven, which she accepted with soft whimpers of gratitude. She would receive no training in witchcraft, and Hulda made that clear to the coven that evening as the girls assembled before her, but Petrina would be provided food and shelter. When Sogg was taken, although Petrina could do little in the way of taking it, she would share in the rule of the land equally with the coven. There would be no squabbling or manifestations of jealousy in the interim. Disruption of coven unity could cause the taking of Sogg to fail, and the incident with Cara, although forgiven, would be the last transgression tolerated.

"From the information developed by your princess," Hulda told the coven, "we now know the enemy's strength, and the state of repairs and fortifications, which increase by the hour. We've no further reason to delay and every reason to press on. Be prepared for departure by morning."

A screeching cheer from the bowels of nine witches tore through the sun-lit swamp. Shrill and piercing it was, like a dagger through armor, and the cold, concentrated power and intent of such undisguised evil caused Petrina to tremble, and she closed her eyes against the horror she was now a part of.

The spirits arrived that fresh summer night in Sogg, and found Mikael. He awakened not to sound, for there was none, and not to the soft wafting of air that the ghosts created in his quarters by their arrival. Perhaps his dream of Old Fallon's spirits had awakened him. It seemed he could hear their grieving wails. They knew their descendants were dying with the river, and that the Fallonese would be no more upon the earth.

Mikael saw nothing amiss in his room as he searched through the dullness of sleep and the duller glow of a half-moon that barely gave him enough light to have his bearings. He felt no danger, but a comfort of sorts, reminding him of his early childhood when he had the peace of his mother's nearness.

He tossed back his coverlet and rose, careful not to disturb Aingeal. Dressed only in his britches, he stepped onto the battlement's catwalk, into the predawn where he encountered Sergeant Barnes. Barnes knew before his captain did that Aingeal had followed Mikael outside.

She held Mikael within the folds of the blanket she wore, and teased him about leaving her bed to go to the city trollops, but sensing his mood, she studied his face as he looked down and across the meadows, remembering Esras and everything that had occurred since his friend's death.

"He's here," Aingeal said. "He woke you—he and those with him."

"Who?"

"Esras."

He was silent for the span of several breaths, understanding now, and the emotion of it weakened him. "Esras," he whispered.

The breeze freshened as the spirits passed by him. His first visual sense of them came as they assembled in ranks on the meadow, no more tangible than the weak moonlight.

"Captain?" Barnes' voice held an odd pitch.

"It's all right, Sergeant. We're safe enough."

The silent and illusory movements of the intangible nonentities seemed less substantial than the mist that would rise at dawn from the dew-laden grass, except here were remnants of remembered life, shifting and shadowless phantoms, the last reality of Old Fallon.

Mikael watched, entranced. Who had called them forth? What force bound them together in purpose, and what abilities in the mortal world could they possibly possess?

So vague was the spectral scene, that numbers could not be established. The lack of solidity and the constant fading and reforming of wisps that often merged with others made counting impossible, but overall, Mikael thought, there were perhaps forty.

All were mounted, and all were armed. Images of lances, axes, bows and broadswords bristled in the moonlight above the heads of horses that probably fell with their masters in some ancient northern battle.

Esras hung in the air just above the grass between the moat and the assembling ghost warriors. Surely it was Esras, and the mare he had named Elsa. Although none of the spirits manifested anything firmer than a limpid fabric of definition, Esras stood out in that his spirit kept itself apart from the others, out front. The mounted death that represented Eras' life moved back and forth in front of the assembled warrior ghosts, as if to straighten their lines.

Suddenly, Mikael knew. Esras had led the spirits here. Somehow, he had made contact with the fallen of Old Fallon and had given them purpose to ride again. A comforting presence, they were. How he missed the old man and his wisdom. Now here was his spirit, and perhaps it had brought guidance, for guidance was desperately needed. Only now, upon realizing that Esras fought on even in death, for Fallon, did Mikael feel the depth of his own responsibility, and only now did he see the utter absence of a means to achieve the impossible. He had fortified the city and the castle, he had made an army, and now he awaited Hulda's advance.

What good was that? Even if successful in holding the witches off indefinitely, where was the victory? The river was still lost, the Fallonese still suffered, and they would continue to suffer until they were gone from the earth. He had been a fool to think he might save them, and the spirits before him now were reminders of his vague value to the people of Fallon Valley.

As he again tried to count the wavering misty forms, he wondered how many spirits were enough, considering they had no hold at all on the physical world. Might there be some power in their coming together like this? Surely not. They were nothing more than the steam rising from decayed life, without even enough substance to cast a shadow. The axes, swords and lances they wielded were not tempered iron, but merely the bearer's recollections of ancient possessions.

Mikael pulled away from Aingeal's blanket and walked back along the catwalk toward the iron door that would let him through to the keep. Aingeal followed. Down the dark spiral staircase he plunged, and then out to the courtyard, and on to the main gate. The sentry there faltered at Mikael's order to let him pass.

So intent was Mikael on his purpose that he forgot Aingeal, and he knew not that she stepped lightly into each footprint he made.

"The portcullis, man!" Mikael shouted at the guard, and the heavy bars lifted to allow him passage.

On the drawbridge now, he peered through the near dark for the wispy forms he had watched from the catwalk. They were still there, and still in formation, as if they awaited inspection. He slowed, and Aingeal touched him. He turned to study her face, expecting a warning, but none came, and the calm he saw in her sweet visage pushed him into the meadow.

"I'll wait here," she said.

Esras seemed to turn Elsa as Mikael approached, although the movement was nothing more than what the summer breeze might have created. Mikael stood beside the spirit now, trying to see a face, or something to reassure him that it was indeed Esras. Perhaps he saw eyes, perhaps just shadows of passing clouds, but Esras was there. He had no doubt now. He could not explain that certainty even to himself, but this was his dear friend.

"Esras," Mikael said.

The spirit's response was instant and silent. Flashes of forgotten occurrences darted behind Mikael's eyes—pictures of the valley, of his mother, their hut, Oriana, the temple, and the river. Jumbled scenes, senseless at first, but then clearer. Nothing he saw was as he left it. A weakened, hollow-eyed people stared at him, and he caught the scent of sickness. Huts were in disrepair and work places were silent. Dusty lanes led from the village to dusty fields that were void of greenery. Summer it was, but no workers tended the gardens. Indeed, there were no gardens, just those barren fields, and the wind played there now, kicking up dust where there had been no dust before.

Mikael gazed at Esras, then reached for him, but his hand found nothing within the mist, not even a chill. Esras turned, or seemingly so, and Mikael found himself at the Aine where it flowed through Fallon. The celerity of deterioration was astounding. The mighty Aine was now a trickle of mud and slime, oozing southward far below its once grassy banks.

Mikael cried out in horror. The river's death was his own as much as it was the valley's. Esras moved away and joined the ranks of those he had brought here. A gesture, Mikael knew, to show him that the Chosen One was not alone, and that the coming battle was perhaps not lost. Not yet.

Petrina stood alone, away from the others, far enough that she could not hear their whispered comments of resentment. The coven had helped her cope with what comforts were to be had in the swamp. The shelter of sticks and leafed branches they had made for her had sufficed, but it was too close to the dens, and too often during the night she heard the girls talking about her—how she had no place here, that she was an outcast even of her own kind. She had endured that, necessarily, because she had nothing else.

She turned away from the breaking camp now and threw up for the third time since daybreak. She was pregnant, with no one to blame but herself. Would Bairre want to know, or was she no more to him than a mistake in his life? If he knew, would he come for her? She shouldn't think that way, she told herself, for she had no hope now from any direction.

All the witches were above ground now, at fires or about duties that would allow them to leave here today unencumbered by possessions. Dens were being sealed, and a certain excitement seemed to exude from the coven as they prepared themselves. Petrina saw Hulda and Kattrin, together as usual, talking with Cara and Vala. Smiles were exchanged, and touching of hands, gestures that only the witches could interpret. Encouragement, probably, for today was the beginning of Hulda's last push toward Sogg. In three days time, the coven would be among the people of Sogg, killing indiscriminately, and death would come to peasantry and noblemen alike. And likely, the dying would continue until Hulda was confident she sat in absolute power as ruler of all Artinus.

By what means the city and castle would be assailed, Petrina could only guess. She had not been told what part she would play in Sogg's fall. But they had saved her alive for some reason beneficial to Hulda, that much was a certainty. Perhaps she would be a guide of sorts, to point out the strengths and weaknesses of the castle.

The half-formed human moved within her, and she thought of running from the evil here, back to Elaine, and presenting herself there for royal mercy that the queen might see fit to grant to a repentant and pregnant servant. Foolish, that thought. The matter of her betrayal had probably already been adjudicated, and her pregnancy would not save her. Elaine would probably not even believe that she was pregnant, for the condition showed only slightly, and would be mistaken for obesity. But what if the child should be born, and presented to Elaine? Then, the queen might think twice before condemning her to death.

Hulda and Kattrin were walking toward her now, both of them smiling. She trusted neither of the witches, especially Kattrin. In the fleeting moments of their approach, a hazy plan fell partly into place in Petrina's mind.

Just before Hulda was close enough to speak, Petrina said, "Queen Hulda, I am ill. Might you help me?"

"A night away from home has not set well with you child," Hulda said, and Petrina caught the sarcasm.

Kattrin's smile was gone now, replaced with green-eyed suspicion.

"I am with child. A little more than half term."

"And how is that a concern to me, Petrina of Sogg. I have given you, an untrained human girl, a place here among my own. And now you say you're pregnant with another human. Am I to pity you?"

Petrina paused to gather her courage. "I am your eyes at Sogg. I'll stand with you and direct your assault so that the heaviest damage can be inflicted in the early moments, making your task easier, simpler." She pauses again to let Hulda consider. "But being ill, I fear you may find me lacking at some crucial moment. So I ask you to bring my child out now, alive, that I may be fully recovered before I'm needed."

"I'm no midwife," Hulda said. Her mouth was twisted in a sneer. "You obviously believe you have some value to me, and perhaps you might, but more to the point, if I need any service from you, why should I bring the child forth to hinder our progress? Why would I not simply kill the thing now, and bring it forth dead, and be done with it?"

"No! You will not. I'll not remain alive and allow that." She had gambled it all with that. She watched Hulda's face for a reaction.

"What say you, Princess?" Hulda asked, without taking her eyes off Petrina.

"Give her to me." Kattrin's eyes were alive with light. "Death before birth. Most intriguing."

"I alone," Hulda said, "stand between you and death. Think you that any here prefer that you live? There's not one, I assure you. They've no inclination to give you a share of anything. Nor do I, except, as you have pointed out, you have an intimate knowledge of the city. So, I'll grant you this thing, but ask nothing more. And know this. If at any time the infant poses the slightest threat to my success, it will be slain."

And then to Kattrin, "See to it, Princess. We'll delay our departure until early evening. Speed her recovery."

As Hulda turned back toward the camp, Kattrin advised Petrina to remain where she was. Petrina sank to the ground and allowed herself to cry. What had she done? Through a haze of tears she watched Kattrin go to the fires, one of which was fed larger pieces of fallen forest debris until it blazed waist high. Several of the witches seemed to be discussing what they were adding to a kettle that was suspended over the flames. Finally, the one Petrina had heard referred to as Alastrina, came to her with a wooden cup.

Alastrina was young and long-legged, without much variety in overall shape. Neither slim nor fat, her body resembled the straight trunk of a tree.

"Drink this when it's cool," the witch said. "All of it."

"What is it?"

Alastrina made no response and returned to her sisters.

Petrina sniffed, then sipped. Some kind of tea. It tasted of the forest. She drank it down.

Petrina's next awareness was the birth. She awakened on the ground, tended by Alastrina and another. Unceremoniously, Alastrina plunked the warm and bloody bundle on Petrina's stomach.

"A boy," she said, and walked away, followed by the other.

Too weak to raise her head and look at it, Petrina clutched it to her bosom. Only the child's feeble movements told her it was alive. It neither cried nor whimpered. Before falling back into unconsciousness, Petrina wondered if her baby would survive. She slept through visions of Bairre, only to be awakened again by Alastrina.

"The child must suckle," the witch said. "The same potion that forced its birth will keep it alive, and that potion is within you. It must feed now, and often." She handed Petrina a ragged piece of dyed cloth.

Alastrina helped the new mother situate herself against a tree and to get the child in place. Petrina gasped when she saw its size. No larger than a half-grown kitten, the boy child sought nourishment with an eagerness that seemed impossible. She covered it with the cloth.

"Bairre," she whispered, then pretended sleep so that Alastrina might leave her.

An hour passed before Petrina was given more of the earthy fluid. Even before Alastrina brought it to her, Petrina was fully revived from the travail of giving birth. She felt refreshed and alive, and she knew her wellness came from the potion. She watched for her chance, and when she knew no one would see her rise, she backed into the forest, holding her son.

Having made the journey twice before, she knew the way, in spite of the spreading waters. How many streams she crossed that first night, she'd never remember. Twice it was necessary to hold the child above her head to keep from chilling it in the polluted and dying waters of the Fallon. But she watched the landmarks and kept her bearings. She slept little and ate nothing, but the boy fed regularly, and never cried. Perhaps it couldn't cry, she thought. Perhaps the premature birth had stopped or prevented certain phases of development. No matter, really. Bairre's son, well or not, would be her salvation.

***

On the morning of the day Petrina knew she would arrive at Sogg, she studied the boy's wrinkled face. The eyes were closed tightly, as if the child was making a concerted effort to keep them closed against a world in which he did not yet belong. She wondered at the color of his eyes. Fire-blue probably, like his fathers. Covering the new life in the dirty cloth, she walked on, alarmed somewhat that her baby would not suckle. But home was near—perhaps another hour.

Weakened from the journey to the point of confusion, she stepped into castle meadows in late afternoon, and a guard soon spotted her faltering steps. She'd only progressed another few paces when she saw a mounted patrol coming toward her. Would Bairre be with them? Time was condensed in her vision, and the horsemen had no sooner crossed the drawbridge than they were upon her. Now she stood facing Sergeant Barnes.

"Sergeant, you will please summon Queen Elaine."

"It's Petrina," she heard someone say. She sensed support from behind, and she stood with less effort.

"I must insist, Sergeant. Now, if you please. I've an infant to care for, as you can see." She threw the cloth back from a pale face with closed eyes.

"The thing is dead," Barnes said, as if he were speaking of some wild creature.

"Dead? How dare you? This is my child. I've brought him before the queen. You'll see to that immediately, sir. Immediately." And she looked down upon the infant in her arms and found no sign of life. The small chest no longer rose and fell, and the tension holding the eyes shut had relaxed.

Petrina fell then, in the summer grass, and wailed. She was still sobbing when the oaken bar fell into the iron brackets of the keep's massive door, shutting her away a second time. No witch would save her this time, and she had no reason to believe her execution would be delayed.

She sat on the silk coverlets of the wide bed, wiping her face with the piece of cloth that she had somehow managed to keep when the dead baby was taken from her. She wondered if it would be buried. Beyond that, she had no concerns left, because life was done. Utterly done.

fourteen

The blood of my existence flows therein, and in him.
—Book of Morrigan

The simplicity of Hulda's plan strengthened the probability of its success. Eight of the ten witches would enter Sogg before dark from four different points, except that the easternmost side, which bordered the castle's meadows, would be left open as an escape route for the citizens. All of the citizen workers assigned to repairs within the castle would have returned to the city before the coven entered. A push toward the city's center would ensue, and all resistors of the coven's approach would be killed outright. Any fortified structure that could be of possible use for defenders would be breeched and the occupants slain. Upon meeting at Sogg's center, the coven would spread out and move toward the castle, crossing the city's entire eastern sector and continuing their search and destroy approach to the meadows. Hulda, Kattrin and Trella, stationed on the city's eastern fringe, would block any escape attempt in that direction. The appearance of ten witches on the meadows would be the earliest warning the castle inhabitants would get.

The summer sun was on its downward arc across a clear sky as the witches waited in the tall grass just south of the city. They were close enough to hear the occasional playful yell of a child, or the hammer fall of a worker. Nervous discussion was absent within the coven; assignments were that definite, instructions that clear, and confidence that high.

Each girl was dressed the same, or nearly so. They wore hooded black

203

robes, the loose sleeves of which fell below the hands and feet. With the hoods in place, one would have to look closely to know whether the thing beneath was human or Elkana. The one slight exception was Hulda. A colored strip of bright cloth ran the length of her robe, a scarlet blaze, front and back, and only in that was she distinguishable from the others. And thus, in the event of an unexpected problem, each coven member would know to whom they should turn for an answer.

Kattrin stood with Hulda now, sulking over the lack of authority she had this day. Even though Hulda had lovingly and patiently explained that the presence of two leaders during the assault increased the likelihood of confusion among the attackers, the princess was hurt. Not only had she been temporarily stripped of authority, but also her chances to witness the easy deaths during the initial thrust had been greatly reduced. She would wait with Hulda until most of the citizens were either dead or in flight.

But still, there was the castle. Those who had imprisoned her in the keep would wish they had not. Mikael of Fallon, in particular. He was her consolation for the indignities she had suffered, and in him she would make up for the killings that had been awarded to the pairs of walking death who entered Sogg ahead of her.

"Now, my own," Hulda said. "Let us take what is ours."

Any watcher from the city would have seen the black-clad evil proceeding off the evening-darkened hill, like bats from a cave, dispersing from a grouping of ten into pairs.

Brenna and Alastrina, human and Elkana, joined in purpose, their race set aside in a common endeavor, entered the narrow streets of western Sogg unnoticed by the middle-class inhabiting that sector. Lanterns were already alight at the intersecting streets and inside the stone houses. Alastrina took in the odors of human cooking, and snorted to clear her senses of the disgusting smell. But Brenna gazed perhaps too long toward the houses from which the odors emanated, remembering her village, her parents, and the life of squalor she had abandoned to serve Hulda.

"Strangers in the street." There was no alarm in the voice from within one of the darkened homes. A wife's passing comment to her husband, perhaps.

They passed that place, recognizing no threat to the coven's purpose. Not so fortunate was the middle-aged man who met them in the darkness—a human returning home from some project that required skills that would be extinguished with his life. A canvas bag of tools hung easily over his shoulder. Brenna heard the clink of iron on iron before she saw the concern in his face. He obviously recognized the witches for what they were, because he stepped to the middle of the street to let them pass, but then made his last mistake by searching beneath the black hoods for facial features. Perhaps the burning gaze of only one would have taken a little longer, but when both Brenna and Alastrina fixed their eyes upon him, death was almost immediate. He fell hard to the stone street, and again the clink of tools disturbed the stillness.

Myronica and Cara, both Elkana, entered the south slums on schedule. The poverty here would give them opportunities the other nine would miss, because homes were less protected and the citizens would see the approach of strangers as opportunity to steal. No few men died that evening in the darkened southern streets.

"A waste, actually," Cara said to her accomplice. "The poor we kill here would not likely stand and fight for the city, but only for their own gain or survival. But who can know for certain? Hulda requires it, and so it is." She paused in both speech and step. "Here now, what's this?"

"It's the river," Myronica said. "One of the new branches. Do you think the city will flood?"

"Hulda would have told us if that were so," Cara said.

As new as the filthy flow of water was to the streets of Sogg, it was yet still shallow, and as if alive, it searched for the lowest places, restless and lost in its mindless movement toward those depths of the earth from which it had been forced.

As they waded across, Myronica and Cara experienced the gentle push, and they suffered the temporary weakness brought on by the loss of their powers, which were inhibited any time they contacted water. They both were glad to step onto the reality of stone pavement on the north side, where they were at least out of physical contact with something a Goddess of whom they had no part had created.

Sergeant Barnes and his night watch stood their posts on the ramparts of the castle of Sogg and peered through the summer night toward the city. Nothing seemed amiss, and no sound foreign to a peaceful town settling in for the night drifted across the meadows to the soldiers. Captain Sveinson had them on the highest state of alert, and every side and corner of the castle was manned. Some who watched tonight were new recruits, pressed into the queen's service, but because of the threat they believed existed, none complained. What they were watching for, they did not know. "Anything unusual," was to be reported immediately, and Mikael himself was to be apprised. Those at the front were especially vigilant, for treachery in the form of a witch had already approached from that direction, and the event was not to be repeated. Any visitor approaching the castle after dark would be challenged, and if satisfactory answers were not returned, the unfortunate intruder was to be fired upon by the bowmen. The only member of the castle's staff not presently secure within the castle walls was the advisor, Sir Bairre, and he was not expected before daybreak. His assignment, as every soldier knew, was to be on the city streets at night. He was Elaine's eyes in those dark places the realm could not visually reach. *A dangerous assignment*, Barnes told himself as he thought of his captain's brother alone in the ill-lit corridors of the injured city.

Bairre's mount favored a right hoof, almost imperceptibly, and Bairre felt the slight loss of rhythm that told him something was amiss with the mare. He dismounted under a street lantern and dislodged a small pebble from the hoof. In his brief examination, he noted the hoofs were untrimmed, and he cursed the stable staff. He would see to that neglect tomorrow. No such thing would have occurred in the days that he controlled the royal mounts. Remounting, he decided to turn south. A ride through the slums would keep him awake and perhaps rouse the citizens a bit. The dullness of the night treks into the city made for long hours, and he would welcome some action to break the monotony. Besides, he had ridden all the way to the inner city, and nothing was out of order. Perhaps in the slums...

He saw them then. Several hooded figures approaching from the west. He counted. Eight in all, and their movements were feminine. He rode toward them. They maintained a steady pace, as if they meant to intercept him. Eight hoods simultaneously were pushed back, revealing the faces of women, mostly Elkana. How very odd. Unless...

The pain that entered his chest came from the witches. He knew that in time. Pulling the reins hard to the left, he whirled the mount and spurred it hard back toward the castle. A ball of fire flung by Donella warmed the air perceptibly as it passed within inches of his shoulder. The chest pain decreased proportionately to the distance he put between himself and Hulda's witches. He had no doubt that he had identified them correctly, and even less doubt that the attack on Sogg that Mikael expected was imminent.

He had ridden faster mounts, but this one ran as if it, too, had sensed the extreme danger that had confronted it moments before. The night air was cool against Bairre's face as he raced for the meadows. His cloak streamed out behind him like a dark specter that followed him through the night. The meadows weren't far now, perhaps another two minutes. He had no way to know that since his departure from the castle an hour before dark, three more witches had slipped into position between him and the meadows, and that they waited there now to slay anyone who attempted an escape from the city.

Mikael awakened abruptly, disturbed by...what? All he heard was Aingeal's gentle breathing from where she lay beside him. He tossed the blanket aside and stood. Perhaps he would walk. He dressed.

"Mikael?" came the sleepy voice of Aingeal.

Not audibly, but surely, he heard now another voice. Oriana's. "Bairre needs you."

"It's Bairre," he said as he grabbed his bow and quiver and bolted from the keep.

The stable master woke to the sound of Mikael mounting Loki. Mikael was at the portcullis within seconds, startling a sleepy guard. Then out and across the just-lowered drawbridge to the meadows.

Two hooded figures faced Bairre at the fringes of the city, blocking his way onto the meadows. A force he couldn't see knocked him from the mare's back. As he came to one knee in an effort to stand, he knew again that deep pain within his chest. He turned to see how close the witches were. One was pitching forward, white fletching protruding from her breast. The other two turned from him to face the threat bearing down upon them at full speed from the direction of the castle. Mikael!

The black-robed forms evaporated. A spray of gravel bit at Bairre's face as Loki's hoofs slid to a stop in front of him. Mikael's arm came down for Bairre, and pulled him to Loki's back. The safety of the night-darkened meadows welcomed them back. As Loki loped toward the drawbridge, a mist developed in front of the riders and began to take the form of a regiment. Mikael recognized Esras and the other spirits.

"What the hell?" Bairre yelled.

Loki's rhythmic gallop remained steady as he ran directly into the insubstantial mass, as if he saw them not at all, or else recognized the ghosts for what they were. Mikael felt the chill of their presence as he rode through, and then, something else. A bumping, as if he had jostled someone. That could not be.

Hulda and Kattrin took possession of the one-story home that they found themselves near upon termination of their instantaneous transportation to this spot, not fifty paces from where Trella had fallen to Mikael's arrow. The queen spoke to her princess over the still-quivering body of the former resident.

"It's true then," she said. "He has the arrows, and he has some ability to recognize danger before it's upon him, else he would not have known to rescue the horseman." She dipped a cup into a thick, warm liquid the homeowner had apparently been preparing for his supper. She tasted it gingerly, then spat her contempt of human nourishment onto the floor.

"We expected this, Queen. We should not delay," Kattrin advised.

"You're correct in that, love, and we shan't. Outside now, and find the others. We'll be within the castle before the night is half through."

The other eight entered. They were ten now—more than enough.

"Spread out as we cross the meadows," Hulda said. "Donella will cross the moat first." She stepped toward Donella and touched her arm. "Burn the portcullis, and then move quickly to the front gate. If the gate is closed, burn that also."

"Yes, Queen."

She spoke to them all now. "Every soldier will die. They will resist at first, and then upon realizing they are defeated, they will attempt to flee or surrender. We'll have none of that. Kill each one. I want no one left alive who has ever had a part of ruling this place. Watch for the one who fires white tipped and white fletched arrows. Take no chances with that one. Whoever among you kills Mikael of Fallon will share equally in my rule of Sogg." A lie, of course, but it would increase Hulda's chance of victory.

As Hulda led her coven to the meadow's boundary, she saw numerous fires burning along the catwalk. She must assume they were preparing hot liquids to fling at her, or fire-arrows, or burning masses of material that would cling to clothing. Fire. How she hated the thought of such a death. Even she, the most powerful witch to have ever risen on the continent of Artinus, had no power to stop fire once it caught her. A witch's weakness, to be sure. She wondered briefly if Mikael would cause his arrows to burn before he launched them. Damn him! This would have been so easy had he not interfered. What was it that drove him to protect this place? His river was spread out all over the continent, polluted and ruined. Was it revenge? A noble motivation, but it would not be enough. Even Mikael of Fallon would have to give way to the hell Hulda was about to unleash.

Theane, one of the two humans in the coven, was the first to sense the presence of spirits. Before she saw their opaque substance, Theane felt their anguish of again being part of the mortal world they had so long ago abandoned to the ages. Well inside the meadow now, she saw them plainly, illuminated in her vision by the energies the ghosts used to manifest themselves. They were mounted, spreading in a line as if to do battle, spreading farther now to match the positions taken up by the witches. Theane sensed only minimal danger. She sought Hulda in the darkness with eyes that witchcraft had enhanced to animal-like efficiency. Hulda felt her gaze and returned it, and Theane knew the queen was also aware of the approaching barrier of specters.

They came together moments later, ten witches and an undetermined number of Fallon dead. Hulda didn't identify the spirits until she was among them, and then the reality of it soaked into her consciousness like river water. Had she disturbed them into action by the earthquake? Being only the energy of remembered Fallon life, the spirits had been awakened to assemble here, to come to the aid of the one they believed could save Fallon. Perhaps Mikael had that much drawing power, that he could summons spirits. But no matter, for spirits were only that. They might rumble the grounds in which their bodies had been buried, as she herself had proven with the quake, but they had no place in the physical world, and no physical ability.

To prove that to the coven, Hulda stood among the ghosts, under their axes, and paused to take upon herself the nonexistent blades. The Fallon dead obliged her with several axes and hatchets made of mist that cut the night air, and upon the contact that could not occur, Hulda fell. She lay on her back beneath the silent thunder of a hundred hoofs that trampled her, and she felt that, too. And then the ancient fighters were beyond her, engaging the other witches. Hulda rose to her knees, feeling the pain of numerous slashes.

Knowing she would find none, she nevertheless felt through her hair for the split skull an axe of the real world would have caused. No gash, no blood. Just pain.

As she got to her feet, Hulda saw others of her coven falling under the pain that had no tangible source. Hulda focused her eyes on the back of a mounted specter, and burned him with her gaze, engaging him intimately enough that a mortal man would have fallen immediately, but the phantom felt it not at all, or it gave no indication of discomfort. It continued to swing the broadsword it had brought here from its ancient grave.

How might one kill a spirit? She asked herself that, and then turned from such thoughts to the business at hand.

"Children," she cried. "The castle."

And the coven obeyed, understanding now as Hulda did, that the spirits were harassers only, without connection to the world of the living. The coven passed beyond the stamping, snorting and ghostly battle horses, and entered upon that part of the castle's closest meadow, directly in front of that spot the drawbridge would fall to give them passage across the moat, the water of which they could not cross by the use of witchcraft. Water. That element of earth so closely akin to fire in its powers to resist and to harm those who had mastered the craft.

Arrows slashed the night air from the catwalk. None found their target, because witchcraft altered the arrows' courses, but Hulda knew that Mikael of Fallon had not as yet launched one of his. Why not?

Hulda stood with her nine in silence now, a silence akin to the moon's vague light that squinted at them through broken clouds. Although a reflection, that light was from Mother Sun. Ten minds locked together as one began to bring the bridge downward against the strength of the huge windlass that now screamed its complaint as it paid out the iron links against its will. Orders from within the castle walls rang out, and then grunts of numerous men working in vain to stop the movement of chains through the pulleys. The descending bridge eclipsed the moonlight, casting the witches into darkness. Lower and closer they brought the bridge toward the meadow grass, and closer still, until it was down. Immediately, the ten were moving across the bridge like rats across a ship's ties to a dock. They took up a position at the lowered portcullis, and applied the same technique.

Fire and hot oil fell through the battlement chutes, followed by pitch and quicklime. By assignment, Cara was expecting the bundles of flaming materials and boiling liquids to hinder their approach, and she was ready.

Cara's arms came up and she held them straight out, as if she would fly, and her head came back to where she faced the falling death directly. The great round flaming spheres and caustic materials altered their gravity-influenced flight, and angled away from the bridge, to both sides, and the steaming, sizzling sound of the moat drowning that energy in the stagnant waters told the other nine witches that Cara was alert.

The portcullis was up now, inviting them in, as if they were visiting dignitaries, welcome at the castle of Sogg.

Elaine argued with him, as Mikael knew she would. Aingeal kept silent and made herself as unnoticeable as possible in the large kitchen. She was still uncertain that Elaine wanted her in the castle at all.

As head of military affairs, Mikael insisted that Elaine retire to the safest place within the castle, which in its present state of repair, would be the keep.

"Have you forgotten, Captain? Petrina is housed there."

"You'll have to take the smaller compartment. And quickly. Have you everything you'll need?"

"I'll need nothing, I hope. This skirmish should be over shortly, do you not agree?"

"Your Majesty, we're set upon by witches, the very same evil that killed your family and nearly destroyed Sogg. I assure you, this will not be a skirmish."

Elaine concealed any fear she might have had. "Be that as it may, sir, I require nothing. If the need arises, I shall send word."

Sergeant Barnes and nine of his soldiers followed Mikael and Elaine up the spiral stone steps. With Mikael's ever-present limp, his broadsword banged more than once against the steep incline, and the sound broke the darkness like a torch, reassuring Elaine that he still carried the king's own sword.

Elaine, in the lead, stopped half way up. "Really, Mikael, there's no need for so many guards. If the enemy progresses to these stairs, I'm done for anyway."

Mikael only grunted. He was fast losing patience with niceties. He had a battle to direct.

Elaine's new quarters were one floor above Petrina's. The small room, recently reconstructed, was as yet unfurnished, save for a rough table the workers had left. The only luxury she would have that Petrina did not was four windows. Petrina had only two because the lower portion of the keep tower was faced on two sides by the castle's forebuilding. At least, Elaine thought, she might keep an eye on the battle's progress.

"And stay away from the windows," was Mikael's parting words to her. Elaine hadn't time to show her resentment, as the door was immediately closed, and she was left with the task of securing it from the inside. How dare he address her so, she thought, then smiled to think of his confidence. The realm could be in no better hands.

Now in the inner courtyard again, Mikael found Aingeal standing perfectly still in the semi-darkness, facing the gate to the outer yard. He touched her shoulder, and she turned. He saw the anxiety in her eyes.

"Mikael," she said, and laid her face against his chest.

"What is it?"

"They've power beyond what I might have imagined. My ability to comprehend it is insufficient. I am… saturated."

"Speak plainly, Aingeal. I've no time…"

"Your arrows are not enough."

"I've an army."

"I see your army dead if you go against her."

"Her?"

"Hulda."

"Then what do you suggest, Aingeal? That we give her the castle and the city? Just walk away?"

"She'll not allow you to walk away. Maybe the soldiers, but not you, and not Elaine. But especially, not you. I sense that she's afraid of you, Mikael, and because she's afraid, she must destroy you, as she has destroyed the river."

"Is the river gone then?"

"She believes it is."

"And you, Aingeal, what do you believe?"

"The Fallon is weakened to the point of death. I feel its sadness. That's what I know about your river. There's that, but also I see that it continues to spread across the continent, and with each new direction, it is further polluted and poisoned. Its disease flows against the current, all the way back to Fallon Valley, and further, to the glacier where it was born. It's low…"

"I haven't time now, Aingeal." He stepped around her, put she touched his arm and stopped him.

"Hear me out, Mikael. Understand that you fight for what you've all but lost. The Fallon, it's low, far below its normal depths. Whatever reservoir held it beneath the earth, must have controlled its flow, for it flows now with the freedom of death, looking for an end, that low place where it might stop. But there's still something left of its old self. In the shallows, I feel the sun warming it, adding to its misery, hastening its demise."

"I've felt the same things, but in a different way," Mikael said. "I'm her lover in a sense. Her anguish is mine, and her death will be mine."

"Captain! They're inside! May Goddess Morrigan save us all." That cry of alarm came from the catwalk. He looked up to see his men staggering backward away from the fires they had kindled. Each man held his chest. Some fell to their knees, others were already prone.

Mikael bolted for the outer courtyard, his injured knee shooting pain to his brain. He met those six soldiers assigned to the gate running toward him. "Back to your post, varlets!"

They ignored him, except one, who paused to look him in the eyes. Mikael saw the apology there, and the fear. The soldier ran after his comrades.

Mikael nocked an arrow and stood facing the raised gate. Why was it raised? Surely, the sentries would not have given entry to something they feared so much. A moment later, a hooded figure appeared in the gateway, a yellow-eyed silhouette caught between torchlight and moonlight. Mikael drew and released, thinking of the creature's heart.

Aife bent her head to look at the white fletching protruding from her breast. Her Elkana snout almost touched the feathers. Blood issued from her mouth like vomit, and Mikael heard it splatter onto the hard-packed ground. She looked up, and Mikael wondered if the yellow light he had thought was in her eyes a second ago had been real, for now it was absent, and she sank as if being absorbed by the earth.

Mikael stood where he was and nocked another arrow. He waited, expecting another witch to attempt entry. Where were his men? Where was Bairre?

Bairre Sveinson found Petrina's compartment in the keep unguarded. She had been forgotten by her keepers because of more pressing matters. Bairre struggled with the bar, and finally, by getting his back under it, he was able to nudge the heavy oaken timber high enough to clear the brackets that held it in place. The bar crashed to the stone floor with enough noise and force to shake the entire keep. Mikael would see him beheaded for this, if the realm egin{center}

survived, which was highly unlikely given the death he had seen thus far. But Petrina should not have to wait as a helpless prisoner until certain death arrived from the witches. They would find Petrina and kill her, and what mode of death they might employ would be leagues apart from the niceties involved in a royal execution. At least that was the rationalization Bairre used to release Petrina.

He pushed the huge doors inward on silent hinges, but did not enter. He stood expressionless, the shock of the scene in front of him taking his voice and his emotions. He felt nothing at first, then rage.

Petrina swung from a rafter by her own cloth garment, her eyes open, questioning even in death why her lover had come too late. Bairre heard the heavy, booted steps of soldiers on the stone stairs above him. The bar falling to the floor must have alerted them. He descended the stairs, taking them two and three at once, only to find Aingeal coming toward him. He turned her around and they entered the inner courtyard together.

Myronica took the next arrow, but her demise was less graceful than Aife's. She screamed, not as one would vent pain, but in rage and bloodlust. Still thirty paces from her killer, she lunged for him, covering ground quicker than thought. Mikael retreated one step and allowed her to fall at his feet. He nocked another arrow and waited.

The castle was suddenly as quiet as it would have been on any previous night at this hour. No orders being given, no sound of running soldiers, no screeches from the witches. Just nothing. He waited.

A scuffing of gravel behind him caused Mikael to turn, expecting attack. It was Bairre, and behind him Aingeal.

"Aingeal, it's not safe. Go back," Mikael said.

"There's no safety within the castle," she responded. "If we're to die today, my place is with you."

"I'll not have talk of dying. Bairre, where've you been?"

Before Bairre could answer, Aingeal said, "Mikael, it's you Hulda wants. I feel her energy toward that end. She wants you as much as she wants Sogg. This silence… they're preparing for something."

Ignoring the warnings from Bairre and Aingeal, Mikael stepped to the gate, his bow ready, and then through to the outer courtyard. The yard was empty, at least as far as he could tell in the near dark. He turned to inform Bairre and found himself inches from Hulda's smirking visage. Kattrin was

214

with her, and suddenly eight black robes surrounded him.

"He's mine," Hulda said.

Deep in his bosom an ache was born, and it grew, and Mikael knew it was from Hulda who held his gaze, the half-smile still on her face. Had she allowed that part of the coven she retained to find his eyes, he would have surely died immediately, but Hulda wanted his life, as Aingeal had said. A fog of disorientation fell around him, fraudulently lessening the danger. Perhaps if he broke eye contact…

The pain diminished slightly, and with that relief Mikael regained some of his reasoning ability. He thought of the falling and fleeing soldiers, and forgave them. He saw an opening develop between Hulda and Kattrin as Hulda moved to catch his eyes, and that dark void between black robes beckoned him. He hurled himself between the two witches, and although in doing so he broke free of the encircling stench, one of them grabbed a handful of arrows from his quiver. He turned in time to see Morrigan's arrows being broken across Kattrin's knee.

He had one left, and that already on the bowstring. He determined to send that arrow through Hulda's heart, even if the others killed him. But he was too close. He'd not have time to draw the bow before they'd be upon him.

He'd not remember dropping the bow and unsheathing Prejudice. A glint of steel might have been seen in the subdued light before it found its first target. Theane fell, her stomach opened and her human blood covering her from waist to knees. Cara was next. The wide blade of the king's sword entered high on her chest and Mikael pushed it through until the bronze hilt stopped it. Mikael was pulling it free when Donella hurled fire at him. He felt the heat as the ball of burning witchery passed closed by him, close to enough to ignite his jerkin. He slapped at the burning material, finding it difficult to extinguish.

Mikael heard a cry of pain from Bairre, but could not take the second required to check on his brother. It was good to know Bairre was in the fight.

And Esras was there, mounted on a ghost-horse, his sword slashing at Hulda. Several witches lay dead on the blood-soaked courtyard. Some of his soldiers had rejoined the battle and had died. Others still lived and fought, Barnes among them. He stepped over the black-robed bodies and thrust his broadsword forward into the bowels of the nearest one that was standing. She screamed, and he realized she, too, was human. Pulling the blade free, he spotted Bairre on his knees. Once called Vala stood above him, her dagger poised. Blood streaked Bairre's face, arms and hands, and his clothing hung in tattered rags.

Vala looked at Mikael as he stepped in front of her and swiped the tip of his sword close over his brother's head and across the witch's stomach. She stepped back, gazing at Mikael as if he had accomplished the impossible. Her pause gave him time to push the blade tip deep into her breast.

"Where's Aingeal?" Mikael asked Bairre. But there was no response, and a quiet settled over the scene.

Looking around him, Mikael realized that all but three of the witches had fallen. Hulda and Kattrin, who he recognized, were still standing, and a third was the fire thrower. The Fallon spirits were less than he remembered, and they confronted the witches now during a sudden lull in the fighting.

"Hold your weapons," Mikael said, and the spirits hovered in silence, taking this order from the living.

"What say ye now, queen witch?" Mikael asked. "Are your visions of power realized? Accept your losses and go."

The force of the three witches' attack was sufficient to push him toward the gate and onto the drawbridge. Bairre was still down, and as Mikael slashed at Hulda and missed, he caught a glimpse of Aingeal kneeling beside Bairre.

Mikael bled from several shallow wounds. If the spirits failed to keep Hulda and her remaining coven busy, they'd concentrate on him and kill him surely with their minds. "Barnes!"

The sergeant appeared at the gate, weaponless, holding a shattered arm. Mikael could expect no help from his men.

But Esras and his few were there, and Mikael heard the muffled clang of steel as the witches held off the ghost weapons with daggers. Perhaps the dead could bring only minimal force into the mortal world. The spirits were being beaten off, driven toward Mikael, and Kattrin was foremost in the advance.

Mikael rushed at her through the spirits, and Kattrin saw him too late. Prejudice entered under an upraised arm and pierced both lungs. The child witch fell, hissing like the demon she was. As Mikael stepped over her to reach Hulda, he heard Kattrin's last words. "Now I know."

Hulda rushed to meet him, and the look of distressed wretchedness in her face at her lover's death was almost to be pitied. In that moment of eye contact, Mikael weakened, and she stabbed him low on his left side. He took the entire length of Hulda's dagger and had to sidestep to pull it free. The pain and weakness took him to one knee, but as he fell, he swung Prejudice fiercely one more time, not even knowing if either remaining witch was in range. The blade cut the night, but before it finished its arc, Donella took a fatal blow in her neck. She clasped one hand to her throat, and Mikael saw the blood spurting from between her fingers. Mikael stood.

With her free hand, Donella flung fire, and this time it found its mark. The flaming ball struck Mikael on both legs just above his knees. Hulda rushed in to finish him with her dagger.

He didn't fall, but the agony of burning flesh stopped him. He dropped Prejudice and beat at the flames with his bare hands. The fire had an unnatural tenacity to stay alive. Already his legs were burned severely.

The flames lapping at his clothing and flesh grew in their hunger, and also in size. Now fire danced on the oiled boards of the bridge, and Mikael saw the blade of the king's sword begin to blacken.

Weaponless and on fire, he faced Hulda. In another second, he would no longer be able to support himself on his ruined legs. He fell into her as she thrust her knife toward his heart. The blade entered his chest and a lung collapsed. Hulda struggled to free herself from his two-armed grip around her torso. If this is how he died, then so would she.

In its greed, the fire began to consume Hulda's robe, and then her flesh. Her screams filled the night. She jabbed at him again, and this time the blade entered adjacent to his collar bone and sank straight down. But he held on.

When Hulda could no longer stand, they fell together. Mikael pulled her toward the edge of the bridge, rolling over and beneath her until they were there. They were a single burning mass of flesh and clothing as they fell the height of three men to the moat. He broke the surface with his back and did not release Hulda until he felt the muddy bottom. He attempted to stand then on legs that could not support him. The waist-deep water hissed around him like a hoard of venomous reptiles, but still the fire clung to his legs like flaming leeches, but its vigor was definitely diminishing. Then it was out.

He fell backward and took more than a little stagnant water into his nose and mouth as he turned and splashed toward the bank. Mikael clawed his way out of the water and onto the grass where he collapsed on his back. The stars winked at him through the broken clouds, telling him he had won, but that he would die. The bleeding pain soaked him from his lower back to his feet, and he knew he could not maintain consciousness against it. He should look at the destruction of tissue, he knew. Maybe he would find no reason to awaken after he fainted. He sat up. The weak moonlight glinted off the bare bones of both legs. More flesh was absent than was present.

So, this was his end. Somehow, he hadn't expected it to be like this. He had never thought that he would die alone. He should have fallen in the frenzy of battle from an axe or sword wound, with his men around him. Ideally, he would have died near his river.

While he could still sit, he looked for Hulda. She had not resurfaced. Fire and water had been her end.

As for himself, if this is what he'd been given, so be it. He deserved it. Morrigan had given him the mission, as well as the arrows and Esras to help him complete it, and he had failed. The river, his only real purpose in leaving Fallon, was lost.

He wondered briefly if Oriana would see his death. He lay back again, this time to die. "I'm sorry," he said to the stars, but they hid themselves behind passing clouds and had no forgiveness to offer.

One of the clouds covered him now, or so it seemed, and it gave him no comfort. It took none of the pain, and kept blessed unconsciousness from him. Now it spoke to him.

"Move, Son of Svein, toward Sogg. She awaits you there." The easy voice was not audible, but still it was there.

"Esras?"

The misty substance began to dissipate, leaving him, but not before Mikael saw recognizable features in his friend's face.

"Who awaits me, Esras?"

But Esras was gone, and again Mikael was alone, except for the pain.

Bairre and Aingeal saw Mikael set upon by the witches, his arrows broken, and his flesh stricken with fire. And Bairre would surely die if Aingeal didn't stop the bleeding.

Mikael was done for; she had seen him fall with Hulda. What had she now? Her father's teachings had been in vain, for she had accomplished nothing with her knowledge, except maybe to find Mikael and to know him again. *Let that be sufficient,* she said in her mind.

And then Esras was there with her, and she saw a little of what she had seen in his face the night he saved her from the blizzard—benevolence when all was lost. And not only Esras, but those with him, the ghosts of Fallon who would willingly die a second death in service to Fallon, if such were possible.

***

Mikael crawled, dragging his useless remnant of bleeding legs across the meadow. Each handful of dew-draped grass he grabbed to pull himself forward was a little closer to whatever it was Esras wanted him to have. "She," he had said. Certainly, he didn't mean Aingeal. Aingeal was inside the castle, as was Elaine. He had no close ties to any other female, other than Oriana, and there could be no doubt as to her location. What could Esras have meant? His answer came from the direction of the city in soft waves that met him in the meadow. The Fallon.

Shallow she was, but deepening as the flow increased. On his stomach, he smelled her spoiled condition. Although polluted by those who should have never partaken of her, she was still the Fallon, and he tasted a bit of the old life that he had once known. Suddenly, she was sufficiently deep that he could immerse his entire head, and he did so.

Here with his river, he could die. Esras had given him that peace. As the waters covered him, his legs cooled and he was comforted somewhat. Mikael Sveinson rolled onto his back, and allowed the Fallon to enter his mouth and nostrils, and to soak into his open wounds. Through her waters, he could still see the stars, and he noted that they were a little brighter, and that the cloud cover was absent.

The water didn't choke him, and he thought that odd. Had he already died? Never had he known such peace, such contentment. His early childhood came to him, and Oriana. He saw the Aine as she had been, full and clear.

"Mikael."

"I'm here."

"Do you know about the Fallon, Mikael?"

"Yes, Priestess. You taught me."

"Not everything."

"No, Priestess, not everything. For I've failed you. The Fallon is lost."

"Almost lost, but no longer. She flows in your veins, Mikael. She has since your birth. And she holds your essence. Tonight, you are joined as never before."

"Priestess, I'm dying. I can do nothing for the river."

"You can, and have, and will, Mikael. Even now, your blood makes her whole. Even now, her waters make *you* whole. Look."

He sat up then, bringing his head clear of the moving stream. He stood, realizing only then that he was naked except for his long shirt and the belt that had held the sword. Only a trace of the previous mutilation was visible in the reflected moonlight. The fire had ravaged him to the point of death, and now he was all but whole. In the passing of his next few heartbeats, he was completely whole. The pain was gone.

He ran toward the castle. Even the old pain from the earthquake injury was absent. He was upon the drawbridge in seconds, and only then realized how far the river had come to meet him. The moat was overflowing now with river water.

Bairre would recover, Aingeal announced at dawn. At Bairre's own request, he had been taken to the stables, where he now rested on a pallet of hay. Already, his color was returning, thanks to Aingeal's ministrations. She had sealed the several lacerations and halted the blood loss. "He won't be on his feet for another day," she told Mikael.

Mikael knelt at his brother's fevered head. "Why, Bairre? You came so close to death. What was it you were fighting for?"

"For Fallon, brother, and our Goddess."

fifteen

And it shall nourish my own during those generations, until that time they return to inhabit the ancient grounds.
—Book of Morrigan

"Captain Sveinson?" Elaine inquired from the catwalk, a little louder than a queen's dignity allowed.

Bairre, just entering the inner courtyard from the kitchen, looked up, trying to see Elaine against the overcast sky. "Yes, my lady?"

"Come to me here, sir. I would have your advice on a certain matter."

As he climbed the stone stairs, Bairre wondered what had brought Elaine outside on such a blustery morning. As he stepped onto the catwalk, he found her standing with Sergeant Barnes.

Elaine's greeting was less than formal. She shivered against a sudden blast of wind from the river before speaking. "How long, Captain, has Eric been a sergeant?"

Eric? Who the hell was Eric? Then it struck him that Barnes had a first name. He hadn't known until this instant what it was. How would Elaine know of such? "Since my years in the stables, Your Majesty."

"Has he served you well? And before that, did he not serve your brother in similar fashion?"

"Of course, Your Majesty." What was she getting at?

"Remember Hulda's assault? Did Eric not stand against that when his subordinates fled?"

"Indeed, he did."

"And during the six years hence, has he not performed above his station? Is he himself not responsible for organizing our elite guard for the Fallon's protection?"

By this time, Barnes had stepped away from the praise, pretending now to have interest in the clear depths of the river that disappeared in the snow-laden ground just east of the castle. He caught a glimpse of one of the old ones as the spirit rode across the meadow thorough the spittle of wind-driven ice crystals.

"The Guard would be far less proficient without his training, my lady."

Still, Elaine had not revealed her meaning. "Have you another to appoint as sergeant?"

Another? Was Barnes being dismissed? Retired? "Yes. Several are qualified."

"Then see to it, Captain. With no objection from you, Eric will be your lieutenant. His sole function from this moment forward will be to oversee the Guard—to make certain the river's departure from the surface of Artinus has the honor and protection Morrigan expects. Your position on that, Bairre?"

Bairre's surprise and pleasure lit his face. "A wise decision, Your Majesty. Mikael will be pleased indeed."

"And how do you imagine your brother has fared through the winter?" she asked.

"I'm sure he is fine. The fall harvest was more than generous to the valley. I left as they were taking in the final stores. With your permission, I'll visit again in the spring."

"Perhaps I shall accompany you. It's time I visit the outlying hamlets along the river, to see how they are adapting to what Morrigan shares with them. And the valley—it would be good to see the children again."

Esras Mikaelson played along the riverbank with the toy boat his father had carved. He pushed it as far as his young arms could manage out into the slow current, and walked beside it through the snow, giving orders to the make-believe crew that manned the rudder and the square woolen sail. Although the gusting breeze jostled the boat, it sat perfectly level on the water, and Esras took not a small amount of pride in that. Oriana would be glad, because she knew how anxious he had been to launch it this first time.

An undine broke the surface between Esras and his boat, almost capsizing the craft and drowning the make-believe men onboard who labored to keep its course straight for their captain.

"Fiona, stop that!" In spite of his reprimand, he smiled to see her so close to the bank.

The concentric rings created by the undine pushed the boat within reach, and Esras picked it up. He dried it on his coat and then laid it on its side in his hands where the winter sun could illumine the smooth cedar lines. He thought of the hours he had spent sitting with his father outside the temple as the boat was carved. It was a warship, his father told him, just like the ones his ancestors had used before the Great Migration. Well, almost like it. A real ship would have a hull of many planks, each overlapping the other. The toy's cedar keel would have been of oak, and the mast of spruce or pine in a full-size vessel. And the hull of an actual warship would have been coated with tar or animal fat.

But his own ship would do for now, and in Esras' seven-year-old mind, the adventures of the early warriors were alive today on the cedar deck. Someday, perhaps he would build a real warship, and sail it down the river to show Queen Elaine. That would be something.

Esras glanced at the sky, seeing where the sun would be if the clouds didn't cover it. His mother would be preparing the midday meal. Perhaps venison and cheese, his favorite. Thinking along those lines, he made his way through the ankle-deep snow toward the large hut situated near the temple. Maybe Oriana would join them for the meal, and he could tell her how well his ship had done on its maiden voyage.

Aingeal met him outside, dry moccasins in her hand. "Your father sent me to fetch you, Esras. He thought perhaps you'd sailed away."

He laughed at the prospect. "Fiona wouldn't have allowed that," he said. "She made the water too rough." This was a good joke his mother had started. Father would laugh.

He found his father at the table, spooning mush into baby Elaine's smiling mouth. "Boat," the child said, pointing at Esras.

"That's right, Lainey." Mikael looked at Aingeal, his pride evident. "So soon. I'd thought she would be older before speaking so well."

Aingeal came to sit beside her husband. She took the spoon from his hand and wiped a rag across Elaine's face. "I think she has her father's resolve."

the end

Printed in the United States
22388LVS00004B/277-324